A SIMPLE *hello*

COOPER TOWN BOYS

BOOK TWO

USA TODAY BESTSELLING AUTHOR

LACEY BLACK

A Simple Hello
Cooper Town Boys Series, book 2

Cover Design by Kristie Leigh, Vanilla Lily Designs
Photographer Eric McKinney, 6:12 Photography
Model Bryan B

Editing by Kara Hildebrand
Proofreading by Sandra Shipman, Joanne Thompson, and Karen Hrdlicka
Formatting by Champagne Book Design

This book is a work of fiction. Any reference to historical events, real people, or real places are used fictitiously. Other names, characters, places and events are products of the author's imagination, and any resemblance to actual events or places or persons, living or dead, is entirely coincidental.

Published in the United States of America.

ISBN-13: 978-1-951829-72-8

A SIMPLE *hello*

CHAPTER ONE

Cade

I WALK TOWARD THE BAR, CARRYING TWO CASES OF BOTTLES SO MY brother can restock, all while belting out a classic Billy Ray Cyrus tune from the early nineties about broken hearts. I lift my chin to the regulars as I pass by, and then paste on a bright, charming smile to a group of ladies standing at the bar, waiting for their drinks.

"Ladies," I state as I walk past, throwing them a wink.

I get the result I'm expecting when I hear their giggles behind me. Setting the cases on the floor, I get to work stocking what's low.

"You don't have to do that, but we appreciate it," Lizzie says as she passes, carrying two drinks for the giggle girls behind me.

Lizzie owns this place now. The Tipsy Lizard. It's been our hangout since we were old enough to legally drink, and maybe even a little before then, until Chuck, the previous owner, would kick us out. Lizzie bought this place back in April, and in the last four months has completely transformed it into a bar everyone wants to hang out at. The best part is, she kept the old-school, classic look with tons of old alcohol memorabilia, and just brightened the place up with some good ol' fashioned cleaning and painting. The place looks great, and because of those changes, it's been busier than ever.

Of course, I don't actually work here. That's my twin brother, Collin. He's worked here part time since returning from the military. Between this and his job as a full-time firefighter, he stayed plenty busy. Didn't take much time for a personal life, thanks to a bitch of an ex who did a number on him when he was finishing his stint in the Air Force.

Then he met Lizzie.

Oh, my brother tried to fight their connection, but it was too strong. He crumbled like a house of cards and fell head over heels in love with her. Now, they are dating and talking about getting a dog. She wants a loyal companion she can bring to work, and he likes the idea of her having one to protect her while he's not here. Rumor has it they're going to the shelter next week to pick one out, and I'm pretty certain that means they'll be living at the same home sooner than later.

Lizzie lives in the apartment above the bar, and even though she's put a lot of time and money into fixing it up, I'm sure she'd much rather move to Collin's place when the time is right. Though, I think they stay upstairs a lot, thanks to the convenience of its location. All I know is my brother's completely smitten with the woman, and even though I don't necessarily have firsthand understanding of it, I'm happy for him.

"Here," Lizzie states, handing me a bottle of my favorite beer after I tear down the cardboard cases.

"Well, if this is my reward for helping out, I'm all yours," I state with a wink and a smile.

She rolls her eyes, clearly on to my game. "Go hit on some poor unsuspecting woman."

With a Cheshire grin, I boast, "On it, Lizard. Don't wait up for me."

Her laughter follows me as I take off to the bin in the dry storage room where they place the broken-down cardboard boxes. Once I've deposited them, I grab my beer and return to the bar. Johnny Cash plays loudly through the speakers as I worm my way to the side where the pool table is located.

A group I know well is over there, playing a game and shooting the shit. Before I even get close enough to hear them, I know the trash talk is high. And the biggest culprit? That'd be my younger sister, Charli. She's ruthless when it comes to running her mouth in a game of...well, anything. Pool, darts, football...everything. She's a menace.

"Hey," I holler when I join everyone in the corner we've claimed.

"Cade!" my oldest friend, Alex, greets. "Get over here. Your sister is kicking Wyatt's ass."

Charli smiles proudly before lining up her next shot and sinking the eight ball with ease.

"She fucking cheats," Wyatt grumbles, dropping his stick on the table. I don't fail to notice there are five or six of his striped balls left on the table.

"Don't be a sore loser, Larimore," she chastises, narrowing her eyes and holding out her hand.

"Whatever, Miller." He pulls a ten out of his pocket and hands it over.

"Thank you," she sings, taking her winnings and sliding it inside the pocket of her jeans. "Who's next to lose ten bucks?"

"'I'm your Huckleberry,'" Quinn announces, quoting the infamous Doc Holliday line from the movie *Tombstone* as he stands up from his stool and makes his way toward the table. Quinn has been our youngest brother's best friend since he was little. Where one went, the other was closely behind.

Quinn didn't come from the best homelife and spent a lot of time with all of us, and because of that, our youngest brother and his sidekick used to love bugging the hell out of us, especially Charli. Quinn is an expert at pushing her buttons, and I can't wait to watch the show, because something tells me these two might come to blows by the end of their game. Figuratively speaking, of course. Neither would ever resort to physical violence.

There are four Miller kids, and I suppose, technically, I'm second in line. But only by five minutes. My identical twin, Collin, was born first, followed very closely by yours truly. Then, three years later, our sister, Charlotte, or Charli as we've always called her, came along. Then, when we thought our family was perfect as it was, my parents announced Camden's addition to our family.

I wanted a puppy, but whatever.

Turns out, I have three best friends for life. We've all been there for each other in ways I'll never be able to truly appreciate. We're tight, and I know a big part of that is thanks to the way we were raised and the fact we're from a great small town, where everyone butts their nose right into your business and doesn't even apologize for it. Sure, it can be annoying at times, but I'd rather live here than some big city any day of the week.

I watch Charli line up her break. "You're not going to do it like that, are you?" Quinn teases.

My sister doesn't even glance up as she replies, "Yep, sure am. Now, shut your piehole before one of these balls accidentally flies off the table and nails you in the giblets."

I bark out a laugh, knowing it wouldn't be an accident at all.

"Protect the McNuggets," Camden hollers through his cackle.

Quinn doesn't seem concerned, however. He just smiles at Charli and waits for her to shoot.

I watch them play, while catching up with Alex. I've been working six days a week, so to finally be able to go out and unwind a little is much needed. When you do road construction, summer and fall are your busiest times of the year, and this season is no different. We've been paving two six-mile stretches of the interstate, all four lanes plus bridge and overpass work. It's a year-long job in total, and it should keep me busy until the snow flies later this year.

"How's work?" he asks.

I take a swig of beer. "Busy."

"I bet, but I drove through earlier this week, and when it's all done, gonna be a damn nice road to travel."

I nod. "It will. That overpass has needed a facelift for a long damn time."

"No kidding," he mutters. "Bet the overtime is nice."

I don't even reply, because he knows it is. Anytime you get a chance to throw a little extra cash in the bank is a plus. I don't spend excessively, but I do enjoy riding four-wheelers with my family and friends. We take a few trips to a couple of riding parks, usually on those long, holiday weekends. Plus, I have a small boat I like to take to a local lake and fish. Not overly expensive hobbies, but it all adds up.

"How's work going for you?" I ask.

"It's not bad. Definitely keeping busy as harvest approaches. All the farmers are getting their shit in order, so I've been doing some machinery repairs," he starts, jumping into a story about a local farmer who needed a pretty big weld on his corn head. Alex is a welder, and a damn good one. He started off working for a local company and eventually branched out on his own. He's crazy-busy himself, working six or seven days a week.

I listen to his story, but my eyes are drawn to the entrance when the door opens. A woman I know from town walks in, but the one who trails behind her has my complete attention. She's…stunning. Long dark hair I can practically feel slide between my fingers and an hourglass body made for my hands. She's wearing cutoff shorts, a navy-blue tank top, and tan sandals, and the best part is she doesn't even look like she's trying. Half the women in here have their tits hanging out, and their clothes painted on, but this woman looks a touch classier, her beauty completely natural.

Then, she laughs, and my heart tries to pound right out of my chest. Even from across the room, I can hear the lightness of her giggle and see the beauty of her smile as she makes her way toward the bar with her friend. As if she can feel my eyes on her, she slowly turns around and scans the room, and I'll never forget the way my breath halts in my chest as our eyes connect.

Brown.

Dark eyes like rich chocolate.

Like a moth to a flame, I'm pulled toward her, almost hypnotically.

"Who's that?"

I blink a few times, registering Alex's question. Without looking away, I reply, "I don't know."

The beauty looks away first, her attention returning to her friend.

"That's Allison Cartright, isn't it?" he asks, referring to the woman I know. She was a few years younger than me in school, maybe the class behind Charli.

"Yeah."

"Her friend is hot."

"Don't even think about it," I state, not even caring if I sound a little harsh.

Alex chuckles beside me and grabs my shoulder. "Well, happy hunting, my friend. If she turns you down, let me know. She's free rein after that."

His stupid comment doesn't warrant a reply. My eyes land back on the beauty at the bar. Lizzie greets them warmly and hands both ladies a drink. Allison hands over some cash and waves off the change. Then, they move farther into the room, finding a vacant small round table off to the side, and like the stalker I apparently am, I continue to watch.

"Yo, brother, wipe your chin. You're starting to drool," Camden announces right before he shoves his elbow into my gut.

I give him my full attention. "Don't make me kick your ass in front of your friends."

He snorts a laugh and shakes his head. "Lizzie would have your ass." He pauses before adding, "You know what? Go ahead and try it. I think I'd like to watch that show."

"Me too," Charli chimes in, smiling widely.

"I've heard enough from the peanut gallery," I say, setting my beer down on a nearby table. I ignore their comments as I head toward where the beautiful woman is sitting. I nod at a few patrons I know—okay, fine, I pretty much know everyone—and even though a few try to engage in conversation, I offer a polite smile and keep moving toward my destination.

When I reach their table, I flash one of my most charming grins. This baby has gotten me out of some trouble over the years—and maybe into a little trouble too. "Good evening, ladies."

The brunette who's captured my attention gives me a friendly smile. "Hi."

Extending my hand, I take hers when she offers it. "Cade Miller."

She doesn't blush or turn on her own charm as I bring her hand to my mouth and place a gentle kiss against her knuckles. "Oaklee."

"A beautiful name for a beautiful woman."

The corner of her mouth curls up. "Does that line actually work?"

She catches me off guard for a slight second, mostly because I can tell she's not asking to flirt. "Sometimes," I reply honestly, pulling out the third chair at the table and taking a seat. To her friend, I ask, "How have you been, Allison?"

"Good," she replies, hiding a smile. "You?"

"Can't complain." I return my gaze back to Oaklee. "Wanna dance?"

She glances around the room. "No one is dancing," she points out, as an old Tim McGraw song plays on the jukebox.

I shrug. "I'm more of a leader than a follower."

"I'm sure you are," she retorts, a faint little smile on her kissable lips.

"So, what do you say, Oaklee? Wanna dance?"

She opens her mouth and hesitates in whatever response she was going to give. "Sorry, but I'm dating someone."

I bring my hand up to cover my heart. "You wound me."

She snorts and glances at her friend. "I highly doubt that."

"No, you do. See, I came over here because you look like you love me."

She barks out a laugh, throwing her head back in the process. My dick twitches in my pants and my hands itch to slide through her hair. It looks so soft and inviting, and all I can think about is feeling it slip through my fingers. "Isn't that a country song?"

I nod. "Sadly, they stole the idea from me."

She shakes her head, clearly not buying what I'm trying to sell. "Copyright infringement is no laughing matter."

"You're right, it isn't. Maybe I'll look into it. Can you file a lawsuit based on a song concept?"

Grinning, she shakes her head. "I don't think so."

I tsk. "Well, too bad for me." I adjust my position in my chair, since my pants feel a little snugger than they did earlier, and ask, "So what brings you to town?"

"A job," she replies, taking a drink of her beer.

"What kind of job?"

"I'm a nurse," she confirms. "Allison and I went to nursing school together, and she called me last week and told me about the vacancy at the clinic here in town. I had an interview with the clinical director earlier today." Dina oversees all the clinics and moves from clinic to clinic throughout the workweek, depending on where she's needed.

"And?" I ask, really hoping she's about to tell me she was offered the position.

"And I'll let them know Monday if I'm accepting the position," she tells me before glancing to her friend.

"She will," Allison states proudly, looking at her friend. "You'll be a huge asset. You have great bedside manner, are personable, and are easy to work with."

"Good bedside manner, huh? Did you know I'm looking for a personal nurse?" Of course, I waggle my eyebrows.

She rolls her beautiful brown eyes. "Charming."

"Thank you," I boast, earning a laugh from both ladies. "So, when you take this job, you'll be working here? Moving here? Both?"

Oaklee doesn't reply for a few seconds, as if gauging how much of her personal life she wants to give out. Honestly, I'd rather her be a bit private and selective than giving all her information to a virtual stranger. "I would be relocating," is all she says.

"Great! I'm an expert on Cooper Town, and I make a great tour guide."

She smirks a little, taking a small drink. "I have Allison, who is also an expert on Cooper Town."

"Yes, but I'm way better looking," I reply with a cheeky grin. Turning to Allison, I add, "No offense."

She barks out a laugh. "None taken, actually. You know, Cade, I've never seen a man work so hard for a phone number in my life."

I feign shock. "I haven't even asked for her phone number, Allison."

"Yet."

Flashing a charming grin, I agree, "Yet." Returning my gaze to Oaklee, I say, "So what do you say? Phone number?"

She turns to her friend and asks, "Didn't I tell him I was seeing someone already?"

Allison nods. "You did."

"Huh, I thought so," Oaklee states.

Leaning forward, I place my elbows on the table and hold her eyes. "I get it. All I'm gonna say is, when that guy singles you up, I better be your first call."

The corner of her mouth curls up. "I think that's another country song."

I huff out a deep breath. "Damn country artists, always stealing my lines."

She leans back into her chair, taking me in. I can practically see her wheels spinning. I'm sure she thinks I'm just another drunk guy in a bar, hitting on her, and while part of that may be accurate, I'm not drunk. I'm just a man who finds her incredibly attractive and would love the opportunity to get to know her better.

But I'm also not one to poach another man's woman. If she's in a relationship, then I'm out. However, I'll be waiting, biding my time, because something tells me that guy has no idea what kind of a gem he truly has. If he did, he would have traveled to town with her and would be here, if anything to keep the assholes like me from hitting on his girl.

Standing up, I give her my full attention. "The best part of my night has been meeting you, lovely Oaklee." I reach for her hand and bring it to my lips, placing a gentle kiss on her knuckles. "I'll see you around."

"Have a good evening," she replies, her smile both playful and full of shock by everything that's transpired. I'm sure it's not every day she has some guy basically throw himself at her.

I walk to the bar and hold up my finger to Collin, indicating I'd like another beer. Leaning my elbow against the bar, I turn my attention back to the table I just walked away from and smile when I see two brown eyes.

She watched me walk away.

In those eyes, I see it.

Interest.

She may have a boyfriend, and it may not happen right now, but Oaklee Last Name Unknown will be mine.

I know it.

CHAPTER TWO

Oaklee

"UMMM...IS THAT GUY FOR REAL?"

Allison snorts before grabbing her drink and sipping. "Oh, he is. Cade is the king flirt and completely full of himself. From what I've seen, he's harmless though."

I glance back over my shoulder, feeling his intense blue eyes on me. He's leaning against the bar, sipping from a beer bottle. His gaze is locked on mine as his twin brother talks to him. He has to be his twin, because they're identical. Well, nearly identical, though their hair is cut a bit different and Cade looks a bit more sun-kissed and weathered than his brother.

"So, tell me about your boyfriend," Allison states, drawing me away from the man who has completely captured my attention.

I stifle a sigh and paste on a wide smile. "He's originally from Cincinnati, the youngest of five kids. He moved to North Ridge for his residency in medical school and stayed."

"A doctor," she replies with a beaming smile. "How long have you been dating?"

I swallow over the sudden lump in my throat. "Six years, off and on."

Her eyes widen. "That's quite a while."

I nod.

"Yeah. I had just graduated nursing school, and he was starting med school. He was awarded an internship in rural medicine and began shadowing the physicians at the clinic I was working at. We hit it off right away, but between his schooling and our work schedules, it's been difficult to maintain our relationship," I tell her, my throat thick with emotion as I think back over the last six years.

If I'm being honest, I've felt like this relationship reached a dead end about four months ago, and I was preparing to end it with him. He started working at North Ridge Medical and moved, leaving me behind in a lonely apartment and surrounded by the dreams I always wanted but kept putting off. We would go days and days without communication. Well, he wouldn't communicate. My texts went unanswered, and my calls not returned for small stretches of time, and I tried not to complain. I knew he was busy. He was working his ass off, every day reaching for the degree he strived to achieve. He rarely invited me to join him for the weekend, because he was either working or wanted to sleep.

Then, during one of our rare phone conversations, he asked me to move.

Not with him, of course, because he has a small studio apartment near the hospital used by medical staff, but whatever.

Finally, I felt like a future staring at us both was within my grasp.

It took a little time to make it all happen. I had to contact my apartment manager and get out of my lease. Fortunately, living near a college and hospital made it easy. They allowed me to break my contract without a hefty fee, so all I had left was to quit my job and pack up my belongings.

When Allison reached out to tell me about the available RN position at North Ridge Medical of Cooper Town, a short twenty-minute drive from North Ridge, where Lance was working and living, I readily submitted my résumé. The smaller, neighboring town appealed to me much more than the bigger city, even though there were job listings posted for the hospital itself. However, I wanted to avoid working directly with Lance.

It's always been important to me to maintain a boundary between personal and professional. Just because I date someone doesn't mean I want to work with them on a daily basis.

I've seen too much reality TV to put myself through that.

"I can understand that. Relationships are hard regardless. I can't imagine adding distance and crazy-busy jobs on top of it," she replies.

I nod, taking another drink of my beer. "How about you? Anyone special you're seeing?" I ask, loving catching up with an old friend.

"Not right now. After my marriage to Zack ended, I've been hesitant to get back on the horse again," she says with a chuckle. "Plus, I know everyone here, and frankly, there's just no single guys I'm interested in."

I glance back over my shoulder toward Cade, who is still standing at the bar talking to his twin brother and the woman bartender. As if sensing my eyes, he glances toward me and smiles. "What about Cade?" I ask, returning my attention to my friend.

"Uhh, no thanks. He always seemed like a good guy, but he's not my type."

Handsome with a killer smile and body isn't your type?

I don't reply, just take a few seconds to enjoy the atmosphere. Allison suggested we get together for dinner and a few drinks, and I'm glad she recommended this place. The other bar didn't sound too bad, but I prefer the casual, laid-back vibe I get from here. Plus, the eye candy isn't terrible either.

The moment I think it, I feel guilty. Lance seems to be making more of an effort lately where our relationship is concerned, and I should focus on that, not the hot guy across the bar. Of course, I'm not doing anything wrong. I turned down every advance Cade made, including his offer to dance, and I told him I'm in a relationship. While he might have flirted a bit, he seemed to respect that enough not to make an ass out of himself or make our exchange uncomfortable. He's just a flirt, that much is evident, and there's nothing I can do about it.

We spend the next forty-five minutes catching up, and I have to be honest, I feel very comfortable here, and I'm not just referring to the bar. The entire town feels like home, and I've only been here since this morning.

When the clinical manager for the hospital, Dina, called me to set up the interview, the doctor in charge of the clinic agreed to meet with me after he was done seeing patients on a Saturday. That worked out perfectly for me, so I wasn't required to take any time off from my other job. Even though they know I'm leaving and relocating, I wanted to avoid putting them in a bind during a workday.

So, I arrived in town just before noon and took a quick little drive through the downtown area before locating the clinic where I was interviewing. In addition to Dina, I met with Dr. Houston, who is the physician I would be working with daily, and it was a great interview. They presented an offer on the spot and granted me the rest of the weekend to think about it, with the promise of calling them Monday to either accept or decline.

I'll be accepting.

The only reason I didn't do it when I met with them was because these types of things truly deserve some thought and consideration, but I have already made up my mind. It's less money than I am making at my current position, but the cost of living is less here in Cooper Town than in the city, but it's still a generous nursing salary.

"Hey, Allison!"

We both look over to the two women who approached the table. "Charli, hi." To me, she says, "Oaklee, this is Charli Miller and Sommer Hughes, two of Cooper Town's lifers. Ladies, this is Oaklee Daniels. I went to nursing school with her, and fingers crossed, she'll be working at the clinic with me now that Ruth has retired."

"Welcome to town," Charli states, pulling out one of the two remaining chairs and taking a seat without being invited.

"Thank you," I respond. "It seems like a good place, so far."

Sommer jumps into the conversation. "It is. I work at the pharmacy here in town, and I just can't imagine living and working anywhere else. Small towns are the best."

"I've only ever lived in the city, so this is a whole new experience for me. But I'm up to the challenge."

Allison's eyes widen. "Does that mean you're going to accept the job?"

I can't even fight the smile. "Possibly," I say, vaguely. If I'm going to accept the job, the clinic should be the first to know.

I'd love to tell Lance, but he's working at the hospital today, and the text I sent informing him the interview went well, and they offered me the job went unanswered. Not that I'm too surprised by that. I know he's incredibly busy, but I thought perhaps he might call me during a break or something.

"I would love to be able to work with you," Allison gushes. "And you're going to love it here in Cooper Town."

"So, Oaklee, what's your story?" Charli asks, her blue eyes sparkling with curiosity.

"Not much to tell, really. I grew up in Anderson Township, a suburb of Cincinnati. I was raised by my grandparents and put myself through nursing school. I've worked around Cincinnati since."

"Why Cooper Town?" Sommer asks, both seeming genuinely interested.

I clear my throat. "A guy, of course," I reply with a chuckle.

Charli's eyes widen. "Oh, this I gotta hear," she states, leaning forward as if to hang on my every word.

Lifting my shoulders, I keep it simple. "I met Lance not too long after I graduated nursing school. He was in med school and doing an internship at the clinic I was working at. We hit it off and started dating."

"So, he's here?" Sommer asks.

"Well, he's in North Ridge. He's doing his residency there."

"That would explain why my brother looked heartbroken as he walked away and keeps staring at you with sad puppy dog eyes." Charli is grinning from ear to ear.

"Your brother?" I ask, confused.

"Cade."

"He's your brother?" I ask, shocked by this revelation.

"Yeah, don't hold it against me," she sasses with a chuckle. "No, he's a good guy. He's the outgoing one, which I'm sure you've already discovered. Collin, the other twin behind the bar, is the quiet, broody type."

Interesting...

"Anyway, I heard he was coming over here to, most likely, hit on you, and now he's standing at the bar looking like someone kicked his puppy."

I roll my eyes. "I'm sure he's fine. His ego is big enough to pad the fall."

Charli barks out a laugh. "Oh, I like you, Oaklee. We're gonna be friends."

I can't help but smile, noticing how she made a statement, as if there was no other option. Honestly? I think I'd like to be her friend too. She's outgoing and blunt but seems friendly enough. I'll probably ask Allison about her, but I can truly see us becoming friends.

And do you know what?

This is what I need.

Friends.

Not that I don't have friends back home, but all of them are married and building families, or they're still single and enjoying a different lifestyle than what I want. I don't mind going out and enjoying an evening, but I realize very quickly The Tipsy Lizard is a little more my scene—not clubs or crowded college bars.

And I've felt stuck right smack-dab between them for quite a while.

"So, are you moving with your boyfriend?" Sommer asks, sipping a mixed drink.

My throat is suddenly dry. "No, not yet," I reply, glancing around the room. "He's in a tiny studio near the hospital, but eventually, that's the plan. I've started looking for my own apartment here, temporarily. If I can sign a one-year rental agreement, that would be perfect."

Something that looks like worry, or maybe confusion, flashes in her eyes, but she quickly hides it. "That makes sense. If you need help, let me know."

"Actually, I might have a lead for you. My parents own a couple rentals, and one of their tenants just moved out. Mom was saying she needed to clean it up and do some touch-up hole patching and painting, but I'm sure it could be available pretty quickly," Sommer chimes in.

"Really?" I lean forward, giving her my complete attention.

"Yep. Hold on," she replies, pulling out her cell phone. "Let me just shoot my mom a message and see if that's still the case. I'd hate to get your hopes up if she's already talked to someone about renting it out."

I nod, trying not to get too excited about having a lead for a rental so quickly. Yes, I've looked online but haven't found too many options listed. I can look in North Ridge or other surrounding towns, but am hoping to find something close to work, so I could walk during the nicer months. I love being outside and try to take advantage of it as much as possible.

"How long are you in town?" Sommer asks without looking up from her screen.

"Until tomorrow. I'm staying at the Cooper Town Inn," I tell them, instantly feeling all eyes return to me.

"Wait. You're not staying with your boyfriend?" Charli asks, clearly confused by this detail.

"Umm, no. He's working all weekend and isn't allowed to have guests like that in their company studios," I reply casually, even though it feels wrong and still irritates me. It's not like I'm looking to stay for a week or two. It's one night, and we're dating. I don't understand why it's an issue. I'm sure if he were to go to the property manager and explain the situation they'd understand and allow it, but he didn't want to ruffle feathers so early in his residency.

"That's stupid," Charli declares, making Allison smile. She'd already made her opinion on the matter clear earlier when we talked about it over dinner but hasn't said much about it since. We became close during nursing school, but our communication became less and less over the years. It wasn't until she reached out and we reconnected.

"Are you interested in meeting my mom at the rental in the morning? She said any time is good with her," Sommer states.

My heart starts to beat in my chest a little harder as excitement fills me. "Of course. I'd love to," I rush out, unable to keep my eagerness at bay.

"Perfect," she states, typing out her reply. "What time?"

"Nine?"

"Yep," Sommer agrees, adding that to her message. "Done."

"Wow, I can't believe that happened," I reply, taking another drink and feeling myself relax even more.

"It's a cute little house," Sommer announces. "One bedroom, eat-in kitchen, and a decent-sized bathroom. There's a laundry room off the kitchen, one car attached garage, and a fenced-in backyard."

My eyes widen. "Wow, I assumed it was an apartment or something."

"Nope. Mom and Dad own a few houses in town. There are apartments, but I wouldn't suggest renting from them. They're a revolving door of tenants, because they're cheaply made and the upkeep is trash. There are also a few condos near the high school, but those rarely have openings. Give me your number, and I'll text you the address."

When I share my contact information with her, Charli goes ahead and asks for it too. "Now we can keep in touch. When you officially move, let us know, and we'll come help."

I smile, slipping my phone back in my pocket and feeling pretty good about my potential move here. You'd never get this kind of warmth in the city. Not only does everyone already feel like a friend, but they're going out of their way to include me. I don't feel like an outsider looking in.

"Excuse me, I'm going to use the restroom," I state before standing up.

"Do you want another drink?" Charli asks.

"Just water?"

She nods. "Lizzie makes delicious nonalcoholic drinks too. I suggest the piña colada, if you like coconut."

"Oh, that sounds good. I'll try that," I reply before making my way to the hallway and slipping inside the restroom. There are two other women in there, standing at the mirror and complimenting each other on their outfits. I move to the available stall, trying not to listen to their conversation, but not really able to avoid it.

"I heard he's seeing someone from out of town," one says.

"Because he's already dated everyone from *in* town," the second replies with a chuckle.

I finish my business and exit the stall. As I approach the sinks, they step out of the restroom, leaving me to it. I wash my hands and dry them on a paper towel, and the moment I pull open the door, I practically walk straight into a wall.

No, not a wall exactly.

A wall of muscle.

"Miss me already?" Cade asks, grinning widely.

"Like a cold," I tease, earning a laugh.

"If you're under the weather, I'd be happy to keep you comfortable and warm," he says, waggling his eyebrows.

I snort and shake my head. "You're incorrigible."

"True story," he replies, sobering. "Here."

"What's this?" I ask, taking the napkin he offers.

He just grins, waiting for me to look. I realize quickly it's a phone number.

His phone number.

"I know you said you were seeing someone, so I'm not asking you for your number. I'm a lot of things, but I don't poach another man's woman. However, if you were to break up, well, then you're free game." He points to the napkin. "And you can call me. Or text. I'm not picky."

I open my mouth, prepared to hand him back the napkin, but nothing comes out.

"When he singles you up, Oaklee, give me a call."

He walks away with a grin, leaving me standing in the hallway, staring after his retreating body. I clear my throat, shove the napkin into my pocket, and head back to my table. Just as I approach it, I spot Cade at the jukebox. He searches the screen for a minute, and the moment the Trisha Yearwood song is over, a new one starts.

I recognize it instantly.

Our eyes connect as the lyrics start, and even though I've heard this song a few times before, it's the first time I actually start listening to the words. The sexiest grin spreads across his lips and he starts belting out the words, drawing everyone's attention. A few people sing along, but my attention is riveted on the man watching me.

"Oh my God, he's got it so bad. He's ridiculous," Charli mutters before laughing.

I'm lost in a sea of ocean-blue eyes with a phone number burning a hole in my pocket. I won't call it, of course, not while I'm dating Lance. I'll probably toss the napkin in the trash when I get back to the hotel. I'm positive I won't ever use it, but it's a bit flattering, nonetheless.

Shaking my head, I try to push all thoughts of Cade's antics out of my head.

That's a tad difficult, considering he's still standing at the jukebox, belting out Jordan Davis's "Singles You Up."

Maybe I'll have another alcoholic drink after all…

CHAPTER THREE

Cade

One Month Later

"You goin' out tonight?" Dalton asks as he finishes loading hand tools into the bed of his work truck.

I can't help but smile. "Yep."

Dalton raises an eyebrow as he glances my way. "There are a lot of issues that arise at a lady's paint night…or is this about the plethora of ladies in attendance?"

The truth is, Lizzie runs a great place. I don't foresee any issues happening, but while Collin is working his other job, I like to make my presence known on the weekends. The idiots do make appearances, especially now that some of Lizzie's special events have garnered so much attention. According to my brother, her paint nights are sold out almost as quickly as she posts them, and the other things she's trying are gaining as much attention, like her Little Black Dress Night, coming soon, and her weekly book club.

"Maybe I'll join you," he says, tossing the last few tools into his truck and closing the tailgate.

I snort. "Bethany won't let that happen. Last time we went out for a beer you passed out naked in the kiddie pool on the back deck."

He makes a face. "Yeah, not my finest moment, but I was hot and wanted to cool off."

"You're lucky you didn't drown," I reply, climbing into the cab of my truck and rolling down the window.

"That's what Bethany said," he grumbles. "Of course, it didn't help Jacob was the one who found me."

I bark out a laugh, loving this story so much. "Maybe next time don't leave the blinds at the sliding glass doors open."

"Anyway, I might be able to come up for a beer. I don't think we have anything planned tonight," he starts, holding up his hand. "No hard shit though."

I snort. "Says the man who orders shots of Fireball the moment we cross the threshold."

He shivers. "Nope. Not happening. I had to tell Bethany no more cinnamon candles in the house. Every time she'd light one, I could taste that shit and want to barf."

Shutting the door to my truck, I fire up the engine. The air blasting at my face is hot, causing me to turn it down. "Don't piss off Bethany, but if you can get out of the house for an hour, I'll be up there."

He nods before throwing a wave and climbing into his own truck.

I pull out of the laydown yard and head for home, ready for a shower and a cold beer. I love my job, and for the most part, the heat doesn't bother me. I'd been in worse conditions when I was in the Marines. Sweating your balls off in the damn desert isn't for the faint of heart, that's for sure.

I'm a heavy equipment operator for the local construction company. While I can jump in just about any piece of equipment we have, I spend the majority of my time on a paver, laying asphalt. It's monotonous most of the time, but I'm damn good at it. I have the focus to keep the machine moving straight, which is actually a lot harder than you'd think.

The late September sun is starting to fall, the temperatures finally starting to drop. "Yeah," I tell him, setting my lunch box in the cab of my own work truck. "Lizzie's doing one of her paint nights tonight at the bar, and Collin is on shift at the firehouse this weekend, so I'll head up later and just make sure everything's okay."

But I'm also damn good in an excavator. When I'm not on the paver, I dig. My time in the military, removing obstacles in our path, usually with some sort of blast, taught me I much prefer to rebuild than destroy. I enjoyed my time as a combat engineer, but being in a machine and helping create something from nothing is exactly where I'm supposed to be in life.

When I pull into my driveway, I park in front of the garage and jump out. We've hit our busy season at work, so even though I've been working six days a week for the last month, and I could easily stay in and sleep until Tuesday, I know I'll head for Lizzie's bar. I probably won't even drink a lot. Maybe one or two and that'll be it. As tired as I am, I don't want to add a hangover on top of my exhaustion.

I run through the shower and dress in a pair of clean jeans and an AC/DC T-shirt. I shove my feet into boots and stop in the kitchen to reheat some leftovers. I'm used to eating a quick ham and cheese or roast beef sandwich on the go at work, so when I'm home, I prefer to cook a decent meal. I love to grill, even if I'm not the best chef. Turns out, throwing a good seasoning on it and slow cooking over open flames can cook about any meat to perfection.

After I eat some reheated chicken and vegetables, I grab my wallet and keys and head back out. It's pushing seven, which means the paint night has already started. It doesn't take much time to get to The Tipsy Lizard in downtown Cooper Town, mostly because this town is less than a mile long from city limit to city limit. A decent number of the four thousand residents who call Cooper Town home live just outside of city limits, thanks to the farms and a few rural subdivisions.

Like the one I live in.

Eight houses in a horseshoe, surrounded by trees and with a creek running alongside the east edge. I'm fortunate to have the house closest to the water, and even though I technically have neighbors, the houses aren't that close. The lots are big, and the tree coverage and landscaping provide space and privacy. It's a great place to live, and I was damn lucky to snatch this house up when it went on the market a year ago.

I make my way into town, the windows down so the warm summer breeze blows through the cab. I love being outside. Camping, fishing, four wheeling—anything I can do to be outdoors. That's probably one of the reasons why I chose the career I did. The heat of summer and the cold of early spring and late fall don't bother me.

What does bother me is not working in the winter. I need to stay active, to keep myself busy. I don't do well with free time, so I keep busy during the off-season with side work. I help my buddy at the farm a lot, which is right up my alley. The only thing I don't like is smelling like cow shit at the end of the day, but I don't complain much. Truth is, I just like working, and I'll do it as long as I'm physically able.

I don't bother trying to find a parking spot on the main drag, mostly because I know they'll all be taken by the women attending paint night. Instead, I park around back where Lizzie and other employees park and then walk around to the front of the building. The back entrance is more of an emergency exit or one used to get in and out of the apartment above.

Fully expecting to hear some classic country playing through the speakers, all I hear when I open the front entrance is women laughing. My eyes scan the room and quickly land on the tables off to the right. They're full of laughing women, all painting their masterpieces while having a drink or enjoying some of Lizzie's appetizers. She always makes a big spread of food for her guests, including some of the regulars in attendance too.

Even though I spot my sister, Sommer, and a few others I know at the tables, I head for the bar to grab a drink. Jani is working and offers a friendly smile. "Hey, Cade. What can I getcha?"

"All American bottle, please," I reply.

As she walks away to grab my drink, I throw a wave to a handful of the regulars at the bar. Tom, Larry, and Gus are there, sipping on their drinks and enjoying a plate of food.

"I started you a tab," Jani says, twisting off the bottle top and setting the drink in front of me.

"Thanks," I reply, taking my first drink of cold beer before heading down to where the guys sit. "Evening, gentlemen."

"Hey, Cade!" Tom hollers, holding up his beer in salute.

"Get over there and try some of Lizzie's food. The little wienies wrapped in bacon are to die for," Larry states, stabbing one with a toothpick and popping it into his mouth.

"I'll do that," I confirm, just as the woman herself walks around the corner from the back carrying a tray of cookies. "Excuse me."

I take the few steps to where she's standing, adding homemade sugar cookies to a platter. "Hey," she practically sings the moment she spots me. "I was wondering if you'd show up."

"I'll always show up for you," I tease in a flirting tone before bending down to place a friendly kiss on her cheek.

She snorts and shakes her head. "Your brother's not here," she replies, the insinuation I only do that to make him jealous heavy.

She's not wrong. I do love to say and do things like that to piss him off. Usually when I kiss her cheek, he comes over and wipes it off before replacing it with a kiss of his own. Makes me smile—and want to do it more every time it happens.

"I know, but word will get back to him," I boast.

Lizzie rolls her eyes. "He's gonna start texting me any minute, isn't he." It's not a question, and it makes me laugh.

"Probably. Tell him I took advantage of him not being here, or that I'm taking good care of you."

She shakes her head. "No way. I'm not poking the bear."

Grabbing my phone from my pocket, I pull up the texting app. "Fine, I'll do it."

She reaches for my phone, trying to pull it out of my hand. "Don't you dare!"

"Fine," I agree, putting away my phone but only so I can grab a plate of food. Teasing my twin will come after I try those bacon-wrapped wienies.

"Help yourself. I always make more than enough."

"I think I'll do that," I say, grabbing a plate and loading it with her delicious food.

"I'm gonna go check on everyone painting. We'll catch up soon," she says, taking the empty container from the cookies with her as she walks off to where the ladies are painting.

Making my way back to the bar, I head toward the opposite end, where there's several empty seats and a baseball game on the television. Just as I sit down and pop my first bacon-wrapped treat in my mouth, the door behind me opens. I glance over and see our youngest brother walk in.

"Hey," Camden greets as he joins me.

"Hey. Lizzie made food." I smear some sort of cream cheese dip on a cracker and pop it in my mouth.

"I'm gonna go grab some. I'm starving. Will you get me a beer when Jani comes over?"

Since my mouth is full, I just wave, letting him know I've got him.

Jani catches my attention. "All American bottle?" When I nod, she asks, "You ready for another?"

"Nope, I'm good," I reply after swallowing my food.

She sets Camden's drink on the bar. "I'll start him a tab too."

"Thanks, Jani."

"Larry told me to grab the little cocktail wieners," my youngest brother states as he sets his plate on the bar and slides onto a stool. "They're almost gone."

"They're pretty good," I confirm, placing a piece of weird cheese with red things in it on a cracker and taking a bite. It's surprisingly sweet and tastes delicious, even though I have no idea what it is. "Where's Q?"

He takes a drink of his beer and starts building a cracker with cheese and salami. "His dad fell and broke his leg earlier today. He's at the hospital with his stepmom. I guess they're going to do surgery tonight to set it."

"Damn, that's too bad."

"Yeah. Let's just hope Q and his stepmom don't get into an argument in the waiting room," Camden mumbles, taking another bite of food.

There's no love lost there. Quinn's parents had a terrible relationship when he was growing up, and it really affected his childhood. His dad has been married a few times over the years, and his latest wife, Staci, is around Quinn's age. Staci has two kids already but doesn't actually have custody of them. Long dramatic story, and I know Q tries to stay as far away from the drama as he possibly can.

"Maybe you should go sit with him," I suggest.

Camden snorts. "Yeah, no thank you. Last time I was with Q and we ran into them, I'm pretty sure Staci was trying to get me to come back to their apartment for a threesome and drugs."

My eyes widen in shock, even though I'm not sure why. Nothing surrounding Jim and Staci surprise me anymore. "Okay, then probably a good thing to stay away."

"Yeah," he mutters, shaking his head. "You work today?"

We spend the next ten minutes or so chatting about work before Charli comes over to say hello. "What are you two doing here?"

"Came to keep an eye on you," I tell her.

She snorts. "How much trouble could I get into during paint night?"

I can't help but chuckle. "Are you kidding? Aren't you the one who called Whitney a walking VD?"

She smiles sweetly and bats her eyelashes. "If it walks like a venereal disease and talks like one, it must be a venereal disease."

Camden laughs. "I don't think that's how the saying goes."

Our sister shrugs her shoulders. "Anyway..."

I listen to Charli tell Camden all about the latest gossip, so-and-so is sleeping with so-and-so behind so-and-so's back, but my attention is drawn to Lizzie as she makes her way to the walk-in fridge, most likely to stock coolers. Getting up, I head toward the door and step inside just as she's about to lift two cases of beer. "I'll get those," I tell her, slipping in beside her and retrieving the cases. They're not heavy, really. I know she's perfectly capable of carrying them to the bar and restocking the coolers, but I want to help.

She puts her hands on her hips. "I can get it."

"I know you can, Lizard, but that's why you keep me around. I'm more than just a pretty face. I'm the muscle too." With a wink, I push out of the fridge and head behind the bar. I don't even wait for her to join me, just open the first case and start stocking the beer.

She returns a minute later with a couple of twelve packs of another popular variety and fills the empty spot in the cooler. "Thank you," she says as I tear down the boxes and reach for the ones she's emptied and placed on the floor.

"You're welcome. I'll run these to the back," I tell her, earning an eye roll.

"You're just like your twin."

I feign disbelief. "I'm nothing like that ogre."

She rolls her eyes playfully once more but laughs. "Obviously," she mutters.

"I'm way better looking," I insist, throwing her a wink before walking to the back of the bar to where she keeps broken down boxes.

Returning to the main bar area, I approach where my seat is and overhear Charli and Lizzie talking. "I'm sad she had to cancel. I hope everything is okay," Lizzie says.

"Me too. I was looking forward to getting to know her better. Allison says she's doing great at work," Charli adds, her words really catching my attention.

"Who are we talking about?" I ask, popping a cracker into my mouth.

"Oaklee. You remember her, right?" my sister asks, smiling from ear to ear.

Oh, I remember Oaklee. The beautiful woman with dark hair and an hourglass figure. I gave her my number before I left that night, but she hasn't used it. Not that I expect her to right away. I mean, she's in a relationship, but that doesn't mean she can't reach out when that's run its course. "I remember."

"Anyway, she was supposed to come tonight, but she had to cancel. And Allison got sick, so she wasn't able to come. Fortunately, it was easy to fill their spots, right?"

Lizzie nods. "It was. I had a waitlist, but I really wish they could have come. I want to get to know them better, especially since Oaklee moved to town. I've only seen her that one time."

I want to ask what time she was referring to, but I already know.

My sister knows too, smirking at me. "Have you seen her?"

"Oaklee? Why would I?" I ask, taking a drink of my piss-warm beer.

"Uhh, because you have a thing for her."

"I don't have a thing," I counter.

"Right," she sings, drawing out the word.

"Maybe we should reach out and see if we can do lunch sometime," Lizzie suggests to Charli.

"Yes! I have Allison's number. I'll text her tomorrow to see how she's feeling and ask about lunch."

They keep talking about the possibility of lunch with Allison and Oaklee, and my mind keeps replaying the night I first saw her. While I haven't seen her since, she's definitely been on my mind more than a time or two in the last month, especially at night. Does it make me an asshole for lusting after someone else's girlfriend? Probably, but the fact remains.

Her memory is still with me.

Like a tattoo on my brain, she's there, silently waiting for me to close my eyes.

Then, she appears, vivid and very memorable.

Like clockwork.

And I sleep like a damn baby.

CHAPTER FOUR

Oaklee

My mind is spinning, just as it has since Friday night.

The night I decided to surprise Lance on one of his rare nights off and ended up being the one surprised.

After I got off work, I ran home and showered. I shaved my legs and threw on some of my sexiest panties, grabbed some food from the Chinese restaurant around the corner from his apartment, and knocked on his door. He wasn't expecting me—that much was obvious. He told me he was exhausted and just wanted to sleep until he had to wake up the next morning for another shift.

So imagine my surprise when the door opened and it was a woman. A woman who seemed just as surprised by my appearance at the door as I was by her answering it. I asked where Lance was. He was in the shower, of course.

And the woman?

Sabrina Dempsey, another resident physician at North Ridge and the woman he'd been sleeping with since he moved to town more than six months ago.

Now, when I look back, I can't help but wonder if I didn't know. Deep down, obviously. If I would have known, I would have ended it. But if I'm being completely honest, I can't even remember the last time we had sex. It was why I was surprising him at his apartment Friday night. I was…in the mood. Had been for a while, not that he'd realize that, since clearly, he was only concerned about his own needs.

But that's how it's always been with Lance.

Lance first, me second.

Always.

Now, here I sit, Sunday afternoon, and I'm just angry. Sure, I was hurt and upset Friday night, but now? I'm furious at him. At him stringing me along, and not just recently, but the entire time. Looking back, I see it now. The rose-colored glasses have come off, and I can see, plain as the nose on my face, that I've always been an afterthought. I should have listened to my gut and broke it off with him a few months back when said gut was telling me something was off.

But then he asked me to move to North Ridge with the intention of moving forward with a life together at some point.

And that's just it.

At some point.

He knew what I needed to hear, even if he didn't mean any of the words he said.

So, I moved, relocated to Cooper Town, took a job, and signed a one-year lease for a cute little rental house. I'm here for a year, whether I like it or not.

The problem is, I do like it.

I like Cooper Town.

I like working at the clinic.

I like my little rental house with the fenced-in backyard and the flower gardens.

I like spending time with Allison and getting to know the others I work with.

I was really looking forward to last night's paint event at The Tipsy

Lizard, but thanks to my douchebag now-ex-boyfriend, I didn't feel like going out. Instead, I gathered up every item I had at my place that belonged to Lance—which, surprisingly, wasn't much, considering we'd been together on and off for six years—and I went and dumped it all out on his Welcome mat. I woke with a one-word text.

Mature.

Mature? Fuck him and fuck maturity.

But that's par for the course, really. Lance did everything he could to blame me for his wandering eye—and penis—as if it were my fault he cheated.

The only silver lining to the entire blow-up was Sabrina ended up leaving, breaking it off with him too, since he had told her he broke up with me months ago.

I don't wish her ill. The poor woman was strung along and lied to as well, but that doesn't mean I want to get together with her and chat over iced coffees and cinnamon rolls. Fortunately for me, she works at the hospital in North Ridge, and while I work for a clinic under the same hospital, neither of the cheaters work in Cooper Town with me.

Thank God for small favors.

My phone chimes with a text, and I pray it's not from him. Not that he's messaged me since yesterday after finding his crap piled in front of his door, but whatever. Since I'd rather he not contact me at all, I'm relieved when I see Allison's name on the screen.

Allison: Hey, just checking on you.

Me: Doing fine.

Allison: That's good.

Me: How are you feeling?

Allison woke up yesterday morning with a bad cold, complete with head congestion, sore throat, and low-grade fever. She was disappointed to have to give up her seat at the paint night, and even though I didn't have a plan to tell anyone about Lance, I ended up spilling my guts via text message after asking her to cancel my seat too.

> Allison: Much better. I think the fever is gone, and I'm taking OTC meds for the congestion and sore throat.
>
> Me: At least it's not the flu bug going around.
>
> Allison: No kidding!
>
> Allison: Anyway, the other reason I'm messaging… Charli sent a text, asking if we wanted to meet her and Lizzie for lunch soon. Doc is off Tuesday afternoon, so I thought maybe we could meet up with them after the last appointment?

Dr. Houston has a few afternoons marked off his calendar to attend appointments with his wife. She was diagnosed with thyroid cancer before I started working at the clinic, and he's determined to be by her side through treatment. I've been told they'll send another physician when he takes the week off for her surgery, but until then, we're just not scheduling appointments during the afternoons he needs to be by her side.

Part of me wants to decline the offer. Yes, I may have told Allison about the whole Lance thing, but I don't know if I want to get into it with my newest friends. I barely know Charli and Lizzie, and I'm certain my relationship will come up at some point in conversation. It always does.

> Allison: You can say no if you want. I understand not wanting to pretend to be fine in public. It's one thing to act that way at work, but completely another when you're surrounded by friends. But if I can make a suggestion, as someone who went through a divorce. Don't sit at home and mope for too long. Yes, grieve the loss of the relationship you once had, but don't drown in the misery it can create. You know he's not at home crying in a bowl of Rocky Road.

I read and then reread her text, her words striking a chord in my brain. She's absolutely right. He's not at home, crying. He's not trying to make things right. He's living his best life, completely oblivious of the hearts he's breaking or the pain he's causing along the way.

The truth is, Lance has always been self-centered and selfish. It was always about him first. He'd break up with me for whatever reason and then come back. He didn't care about my needs, my time, or my feelings. He used me, plain and simple.

And that realization hurts more than the actual breakup.

> Me: I'd love to go. I don't plan to leave Cooper Town now, and I want to get to know Charli and Lizzie.

> Allison: Yay! I told them we'd meet at the diner, since it's in the middle of town. Easy walking distance for all of us.

> Me: Perfect. See you tomorrow morning at work.

> Allison: Have a great rest of your Sunday. If you get bored at home, call me. We can go for a walk or shopping or something.

I glance around my little rental. There are still boxes that need unpacked and laundry that needs washed. Not to mention I need to purchase a lawn mower. I didn't have to worry about it before when I lived in an apartment, but now I have a lawn to take care of. Making my decision, I fire off a quick text to Allison.

> Me: Actually, I do need to do a little shopping. Want to go shopping with me?

> Allison: Absolutely! I can be ready in thirty minutes. I'll even buy lunch.

A smile spreads across my face and my fingers move across the screen.

> Me: I'll pick you up in about thirty.

> Allison: See you soon!

I set my phone on the counter and head to my bedroom. I might have just had my heart ripped from my chest, but I refuse to go out in public in my cleaning clothes. Instead, I put on a pair of cute denim shorts with lace around the leg holes and a loose-fitting tank top in a deep blue color. I slip my feet into a pair of brown sandals and then head for the bathroom to make myself presentable.

After straightening my hair and putting a little eye makeup on my face, I return to the kitchen and grab my things. I exit the door off the laundry room and enter the attached garage, where my Jeep Cherokee is parked. It's older, with high miles, but it's a solid, reliable vehicle. And it should have enough room in the back, especially if I put the back seat down, to fit a push mower.

I head over to Allison's place across town. She lives in the small two-bedroom house she got in the divorce and is saving to have the siding redone. It's currently canary yellow, a color her ex-husband was fond of, and she hates it with a passion. But siding isn't cheap, that's for sure, and she'd prefer not to take out a loan or put the expense on credit cards, like most homeowners would do. There are a few broken pieces that really need replaced, especially around the front porch, or she'd just repaint it. She says she can live with the color until she can pay for it outright. Until then, she'll save where she can.

A quick text lets her know I'm close, and when I pull into her driveway, she's standing on her front porch. "I could drive if you want," she offers as she climbs into the passenger seat.

"No, I don't mind. I need to buy a lawn mower, and it's probably easier to put it in my Jeep than your car," I tell her, slowly backing out of her driveway and pulling on to the street.

"Oh! An adult purchase. Where are we headed?"

"Well, there's a couple of places in North Ridge we can check out."

"Yep," she says, setting her purse on the floor. "Do you like hibachi? There's a great little place near the Menards over there."

"I love it," I tell her, my stomach growling at the mention of food.

Laughing, she replies, "Well, let's grab food first. Then we can shop."

"Sounds like a plan."

"What about this one?" Allison asks, stopping in front of a red mower that looks a lot like the other four on display.

I look it over, wishing I knew what the differences were, besides the price. The motor area looks completely different, and I'm not exactly sure why. Not that I know anything about sizes of motors on push mowers. I read over the tag, but it's practically in a foreign language to me, and we have yet to find an employee who can help us.

"I'll go look for someone to help," Allison states, clearly reading my distress.

She walks away, leaving me to mull over the decision I face. Honestly, I could probably just buy one and it would be fine, but I'd like to understand what I'm spending my money on.

"You look lost."

I spin around, recognizing that voice immediately, even though I've only heard it one night a month ago. "Hi."

Cade flashes a sexy little grin, his blue eyes sparkling under the fluorescent lighting. "Whatcha doing?"

"Shopping," I reply, catching the way his eyes slowly peruse down my body like a caress. Goosebumps instantly pepper my exposed skin, and I refuse to acknowledge what's happened to my nipples. I just pray he can't see them through my shirt.

"In the market for a new mower?" he asks, setting the handheld basket he's carrying down on the floor.

"Yeah, I need one for my new place. Allison went to find an employee."

He takes in the selection. "What are you looking for it to do?"

My eyebrows shoot toward the ceiling. "Uhh, mow my yard?"

He flashes a quick smile. "I know that, but each one of these is a little different."

"I figured, but I don't know what."

"Are you looking for an electric mower?" he asks.

"They make those?" I ask, completely dumbfounded by this news.

Not that I should be, considering they have electric cars and motorcycles, but I suppose I didn't realize mowers can be electric too.

"They do. This model is electric. If you don't want to deal with gas while you mow, it's a decent option. It's a twenty-inch cut, which is average for push mowers. The batteries last up to fifty minutes, so if you have a smaller to medium sized yard, that would be about perfect."

I glance from the mower to the man standing beside me. "Are you a lawn mower salesman in your spare time?"

He grins widely. "No, but I know equipment. I'm a heavy equipment operator," he states.

I read the tag details once more and check the price. "I'm not afraid of a gas mower, but it would be nice not to have to store a gas can and have to run to fill it all the time."

"Agreed. If you like the electric option, this one is self-propelled. It's more expensive, but you get the best of both worlds and it's easier to use. Plus, electric mowers are considerably quieter."

I nod in understanding, contemplating the choices. I spend a couple of minutes looking them all over. Cade stands nearby, but doesn't say anything. He lets me work through it in my head, which I appreciate so much. I realize how important that is, and not just because of his push mower knowledge, but because he's not overwhelming me with his own thoughts and opinions. The man I won't mention would have told me which one to purchase, whether it was the one I wanted or not.

"Found someone, finally!" Allison announces as she approaches. "Oh, hey, Cade."

"Hi, Allison," he replies.

The moment he turns back to the mowers, she smiles at me and waggles her eyebrows. I, of course, roll my eyes at the other woman and turn my attention to the associate who is trailing behind my friend.

"Can I help you?" the young kid asks.

"I'd like to purchase this mower," I state, pointing to the electric self-propelled model.

"Okay," he states, grabbing the tag. "I'll take you at the counter."

I start to follow but stop and turn around. "Thanks for your help, Cade."

He flashes a quick grin and grabs his basket. "Holler if you need help getting it out of your vehicle. You have my number, right?"

My throat is dry, but I manage a nod.

"Good. Use it anytime you're ready, Oaklee." With that, he turns and walks off, his ass looking very amazing in the loose-fitting, well-worn jeans.

"Wipe your chin, girl," Allison mutters beside me, causing me to blush.

I'm hit with a wave of guilt, and the realization of how unwarranted it is now is like a bucket of cold water over my head. The reason I would feel guilty for checking out another man is gone. He clearly didn't have the same problem, not only looking but touching too. Now, we're not together, so I should have absolutely no guilt when it comes to checking out a fine man's ass.

Holding my head up high, I shrug at my friend. "What can I say? He has a nice ass."

She barks out a laugh and nods in response. "That he does." Linking her arm through mine, we walk toward the counter where the sales associate went. "Let's go purchase you a mower, shall we?"

"We shall."

"And then we can talk about the number you have in your phone and when you're going to use it."

I roll my eyes. "I'm not going to use it."

She gapes at me. "Why not?"

"I've been single for like...forty-eight hours."

"So? Single is single, my friend."

"That may be true, but I'm not ready yet," I insist, stepping up to the counter and pulling out my wallet. I'm going to need my credit card for this purchase.

I pay for my purchase and am told which door to drive to so they can get me loaded up. Before we know it, we're all set and heading back to Cooper Town. As Allison talks about what she needs to do when she gets home, my mind drifts to the man who appeared out of nowhere earlier. He was incredibly helpful when it came to talking me through the purchase, even though I probably would have gotten the same assistance from an employee.

I wasn't lying when I told Allison I wasn't ready for anything more. Not from Cade or anyone else. I'm two days out of a relationship I've had for most of the last six years. I'm not ready for anything more than a basic friendship, at least right now.

That doesn't mean I can't look, right?

Because Cade is awfully pretty to look at. And I'm not just talking about his ass, which is pretty fucking nice. His blue eyes are so alluring, and his smile is contagious. He's charismatic and one of the biggest flirts I've ever met, but something tells me there's a lot more to him. In a nutshell, he's romance book-worthy eye candy.

What's a newly single woman to do?

CHAPTER FIVE

Cade

I LOOK OUT THE WINDOW AND SIGH. I HATE RAINY DAYS. I'D MUCH rather be working. But I do admit, having a rare day off during the week, after working six days a week, is a welcome reprieve. Unfortunately, because of the rain, I can't do anything outside, like I'd prefer. Instead, I spend a little time cleaning up my place before heading out to my two-car garage and turning on the radio. I keep my work truck parked outside, and my personal one in the garage. That leaves space for my four-wheeler and whatever project I want to tinker with.

This particular time, it's an old dirt bike I picked up from a friend for a steal. It wasn't running right, but I knew I could get the engine tuned up with a little work. I've spent the last few weeks cleaning it up and replacing a few parts, including the carburetor. It fires right up now and runs smoothly, ready to hit the trails. Now, I need to decide if I want to keep it or sell it.

Just as I start to clean up what little mess I have, my phone chimes with a text notification.

Collin: Rained out?

Me: Yep. You working?

Collin: At The Lizard today.

I glance at my watch and notice it's near lunch.

Me: Want some company? I could bring food.

Collin: Yes to both.

Me: See you shortly.

I slip my phone into my pocket without reading his reply and go looking for my truck keys and wallet. Once I have everything, I return to the garage, climb into my truck, and back out of the driveway. It only takes a few minutes to get to town, and when I turn onto the main artery through Cooper Town, I find it alive with people. Even on a rainy, crappy September day, there's still people out and about over the lunch hour.

I park near the bar and walk a few doors down to the pizza joint.

"Hey, Cade," the owner, Mario, greets when I enter. "Dining in?"

"Nope, taking it to go. Collin's at the bar, so I'm gonna eat with him," I tell him, pulling out my wallet.

"Sounds good. Want me to run it down when it's ready?"

"You don't have to do that," I reply.

He waves off my comment. "It'll take two minutes, tops. What can I getcha?"

"Let's do a large mega meat pie with breadsticks."

"Marinara?"

"You know it," I reply, grabbing my credit card.

"Salad?"

"Let's skip it this time," I reply. Sometimes it's just easier to not deal with plates and forks when eating at the bar.

Mario taps on the computer screen. "Thirty-one sixteen."

Handing over my card, I sign the slip when it's given to me. Since he doesn't add a delivery fee, I make sure to add a ten-dollar tip.

"Give me twenty, and I'll have it over to you."

"Sounds good, Mario. Appreciate it."

"No problem," he replies, ripping off the order slip and handing it off to the kitchen staff. "See you soon."

I step outside, grateful the rain has let up to a light drizzle. Just as I approach the bar, I catch movement down the street. I don't know what grabs my attention exactly, but I instantly realize it's Allison and Oaklee. They exited the clinic and are hurrying down the block to the diner. Even though Oaklee has her head down, I'd recognize that long hair and curvy body anywhere. She's in shapeless scrubs, but she might as well be wearing lingerie, because even in her daily medical outfit, she looks sexy as fuck.

Unfortunately, she disappears inside the diner. A wave of sadness washes over me, and I'm tempted to run over and cancel the pizza order and replace it with something from the diner. Or maybe I'll go down and order a second option for us to have. You know, leftovers for later?

Realizing I've completely lost my mind over a woman I've seen exactly two times, I finish walking to the entrance of the bar and pull open the heavy door. The room is dimly lit, though it's significantly brighter than it was before. Lizzie has done a number on this old place and transformed it without completely changing the vibe. It still has the old, classic feel, and I know a lot of people appreciate that.

"Hey," Collin says when I step inside.

"Hi. Pizza will be here in twenty."

"Mario's delivering?" he asks, wiping down the bar top.

"Yep."

"He's been doing that for Lizzie and me any time we order. Pepsi?"

"Yeah, that's fine," I state, taking a seat at the end I usually gravitate toward. Of course, I have the pick of the bar, considering no one is here. Not that I expected the place to be packed or anything. He did just open it at noon.

"Where's Lizard?" I ask once he sets my drink down in front of me.

"At lunch with the women. I was supposed to work this evening, and she this afternoon, but we switched so she could go meet Charli, Allison, and Oaklee at the diner. Then, I guess she and Charli are running to the bookstore."

I snort and shake my head. "You say you've switched shifts, but I know you'll be here all evening. You'll leave when she leaves."

He flashes a rare, easy smile. "That's what you do when you're in love."

"I'll take your word for it," I mumble.

"One day, brother," he practically sings, but to me, his comment doesn't warrant a reply.

"So...Oaklee," I start, knowing it'll catch his attention. I'd love for him to share what he knows about her, which is probably less than what I do, but a guy can hope. I mean, his girlfriend has befriended her since she relocated to town, so maybe he's heard some talk or something.

He levels me with a pointed, somewhat annoyed look. "Ask what you want to know."

"Lizzie talk about her much?"

"Nope," he replies right away. "As far as I know, today is the first time they've met up."

I nod.

"Listen, this woman clearly got your attention. Ask her out," my brother says, as if I hadn't already thought of that.

"I did."

He grins from ear to ear. "She turned you down?"

"Yes, because she's seeing someone."

"Oh." He leans on the bar. "That sucks."

"Yeah," I reply, taking a quick sip of my Pepsi. "I did give her my number though. Told her to give me a call when she's single."

He chuckles as he reaches for my glass and refills it with the soda wand. "Of course you did."

I shrug and point to the remote. "Hand it over. Anyway, she took my number. Who knows if she'll use it."

"I remember her that night," he starts, setting the remote down in front of me. "You watched her until the moment she left."

I turn on the TVs and start looking for something interesting to watch. "Your point?"

"She grabbed your attention and hasn't let go."

"It's probably because I saw her Sunday buying a mower."

"Or it's because you can't have her and that bothers you."

I snort.

"You've never had anyone turn you down like that," he reasons. "And it's bothering you."

Is it? Is that really the issue?

I don't think so. I don't see Oaklee as a challenge. I am genuinely drawn to her, and I can't figure out why. She's attractive, yes. But it's more than that. There's this light about her, a glow that seems to cast a bit of her goodness my way.

Fuck, what am I talking about? I have no idea what kind of person she really is. However, something tells me she must be good if she's a nurse. She's devoted her life to helping people, so that has to count for something.

Well, hell, what do I know? Maybe that's exactly it.

From the time I was sixteen, girls just sort of...flocked to me. I've had plenty of casual girlfriends over the years, and even a couple who I dated a bit longer and exclusively. Finding a woman to warm my bed hasn't ever really been hard, if I'm being honest. Maybe that makes me sound douchey, but it is what it is. I like women. They like me. The fact I would have taken Oaklee home with me—no questions asked—and she turned me down because she was dating someone is probably what's causing my thoughts to constantly turn her way.

She's different than the rest because she *didn't* jump into bed with me.

And because of that, I'm attracted to her more.

I've always liked a challenge, and maybe that's exactly where this infatuation stems from.

She said no.

Fortunately, I'm saved from having to continue this deep dive into my inner soul by the arrival of our pizza. "Lunch is served," Mario announces as he heads toward me, two boxes in his hands that smell delicious.

"Thanks, man. Appreciate you bringing it over," I tell him.

"You're welcome. I like coming over and seeing what updates Lizzie's made. She's really transformed this old place, hasn't she?" he asks, glancing around the empty bar.

"She sure has," I confirm.

"Thanks for delivering, as always," Collin states as he opens the smaller box on top and sets it to the side.

"You're welcome. I better get back over there. Have a good one, guys," he says, turning and heading for the door.

My twin and I both holler our goodbyes before immediately stuffing our faces with food. One of the hardest habits to break when you come home from the military is not shoveling in the food when it's in front of you. At times, you never knew when your next meal might be or how long you'd get, so you quickly form a habit of eating fast, especially when you're on the go.

"You know, you should just ask Lizzie to move in with you," I say as I swirl a breadstick in some marinara.

"You don't think it's too soon?" he asks, not looking up from his pizza. The fact he asked that question and didn't argue about the fact it's too soon tells me he's thought about it.

"No, I don't think so. I mean, I know it's only been a few months, but you two are solid. And I can see you're happy."

He grins just a bit. "I am. Never been happier, actually. When I think back over my time with Whitney, I can see a difference. Not just in the relationship itself, but how I feel. I'd like to think a part of the demise in my first big relationship was the distance. I know it wasn't easy on either of us. The miles and the separation took a toll. But that doesn't warrant cheating. If you're unhappy, then break up. I wouldn't even have cared if it was in a fucking email, you know? But don't go on with your life with someone else, all while stringing me along and letting me think we were still happily together."

He wipes his mouth with a bar napkin. "Anyway, now, I just feel…settled. I guess that's the only way to describe it. I'm relaxed, and you know that's huge for me. I'm never relaxed," he says with a snicker. "But everything with Lizzie feels right. Easy. Like we've been together for years, not months. She's the best part of my day, man. The best part. I can't wait to get back to town after a shift, and not because I'm anxious to get to bed. I can't wait to see her, even if just for a bit."

I find my own smile spread across my face. "I'm happy for you, Collin. Truly. I like Lizzie, and if you were to take the next step, I know our entire family would be behind you."

"Thanks," he says softly. "I don't know if we're there yet, but it feels like it's moving in that direction. I stay with her upstairs on nights either of us work, and if we're off, we're at my place."

"Sounds like you're practically already living together," I state, taking another slice of pizza.

"Pretty much, but I guess it's considered unofficial. Making it official would be...big."

"It would be," I confirm. "But if anyone is ready for that next step, it's you."

He nods, seeming to consider my words. After a bit of silence, where we both turn our attention to the car show playing on the TV, he asks, "Did Wyatt call you about Saturday?"

"I got a text from him earlier this morning. Sounds like a good time."

Collin nods.

"You gonna be able to go?"

"For a little bit. Lizzie and I are both working Saturday night, so we'll go for a bit in the afternoon for the fish fry part. We'll have to skip the bonfire."

I nod. "I hope we're done by noon this Saturday, but it might be midafternoon before I can get there."

"Take the overtime while you can," Collin says, and the conversation quickly turns to work.

Before I know it, the pizza's gone and the owner of this fine establishment is returning from her little lunch and shopping soiree. "Hey," she hollers when she enters through the back entrance and sees us both.

"Hey, baby," my brother coos, his entire demeanor changing at the drop of a hat. He instantly smiles and moves toward her, taking the bag from her hand and pressing his lips to hers.

A ping of something I don't like swirls in my gut.

I've never been a jealous man, but watching my brother—my twin—with Lizzie causes the ugly green monster to stir. Not because I want Lizzie, mind you. Because he has something special, something I've secretly longed for my entire life. Ever since I was old enough to notice the relationship my parents have. The kisses hello when he'd get home from work, the way he'd touch her hand when he was helping her in the kitchen, him watching her walk away with a hint of a smile on his lips, as if he still couldn't believe she was his after all these years.

"Hi, Cade," Lizzie says as she approaches, a warm smile on her face.

"Lizard. What'd you buy me?" I ask, referring to the large bag my brother sets on the bar.

"Books!" she proclaims, her green eyes sparkling with excitement and energy.

"Eww," I grumble, fake shivering to punctuate my point.

She rolls her eyes and dives into the bag, pulling out book after book.

"Jeez, Lizard, did you leave any books at the store?"

"Nope," she smarts off, placing them in stacks in front of her. "I got my top five TBRs in each of three categories I enjoy reading."

I glance at my twin. "TBRs?" I mutter, earning a shrug from him.

"To be read. Stay with me, Cade. Anyway, I picked out my top five in contemporary romance, autobiography, and true crime."

My eyebrows shoot up. "That's quite the variety. Romance and true crime? Remind me to always stay on your good side."

With a pointed look, she replies, "You'd do well to remember that, mister."

"What did I miss?" Charli asks, slipping out of the restroom and joining us at the bar. "I had to pee so dang bad. Oh, I can't wait to hear which one you read first." She jumps from topic to topic so effortlessly, it's hard to keep up with our sister at times.

"I think I'm going with this one," Lizzie announces, handing over the hardback book she plans to read. "I think it'll be perfect for the next book club."

"Definitely! And I love the fact Vivian is going to make sure she has plenty of copies in stock of whichever book you want to read and discuss next."

"I don't understand. Why do you need a club to read books?" I ask, reaching for the closest stack and checking out the covers.

"Wouldn't you like a group to share and talk about your favorite hobby?" Charli asks.

I shrug and slide the romance books back toward them. "Believe it or not, guys over the age of twenty don't usually sit around and talk about sex."

That comment earns me two sets of eye rolls and a snicker from my brother.

"You're gross," my sister argues.

"Why? Because sex is my favorite hobby? Sister, if it isn't yours, they're doing it wrong." Realization hits me. "You know what? Never mind. You're not allowed to have sex."

"Oh my God," she grumbles. "I'm not sixteen."

"Still. Let's just pretend you don't have sex. Ever," I mutter, taking a drink of my Pepsi with a splash of cherry and suddenly wishing it had some Jack in it.

"Oh, I have sex," she sings.

"All right, friends, let's change the subject before this turns into some family brawl worthy of *The Jerry Springer Show*. I'm gonna run these books upstairs, and then I'll be back," Lizzie informs us, placing another kiss on my twin's lips before rebagging the books and taking them away.

"How was lunch?" I ask when my sister plops down beside me.

"Good," she states, lifting the lid on the empty pizza box. "How was yours?"

"Mario makes the best pies," I confirm.

"He does."

Before I can even stop myself, I casually ask, "So, just you and Lizzie go?"

She slowly turns my way, and the look on her face lets me know she's not buying what I'm selling. "Just ask instead of beating around the bush."

"Just making conversation," I mumble, taking another drink of my Pepsi.

Charli huffs out a deep breath. "You know Allison and Oaklee were there too or you wouldn't be asking.

"How are they?"

My sister laughs. She actually laughs in my face. "What you really want to know is how Oaklee is doing, and I'm not going to give it to you. If you want to know, ask her."

"Maybe I will."

"Good," she counters.

I don't say anything else, just turn my attention to the TV. Cade gets Charli a drink, and before we know it, the regulars are showing up for their afternoon of hanging out, enjoying a drink, and watching TV. Of course, there's a lot of gossiping going on down on that end of the bar, but I don't pay them much attention.

My mind is focused on Oaklee.

On the fact there was something in my sister's tone I can't quite put my finger on.

I'm not sure what it means, but I do hope I run into the beautiful Oaklee sometime again soon.

Turns out, it's the best part of my day.

CHAPTER SIX

Oaklee

MY DAY HAS COMPLETELY TURNED TO SHIT.

Not the lunch with Allison, Charli, and Lizzie. That was pretty great. In fact, I really hope we can do it again soon, because it was a lot of fun and the hour flew by in the blink of an eye. Honestly, I didn't even want to go back to work but didn't really have a choice. When you have bills to pay, especially after just moving to a new place, and a new job, you don't really have the luxury of skipping an afternoon of work. Not without being reprimanded.

That's why I had to stay put instead of traveling back home when my grandma called me. Grandpa fell at home. Not only does he have a gash on the side of his head that required some stitches and a few staples, but he has a concussion too. Apparently, when he fell, he hit the coffee table. She had to call an ambulance because it was bleeding so badly and he was a little disoriented.

My grandparents are still agile, even as they hit their early seventies. They've stayed active, and to think about him being rushed to the ER in an ambulance is difficult. Especially since I'm not right up the road, so to speak, anymore. Anderson Township is a few hours away, and while I could easily jump in the car after I get off work and drive back home, Grandma insists I don't.

He's already released and home resting.

But that doesn't stop the worry and anxiety from taking over.

When I left Cincinnati, it was harder than I expected to leave the two people who were the most stable and consistent people in my life. The problem is, every time the woman who birthed me would drop me off on their doorstep, I saw the hardship flash across their faces. It wasn't easy to raise their granddaughter, not when they both worked full time. Every time she'd show up on their doorstep, me and a single bag of belongings in tow, it completely disrupted their lives. Even as a young girl, I saw it.

I saw their struggle.

Every time my mother would bring me back, unable to be the mom she promised to be, they'd do their best to pick up the pieces of my young broken heart. Of course, the court system seems to believe a woman with many issues can change over and over again and kept putting me back in her care. She'd get picked up, go to rehab, and then get clean for a while. So I'd be sent back to her. The cycle repeated so often, it was sad. Disgusting, even.

When I was thirteen, she didn't even have the decency to take me back to my grandparents before she took off. She left me—alone—in our run-down apartment until the school called for a welfare check. When the officers arrived, finding me there with no power, no water, and barely any food, my grandparents were finally granted a permanent guardianship until I was eighteen. It probably saved my life, if I'm being honest, because staying with my mom would have eventually killed me, or turned me into something that reflected her own sad existence simply because I barely knew better.

My heart hurt all afternoon, even after I spoke with my grandma and she insisted I not come. Realization was heavy as I thought about those two people being the only ones I've truly had in my corner most of my life. The moment I could, I went off to nursing school, determined to make a life that's my own, where I can take care of people who need it. I never wanted to be a burden to anyone ever again, that's for sure.

"Hey, you all right?" Allison asks as we prepare to close down the clinic for the day.

"Yeah," I reply, flashing a quick smile.

"What's the latest?" she asks, referring to my grandpa.

"He's home and resting. Grandma told me not to worry about coming home. There's nothing I can do, but part of me feels like I should, you know?"

"Sure."

"I'll call my grandma again when I leave here, just to see if they need anything."

"I'm hoping the network gets back online soon, or tomorrow's going to suck too," Allison states, referring to the internet network the clinics and hospital use. It went down about two o'clock this afternoon, and IT hasn't been able to get it back up yet. Everything basically came to a halt. We couldn't discuss test results with patients or even order prescriptions. It's been a mess, and all I can hope is it works properly tomorrow.

"Big plans tonight?" I ask after we say goodnight to the office manager, Fiona, and head for the back exit of the clinic.

"Dinner with my parents," she replies, making a face. "I hope they can get through a meal without fighting, but I highly doubt it. The part I'm looking forward to the most is seeing my niece." Clara, her niece, is four and Allison dotes on her. She spends as much time as she can with her, including dealing with her bickering parents. "You?"

I stop in the middle of the small lot and glance around. "Honestly? I'm thinking about grabbing some queso and chips and a bottle of wine and drinking the night away."

She snorts a laugh. "I'd totally do that with you, if it weren't for this dinner. It's my brother-in-law's birthday, so I can't skip it."

I wave off her comment. "Go enjoy your niece. I'll probably be in bed by eight anyway, especially if I drink wine."

Allison moves to her car and opens the driver's door. "Don't drunk call anyone."

I bark out a laugh. "Doubtful."

"Or, you *could* drunk text Cade. You still have his number, right?"

I told Allison about him giving me his number the night we met more than a month ago, but it hasn't been discussed since. "I'm not drunk texting Cade."

"Why not? You're single now. You could totally text him."

"Not happening," I argue, opening the door to my Cherokee and preparing to climb inside.

"It could," she sings, giggling as she climbs inside and shuts the door. Before I can slip inside my own vehicle, her driver's window rolls down and she hollers, "Make sure you share all the details tomorrow."

"There will be no details to share," I yell, shutting my door and shaking my head.

I pull out of the small lot the employees use and head toward the small grocery store. It's not much, carrying the basics you'd need and prices higher than you'd find at a big box store, but it serves its purpose. I've caught wind that many residents try to support the small mom and pop store as much as they can, while still taking advantage of the cheaper prices when needed. After living here a short time, I've found myself shopping there a handful of times for a night or two of dinners or to get a few things to take to work for my lunch.

The grocery store is only a block off the main road and has its own parking lot. Since it's just after five, the lot is fuller than usual, most likely thanks to other residents doing exactly what I'm doing—stopping on their way home from work.

I park in the second row and head for the front entrance. Once inside, I retrieve a basket to carry my purchases, knowing I won't need the capacity of a cart. I really only need a handful of items, and I take off in search of those.

My first stop is the chip aisle. Usually, I wouldn't mind making a homemade queso dip, but to be honest, after the long afternoon and heavy emotional baggage I've been carrying, I want something quick and easy. So, jarred dip it is. I find what I'm looking for and grab a bag of tortilla chips to go with it.

But then an idea hits me, and I make my way to the meat section. This is totally cheating, but if my goal tonight is a quick and easy meal, then this option will suffice. I move to where they keep prepackaged, prepared meats and find what I'm looking for. It's a container of pull pork coated in Jack Daniels barbecue sauce. If I had time to cook my own pulled pork, I would, but unfortunately, that's not in the cards tonight.

So this will have to do.

I head toward the back of the store next, grabbing a small container of sour cream before walking to the fresh vegetables and finding two jalapeños that are perfectly ripe. My stomach growls at the thought of the pulled pork nachos I'd be having for dinner, even after enjoying such a large, homemade lunch earlier at the diner. Usually, I might have something small, like a chicken salad sandwich or an egg and cheese sandwich, but I'm about to engage in eating my feelings, and that requires a big plate of comfort.

Once I have everything I need, I make my way toward the last aisle near the register. Originally, I was going to grab a bottle of wine, but as I scour the selection of liquor, my eyes settle on a bottle of tequila and the strawberry mix sitting beside it.

"I'm more of a lime or peach man myself, but I guess I could settle for a strawberry margarita instead."

"Salt or sugar?" I ask, turning to face Cade.

He makes a face of horror. "People ruin a margarita by rimming the glass with sugar?"

I nod in confirmation.

"That's a travesty."

"Agreed," I reply.

He looks down at my basket. "Taco Tuesday?"

"Isn't every night Taco Tuesday?" I ask. Mexican is my absolute favorite, and I'd eat some sort of Mexican entrée every night if I could.

Cade's face shows surprise as his mouth gapes open. "Marry me."

"What?" I ask with a bark of laughter.

"I'm in love with you," he states, earning an eye roll.

"You're nuts."

"Surprisingly, you're not the first person to tell me that," he replies, offering a cheesy grin. "On a serious note, I take it it's a nachos and tequila kinda night?"

"Yeah." I turn my attention to the alcohol, noting the four different brands of tequila.

Cade steps forward, standing directly beside me. His woodsy scent tickles my nose as he reaches up and points. "If I might make a suggestion, get this one. It doesn't burn like the cheap shit and doesn't cost an arm and a leg like that one."

I take in the brand he's suggesting and nod. "Thanks," I say, reaching for a bottle and then grabbing the strawberry mix on the shelf beside it.

When I have everything I need, I turn to face him and find his eyes sparkling. "So…taking Taco Tuesday to the boyfriend?"

His question makes me shift uncomfortably. "Not tonight."

He seems genuinely surprised by my reply. "No?"

I lift my shoulders and shift on my feet once more. "He's…busy."

"Huh. So…you have no one to share Taco Tuesday with."

"What if I'm still dating someone?" I ask.

"Are you?"

I open my mouth, fully prepared to lie, but that's not what comes out. "No."

Again, he seems shocked by my answer. "You're not?"

"It's a recent development," I mutter, looking away as a new wave of anger washes over me.

"Well, then, tequila is the right choice, but not with that fruity mix. We're doing shots," he states, glancing around, like he's searching for something.

"We?"

"Of course! I never let a girlfriend suffer by herself. We'll curse him together."

"I'm not your girlfriend, and I don't need your help cursing him," I counter.

"No, of course you don't need my help." He snaps his fingers. "We could do one of those boyfriend hexes, like a spell."

"A what?" I ask, chuckling.

"It's a thing."

"If you say so," I mumble, shifting my basket to my other hand since it's getting heavy.

"I do. I know these things."

Fighting a smile, I ask, "You know a lot about breaking up with a boyfriend?"

"Of course I do. I'm a boy and a friend. I'm better than a boyfriend, because I cause less bullshit. Plus, I'm usually better looking than a boyfriend, which helps a gal friend get over the douche faster." He waggles his eyebrows and grins mischievously.

"How is that?"

"Because when you're thinking about how good-looking I am, you're not thinking about the asshole. See?"

I shake my head, not at all surprised by his antics. "Not really."

He sighs, reaching into my basket and snatching the bottle of tequila. "Because I'm a good boy friend, I'm going to bring the tequila."

"I don't—"

"What do you say, Oaklee? Ready to banish his memory for good?" he asks, swinging the bottle of tequila in front of me.

"I..."

I shouldn't, that's for sure. Sharing tequila with Cade is the very last thing on the long list of things I should do this evening. Well, maybe not the very last. That would be reconnecting with Lance. But it's not near the top. It falls after cleaning my entire apartment with a toothbrush and licking all the dirty dishes clean.

Yet...I'm considering it.

It's as if Allison is standing beside me, whispering, "Do it, do it."

"Come on, Oaklee. I pour a mean shot of tequila."

"I have no doubt about it," I mutter, wondering about the long line of brokenhearted women he probably has trailing in his wake.

He stands up straight and lifts his chin. "I'll be a perfect gentleman. I won't grab your ass or cop a feel. Unless you want me to."

I roll my eyes and shake my head. "You're incorrigible."

"That's code for amazing."

I snicker at his obnoxiousness. "Fine, but we're buying the mix too. I'm not downing a bunch of shots of tequila. I have to work tomorrow."

"Fine, fine. One shot. We'll banish the loser and then toast to your new boyfriend with margaritas."

"You're not my boyfriend."

"Man friend? Yeah, I like that better. I'm all man, anyway."

My eyes completely betray me, dropping to take in his jean-clad legs and fitted T-shirt that hugs every muscle he has.

"Eyes up here, Oaklee. You start objectifying your man friends and they'll get the wrong idea," he states with a wink. "Anything else you want with your nachos and tequila?"

I glance in my basket. "Cookies."

"Done," he replies, not even questioning the request. "I'll be ten minutes behind you."

My jaw drops open, ready to stop this entire farce, but nothing comes out.

"See you soon, Oaklee."

Before I can say anything, he takes off to get cookies, holding a bottle of tequila. I watch him until he rounds the corner at the back of the store and disappears.

This is a huge mistake.

I should go find him, take the tequila I was planning to purchase, and head home.

Alone.

Yet, that's not what I do. I slowly make my way to the register and place my basket on the conveyor belt. The young woman rings up my purchase, and without giving it a single thought, I swipe my card while she bags my groceries.

"Thank you," I mutter, grabbing the two bags and heading for my Jeep.

As I place the two bags in the passenger seat and climb behind the wheel, I know exactly what I should do. I should wait for him to come out and decline his offer. This has bad idea written all over it with Sharpie marker.

But, again, that's not what happens.

Instead, I put my Cherokee into reverse and back out of the spot. I drive a little faster to get home, hoping I have a few extra minutes to pick up and freshen up before he gets there.

Wait.

Just as I pull onto the main route through town to head to my little rental house, something hits me.

How in the world does he know where I live?

CHAPTER SEVEN

Cade

The moment she opens her door, I ask, "How many times have you thought about canceling?"

"How did you know where I live?" she counters with her own question.

"Easy. Everyone in Cooper Town knows where everyone lives." I make no move to step toward her as she stands in the middle of her doorway, holding open the screen door.

She stares at me, waiting.

"Charli," I confess, holding up my hands. "But in my defense, it was casual conversation. She didn't come to me specifically with the details, nor did I ask. I overheard her and Lizzie talking about you renting from Sommer's parents and it just came out."

It takes her a few seconds before she nods. "I'm not used to this small-town thing."

"I understand. It's a lifestyle, and if you're not used to it, it can seem like a lot."

She snorts. "No kidding."

We both stand here for several more seconds before I finally hold up the bottle of tequila with one hand and a bag containing dessert. "So, am I leaving this with you, or…"

She glances at the bag. "What'd you bring?"

"Well, I didn't see any fresh cookies in their bakery that looked good, so I grabbed some edible cookie dough and fudge swirl ice cream. I even bought a bottle of chocolate syrup."

Her eyes brighten with excitement as she glances up at me. "You brought cookie dough?"

I shrug, hoping I did the right thing. "Charli says ice cream and cookie dough heals a broken heart, so I took a shot that it works for all women."

Oaklee grabs the bag of sweets and looks inside. "I've never had the edible cookie dough like this."

"We can bake it too, but the package says it's okay to eat raw."

She steps back, granting me entrance. "All cookie dough is okay to eat raw."

"It is?" I ask, stepping inside her space.

"Well, probably not, but I've never had an issue. It's like drinking hot coffee or taking medicine. In this society, you have to put warning labels on everything now."

"True," I state, glancing around the living space. It's an open floor concept with the living room taking up the majority of the space, along with the kitchen and small dining area between them. "Nice place."

"It is," she confirms. "Brenda painted the living room, bedroom, and hallway before I moved in. She said the previous tenant must have hung a thousand pictures on the walls."

I step back and think. "Huh. I think I have two."

"Two pictures in each room?"

"No, two pictures total."

"Seriously? How is that possible?"

I lift my shoulders and return my gaze to her. "Easy. One picture is of my entire family on the day I returned home from my first tour overseas, and the other is of me and Collin last summer when we were camping and four-wheeling at a big park in Indiana. We're both covered in mud and wearing matching smiles."

She's grinning. "That sounds fun."

"Ever been on a four-wheeler?" I ask.

"Come on, let's go in the kitchen so I can finish prepping the nachos," she answers.

I follow behind, casually stealing a glimpse of her ass. She's wearing black leggings and an oversized T-shirt now, having changed from her work scrubs. "Can I start the margaritas?"

She glances over her shoulder, her long hair making my hand itch to touch. "I thought we were doing shots?" she jokes.

"That's still an option," I inform her, setting the bottle on the counter beside the strawberry mix, blender, and salt container. "You have ice?"

She nods. "In the freezer."

I get to work on a batch of margaritas. I might add a splash more tequila than I should, but I figure it'll help her relax. Since I'm driving, I'll only have one and then switch to water.

"So, you never answered my question," I say, adding the ice.

"Which question?"

"Four-wheeling. Ever been?"

"Nope, but I love being outdoors. Maybe someday," she responds casually, cutting up the jalapeños.

I'm ready to open my mouth, to invite her to go with me sometime soon, but quickly think better of it. The last thing I'd want is for her to feel like I'm pushing my way into her life, especially after what sounds like a very recent breakup. I don't mind being a rebound guy, but usually that involves just sex. Asking her to go do one of my favorite pastimes isn't exactly keeping it casual, if you know what I mean.

I turn on the blender, watching as the liquids blend together and the ice is devoured, making a pretty great mixture of alcohol and taste. "Glasses?" I ask, not wanting to open up all the cabinets in search of what I need.

"To your right, by the sink," she tells me, just as she moves toward said sink to rinse the spicy peppers. We're standing directly beside each other, a fruit scent ebbing from her body.

Is it the margarita mix?

Is it her?

There's only one way to find out.

I bend down, practically shoving my nose into her neck, and inhale.

"What are you doing?" she whispers without moving.

"Smelling you. I caught a whiff of something fruity, and I was seeing if it was you," I tell her casually, though what's happening in my pants is anything but.

"Umm, you're making strawberry margaritas."

"It's not exactly strawberry I smell. It's sweet and fruity, yes, but with hints of vanilla."

I watch as she swallows hard and turns her head to meet my gaze. "That's my lotion." She's trying to be casual, but it's not working.

Desperately needing to put a bit of distance between us, I step back to the left and grab the two glasses I was retrieving before I was distracted. "Huh. Well, it smells nice."

She clears her throat, eyes focused on the peppers. "Thanks."

I hum an old Hank Williams tune as I coat the rim of the glasses in the salt and pour two perfect margaritas. I take a quick sip of the one I'll keep, savoring the sweet strawberry mixed with the punch of tequila. We're talking high-quality presentation and superior taste, if I do say so myself. "Damn, I'm good."

She chuckles and puts the chopped jalapeños into a bowl. "I think this is ready too," she says, moving to the fridge to grab the container of sour cream.

I take our glasses to the table and join her at the counter. "You did all this, plus changed and freshened up before I got here?"

She shrugs her delicate shoulders and blushes. "Well, this is pretty simple. The meat takes like two minutes to heat up, and the cheese dip is just microwaved until melted. Cutting the peppers took the longest," she says with a chuckle.

"It looks delicious."

"It's not authentic or gourmet," she counters.

"It's perfect. I usually just throw some meat on the grill or cook some vegetables. I'm pretty simple when it comes to food," I tell her, taking the plate she offers. "No, you go first."

"But you're my guest."

"Ladies first, Oaklee. Always." I give her a wink and step back, allowing her to make a plate first.

I don't miss the way she blushes, obviously picking up on the innuendo I wasn't even trying to aim her way. But now that the comment is out there, I won't take it back. She would always come first, in every way that matters, including in the bedroom.

She piles a mound of chips on her plate, followed by a healthy scoop of barbecued pulled pork, queso cheese, some jalapeños, and a dollop of sour cream.

"Spicy doesn't bother you?" I ask, reaching for the chips and forming the base on my plate.

"I love things a touch spicy, but jalapeños are the hottest I go. A friend of mine used to use ghost peppers on her tacos and I almost died just by smelling them," she says, taking her plate over to the table. "My eyes would water through the whole meal."

I chuckle, scooping my first chip in the barbecue pork and cheese mixture, making sure to grab one of the jalapeño slices and a touch of sour cream as I do. "Damn," I mutter, chewing and savoring the spicy, tangy taste. "This is good."

"I could eat this kind of food every day. Dips too. I don't need meat and potatoes, though I do appreciate a good steak too. Usually, if I have time, I make this Velveeta and RO-TEL dip that's amazing."

If my mouth wasn't watering before, it would be now. "That sounds delicious."

She shrugs, scooping a chip in the topping and popping it into her mouth. "It is. Easy too. I've even made it before where I'll add a pound of sausage or ground beef and call it a meal. I think it all stems from nursing school. My roommate and I would have to eat on the fly around classes and work, so you just do what you have to do."

"Makes sense," I interject. "I'm so used to eating on the fly during the day because of my job and being in the military, so I try to make better meals at night."

"I know you are a heavy equipment operator, but what exactly do you do?"

"I work on roads and bridges mostly. It's pretty cool."

She grins. "You were a Matchbox Car kid, weren't you." It's not a question, and her comment makes me laugh.

"Absolutely. I was a messy kid, always playing in the grass and dirt."

"I can see that." She shifts in her seat, looking up and meeting my gaze. "And…thank you for your service."

I nod, never really knowing what to say when someone thanks me for my service. I remember early on in my career, a man walked up to me in the airport when I was catching a flight home and thanked me. I just nodded and shook his outstretched hand. But that show of appreciation went a long way for me. I never say you're welcome, I always just nod. Why? Because it's what I do—or did—and I'd do it again a thousand times over. I was only one small piece of the massive puzzle that is our armed services, and I was proud to do what I did. Still am.

I'm a proud U.S. Marine Veteran.

We make small talk about easy stuff, nothing heavy like pasts and families. Though, my family is anything but heavy, I sense there's a little more weight to hers, based on the few things she's mentioned. So, we talk about our jobs mostly, and I find it fascinating to hear her talk about nursing. She doesn't go into any specifics, thanks to the HIPAA laws in place, but the occasional nameless funny story is appreciated.

"He was six, and he asked me if his mommy was going to poop out his baby brother like she did him," Oaklee states through her giggles.

The sound is…refreshing, and a little erotic.

"Classic," I reply with my own chuckle.

"Anyway, that little guy was a handful. I'm pretty sure the mom wanted to crawl beneath the table and hide. The moment the doc sent in her prescription for an antibiotic for her chest cold, she hightailed it out of there, practically dragging him behind."

Our plates are empty and so are the glasses of margaritas. "Kids say the darndest things."

"That they do," she confirms, standing up to collect the empty plates. "Do you want more?"

"No, I'm full, thanks. It was delicious."

"You're easy to impress," she quips as she throws our paper plates in to the trash can and moves to put the leftovers in the fridge.

I get up and move to the blender. Instead of pouring what's left in the blender into our glasses, I decided to pour two shots of tequila. Since she only has one shot glass, I pour a shot and dump it into my glass and refill the tiny glass with liquid for her. Carefully, I take the glass, shot, and bottle and head for the living room.

There are still a few boxes stacked in the corner, but for the most part, she has everything set up from her move. I set the items down on her coffee table and smile when she joins me, a hesitant look on her face.

"I thought we weren't doing shots?"

"The margaritas were for the easy stuff," I tell her, holding out the shot glass for her to take. Now, if she tells me no, I'm not going to press or force her. She doesn't want to do it; she doesn't have to. But sometimes you need a good stiff shot of liquid courage to say what's on your mind.

She joins me on the couch, sitting toward the front. She looks a little stiff, even after the margarita, and I understand that. She doesn't really know me, even if she did allow me into her house.

"So, what's the hard stuff?" she asks as I take my glass with my own shot and hold on to it.

I lean back, kicking an ankle over my knee. I'm trying to show her I'm not threatening in any way, and she holds all the cards. "First off, you don't have to do anything you don't want to do, including drink that shot. Understand?"

She nods, her beautiful eyes laced with nervousness. "I understand."

I pull out my phone and press a call to one of my first contacts, putting it on speakerphone. "What's up, numbnuts."

I hold Oaklee's gaze as I answer my brother. "I'm at a friend's house. I'm gonna send you a pin drop location. Come pick me up in fifteen minutes."

"Uhh, why?"

"Because I've been drinking and shouldn't drive."

"Oh, gotcha. See you in fifteen."

"Thanks," I reply, disconnecting the call and firing off my location. "There. Now you don't have to worry about me overstaying my welcome or trying something hinky."

Her eyes dance in humor. "Hinky?"

"It's a word," I counter.

"I know it's a word. I just haven't heard it used since 2004." Her smile stretches across her face, almost rendering me speechless.

I take a deep breath and down my shot. The tequila burns as it goes down, but it's definitely smoother than the cheap shit. "All right, I'll go first. I've never had a long-term girlfriend."

Confusion mars her features. "What? Not one?"

"Nope. Not unless you count the woman I took to my senior prom. We hung out a bit before and after, but there were no titles given. She knew I was going into the military after high school and had no plans for any entanglement back home."

She nods. "That makes sense. At least you didn't give them false hope."

"Nope, I'd never do that," I tell her. "I'm honest to a fault when it comes to women. I'd never say something just to get someone into bed."

She watches me, gauging my sincerity, I'm sure. "So, why not now? You've been out of the military for a while, right?"

"I have, but I guess, I've just preferred to keep things light."

She cracks a slight smile. "Is that a polite way to say it's just sex?"

I lift a shoulder, holding her gaze. "Perhaps. Sometimes, that just makes life easier, you know? But I'm always up front about it. I'd never tell a woman something just to get her into bed, remember?"

She nods in understanding before she takes a deep breath and downs her shot. She makes a face and sticks out her tongue. "Smoother, but still kinda gross," she says, making me chuckle.

Then, she takes another deep breath and levels me with an intense look. "I've dated Lance off and on for six years. Last Friday, I went to his apartment to surprise him, and a woman answered the door. He has been cheating on me."

I try to keep my face neutral, but I already know I fail. Anger washes through me in a way I rarely feel. The last time I wanted to hit someone this badly was when some asshole wouldn't take no for an answer with Charli and tried to get a little handsy. Before I could even take him outside and give him the proper ass-whoopin' he deserved, she kneed him in the balls and dropped him like a bag of hammers.

"I broke up with him immediately and dropped all his shit I had at my place on his Welcome mat."

"Fuck him."

She nods and gives me a small smile.

"I'm sorry you're going through that."

"Thank you, but I should have seen it coming. He was always…distant. Never had time for me, and I always made excuses for him since he was in med school."

"Fuck him," I state a second time with a little more heat.

Her grin widens. "Fuck him," she repeats.

"Atta girl," I say proudly. "Anytime you find yourself starting to make excuses for the cheating bastard, I want you to repeat after me. Fuck. Him."

A giggle slips from her mouth, making my cock twitch in my pants. "Fuck. Him."

I nod and stand up, watching as she does the same. "Lock up behind me."

Confused, she asks, "You're leaving?"

"Yep. My brother will be here in a few minutes to pick me up. My truck is parked on the street, so it shouldn't be in your way. I'll grab it tomorrow night after work, if that's all right."

She looks even more confused. "How will you pick it up?"

"I'll have someone drop me off."

Nodding, she follows me to the front door. "Thank you for dinner," I tell her, pulling open the door.

"You're welcome. Thank you for the tequila. Do you want to take the bottle with you?"

"No, I'll leave it here. You never know when we're gonna need some liquid truth serum again," I state with a wink.

Smiling, she steps up to the door as I exit her house. "Thank you for the company."

"I'm always available to keep you company, Oaklee," I say. "All you have to do is call."

The ball is in her court.

Again, she nods just as my twin's vehicle pulls up to the curb and parks behind my truck. "That's my ride. Lock up behind me."

"I will."

"Sleep tight, sweet Oaklee."

"Thanks to the tequila, I think I'll sleep like a baby," she informs me with a little giggle.

"See ya soon," I say, and without waiting for her to reply, I head for my brother's truck, hands shoved in my pockets. I don't look back, even though I want to. I mean what I said. The ball is in her court. What happens next is her decision, and whatever that is, I'll honor it.

Even though I'm really good at dropping little nuggets of persuasion…

Ideas are already forming as I climb into the truck cab and close the door.

I'm smiling from ear to ear as he backs up and pulls away from the curb. "So…Oaklee…"

I lean my head back, visions of the beautiful nurse filling my mind. "Yeah…Oaklee."

CHAPTER EIGHT

Oaklee

"GOOD MORNING," I SAY AS I ENTER THE BACK DOORWAY OF THE clinic.

"Hey, morning," Allison sings, sipping a cup of something iced from the coffee shop down the block. If I had to guess, it's an iced mocha coffee with extra cream and caramel cold foam, one of the many delicious drinks I like to get when I need a little kick of caffeine to start my day.

The moment I spot her drink, I wish I would have given myself an extra few minutes to go down and secure my own. You'd think consuming a bit of tequila last night would have helped me sleep, but it didn't. In fact, it seemed to have the exact opposite effect. I was up half the night, replaying over and over again every second with Cade. In fact, I picked up my phone twice to send him a text, but every time I'd start the message, I'd delete the few words I'd started with and set the phone back on the charger.

"You look tired," Allison says as I hang my purse on a hook behind the door in the nurses' station.

"Didn't sleep well," I tell her, taking another look at her drink with longing.

"You should have texted me, and I would have picked you up one," she says, obviously catching the fact I'm practically drooling just by looking at her coffee.

I wave off her comment, even though I wish I would have too. "I'll just grab something with caffeine at lunch," I tell her, already thinking about walking down and buying a coffee and an Italian chicken wrap from the diner.

"You know, Doc probably won't be here for another fifteen minutes or so. You could run down and grab something. I'll check in the first appointments," she offers, but it falls on deaf ears. I'd never agree to that, letting someone do my job, just so I can grab a drink.

"Thanks for the offer, but I'm good," I insist, heading toward the front office area to say good morning to the others.

Fiona, the office manager, is already at her desk working and offers a wave and a smile without removing her eyes from her computer screen. Becky, the front desk clerk arrives moments later, always teetering on the line of being late, and flies through her morning routine of powering everything up before our first patients arrive.

I walk through the exam rooms, making sure everything is ready to go, even though they should already be set. The last thing we do after a patient vacates the room is prep it for the next one, and that includes the last patient of the day. But we always make sure the rooms are clean and ready, which they are.

Finally, I take today's patient list from Allison and check them over. Dr. Houston is a GP, or general practitioner, which means we see a variety of ages and ailments throughout the day. He does have a few maternity patients, but not many, since most of them drive over to North Ridge and see the obstetrics practice over there. It looks like one of his expecting mothers is on the schedule this morning, and I admit, these appointments are some of my favorites.

When patients start to arrive, I get to work, checking them in. There are three exam rooms, and we schedule them in rotation fifteen minutes apart. Sometimes we get behind, but usually not too bad. At least, we haven't since I arrived here.

What I love most about working at a small-town clinic, as opposed to the city one I came from, it feels so much more personal. In just a short amount of time, I feel like I know the patients on a more personal level, as if we're becoming friends. I've discovered an older woman named Gladys brings homemade bread to every appointment she has. Last week, it was zucchini, and I was told the time before that, strawberry banana. Allison said her pumpkin loaf is one of the best she's ever tasted, and I honestly can't wait for that.

The patients share stories about their families, work, or everyday life in Cooper Town, and as someone who recently moved, it gives me a look into the lives of those here. I feel like a part of it all, even after just a short amount of time, and I appreciate the vibe I get here.

When all three of the first appointments are situated in rooms, Dr. Houston comes in, looking a bit frazzled. "Good morning," he greets, moving quickly into his office and preparing to see patients.

"Good morning, Doctor. Your first appointments are ready," I tell him.

He nods, wrapping his stethoscope around his neck and making sure his pockets are filled with what he needs. "Janice Dorshe will need blood work. Can you go ahead and do the draw?" he asks, clearly having already checked his morning schedule before arriving.

"Allison is already on it," I tell him, earning a warm smile.

"Thank you," he says before grabbing the chart outside Room 1 and knocking. He slips inside and offers a warm greeting to the patient before enclosing them inside the room to conduct the appointment.

Just as I turn to head to the nurses' station, Becky hollers from the doorway, "Hey, Oaklee, someone's here to see you."

Curiosity piques immediately, because I can't imagine who might be here. Everyone I know is either here at work with me or the few friends I've made since I arrived in town, but they all have jobs and wouldn't just drop by to my knowledge. Text messages, sure, but stopping by the clinic? I don't think so.

I move to the front check-in area and find the young woman who owns the coffee shop down the street. "Hi," I greet when I reach the counter.

"Hi, Oaklee. I'm here to make a delivery," she says, placing an iced coffee and a white bag on the counter.

"A delivery?" I ask, wondering if Allison had made a call.

The woman smiles widely. "Yep! He left me very specific instructions to bring this to you and wish you a good morning."

My mind spins.

Did Lance do this?

But as soon as that question enters my brain, I dismiss it completely. Lance never worried about me eating breakfast or getting a morning coffee while we were dating, let alone after we've broken up. In fact, I'm pretty sure Lance wouldn't know how I took my coffee to be able to order something for me.

Which leaves the question…who?

"He said to tell you, you have his number." Then, she turns to head out.

"Wait," I blurt out, causing her to stop and spin around. "Let me get you a tip. I didn't realize you delivered."

She smiles and waves her hand. "I don't but did this as a favor. And the tip has already been covered, thank you. Have a great day, Oaklee."

I watch her walk out of the clinic, feeling the eyes of those around me.

"Umm, someone sent you breakfast? That was so sweet!" Becky proclaims from her position at the counter.

"Oh, yeah," I say, grabbing the bag and the coffee.

Before I can exit the front desk area, she asks the burning question, "Who?"

I pause and realize I'm smiling. "A friend."

"A guy friend, I'm sure," she replies with a wink. "He did good, whoever he is. No man has ever sent me my favorite coffee."

I just smile and return to the nurses' station, my heart thundering in my chest. By the time I reach the little area Allison and I work from, she's there, having completed the blood draw. "Oh, look at you, running down to the coffee shop."

"Uhh, no, it was delivered."

Allison stops and looks up at me. "They delivered it? I guess I didn't realize they did that, and I've been a customer since she opened."

I shrug and set it down at my station. I take the paper covering the end of the straw off and sip the cold, icy drink. The vanilla and caramel flavors hit my tongue, and I instantly feel better.

"Wait a minute. Oaklee, do they deliver?" Allison asks, watching me intently. There's no missing the gleam in her eye.

I sigh and scoot closer in my chair so no one can hear. "It was sent to me…from Cade."

She gasps. "I knew it!"

"How?"

"Because I know Catie doesn't deliver," she points out. "Not unless you make a special request. So, was there a note?"

"Just a message to tell me good morning and I have his number."

She grins. "You should use it."

I open my mouth, prepared to tell her I almost did, but close it just as quickly. I'm still a little torn about what to do where Cade is concerned. After all, I did just break up with a long-term boyfriend. It's been less than a week, hardly long enough to entertain the idea of seeing someone new. But then again, Cade has pretty much confessed he's not that type of guy anyway. He doesn't date. If I were to text him, there's only one direction it would go, and that's strictly physical.

Yet, that thought is…appealing.

Probably because it's been a while since I actually had sex. Lance was always busy, at least for me. Proof that he was getting it elsewhere answered the door last Friday night, right? So, why not entertain the idea of having a little fun with Cade? One, he's good-looking. Like really, really good-looking. Two, he's let me know he's very much available. And three, it's just sex. No emotions. No strings.

For the first time, I want to do something for myself.

That might be selfish, but it's true.

The last time I put myself first was when I went to nursing school.

I pull out my cell phone and tap the texting app.

"Yeah, girl," Allison murmurs with a giggle before returning her attention to her computer screen.

Taking a deep breath, I type my message.

> **Me: Thank you for the iced coffee and muffin. It was a thoughtful and welcome surprise.**

He doesn't reply, but that's okay. I know he's busy at work. He talked a little about what he does, and I know it's both dangerous and time-consuming on the interstate, where he's working. His job on the paver requires complete attention, and he doesn't take phone calls or check his phone until he gets to a stopping point.

Of course, I think about the truck still parked in front of my house. I admit, the first thing I did when I got up was go peek out the front door and see if it was still there. He said he'd be by after work to get it, and I can't help but wonder what the neighbors thought. Do they recognize his truck? Are they already talking because it's still there?

Not that I care.

At least, that's what I keep telling myself.

I hear a door open and get up, preparing to meet Doc in the hallway. "Go ahead and eat. I'll get this one," Allison says, standing up and leaving me alone in the nurses' station.

I unwrap the chocolate chip muffin tucked securely inside the white paper bag and take my first bite. The chocolatey goodness explodes in my mouth, and I quickly devour the rest of the sweet treat. By the time Allison comes back and lets me know the next patient is here, my breakfast is gone and I'm smiling.

I'm just not certain if it is the chocolate muffin or the man who took the time to send it to me that has the effect on me…

My phone vibrates in the pocket of my scrubs, but I don't retrieve it.

"Got a minute, ladies? Doc wants to talk to us up front," Fiona states after popping her head inside our little station.

"Of course," Allison replies, giving me an odd look.

Without saying another word, we follow the older woman up to the front and find Becky already there, waiting. The office just closed, the last patient left only minutes ago, so the fact we're being summoned to an impromptu meeting is a tad concerning. At least it is for me. Maybe this is normal, but gauging by the odd looks on both Allison and Becky's faces, I'm assuming it's not.

"All right, I'm going to make this fast. I know you all want to get out of here for the evening," Doc says as soon as he rounds the corner and finds us all waiting.

Becky is sitting on her office chair, as is Fiona, while Allison and I both lean against the back counter.

Dr. Houston exhales. "Well, I won't drag this out. You know Cheryl has been to an oncologist for her thyroid cancer. They're going to do surgery this coming Monday to remove her thyroid and some lymph nodes. They've discovered the cancer has spread, and we're being aggressive. I'm going to take the next month off to be with her as she has surgery and radiation."

"Oh, Doc, please send our love to Cheryl," Fiona says, her eyes filling with tears.

"They feel they caught it early enough, and we're both happy with the plan of attack her oncology team has come up with. I'll be here through this Friday and then will return in about thirty days," he says.

"Who are they sending to cover for you?" Allison asks.

He sighs. "Well, my usual backup is Dr. Martinez, but she just opened the new clinic in Haven. I'm told they're going to shift physicians from both the hospital and other clinics to cover. It won't be the same physician every day, but we will have the schedule the week prior. Their goal is to keep it to two or three doctors in our office rotation, so it's not confusing to patients and staff."

He gives his attention to Becky and adds, "When we call to confirm appointments, we'll want the patient to be made aware of the change in physician. I made it very clear to Dina, the clinical manager, I want us to know the week prior who will be seeing patients that next week. If a patient doesn't feel comfortable seeing another physician, then we can reschedule them for when I return if we feel the appointment can wait. But I have my utmost confidence in whoever they send here to help cover. We have some of the best physicians and medical staff in the area."

"We do," Fiona agrees.

"And Dina will be on-site two days a week for the next month. I know she usually makes appearances for a half day or full day as needed, but to help coordinate physicians, she wants to be here more." He clears his throat and continues.

"This is probably a good time to also tell you we're going to add specialty services to our calendar soon. It's part of the reason they insisted on hiring another nurse again instead of a medical assistant. They're bringing in a rotation of specialists two days a week to start. Dina will dive into it more when she's here next week, but the back two exam rooms we use for emergencies will now be used for those specialists."

"So, we'll be seeing twice as many patients those two days?" Becky asks, clearly realizing her work load those afternoons will increase.

"We will, but they assure me it's nothing you all can't handle. The clinic in Rutledge already does this, and their existing staff manages just fine," he states.

No one says anything else as we all process the news Doc shared.

"Things will be a little different, especially with me being out of the office for the next month, but I trust you all will manage and adapt just fine. Dina will be here to help as much as she can, and if she's not in the office, she's a call away. Fiona can call her for anything," he adds.

We all nod, processing the information he's shared.

"I'll let you all get finished up. If you have any questions, come see me or Fiona tomorrow. Dina's planning to be here Friday, I believe, and she can answer any additional questions you have too."

"We'll be praying for Cheryl," I say, returning the topic back to his wife. I've met her once, when she stopped by with lunch to share with Doc. They're a wonderful couple, recently celebrating their twenty-fourth wedding anniversary. They share two sons, nineteen and twenty-one, who are both in college, and from what I've gathered in my short time in town, the entire community loves them.

"Thank you," he replies with a hard swallow.

"Please let us know how the surgery goes," Allison adds.

"I will."

With that, we disperse from the meeting and get to work shutting down the clinic for the night. I get the rooms prepped for tomorrow's first patients, while Allison finishes computer work and sending the last round of prescriptions to the pharmacy. When everything is complete, I grab my purse from the back of the door and meet Allison near the doorway.

"Ready?" she asks.

"Yep."

We step outside, the gorgeous late September air still holding a touch of the warmth from the day. "Have you heard from him?"

I think about the phone in my pocket, the one that vibrated right before the staff meeting, and pull it out to check the screen. When I see his name, I smile.

"I'll take that as a yes," she replies. "I better hear all about this tomorrow morning."

I shared a few breadcrumbs over our lunch hour about running into him last night and sharing nachos with him.

"Good night, Allison," I say before climbing behind the wheel of my vehicle and firing it up. Then, I tap on the phone screen and read the message he sent.

Cade: Sorry for the delay. Work was crazy today. You're very welcome. Dinner?

Smiling, I don't even give any thought to my reply. It's instantaneous and feels right.

Me: Where?

CHAPTER NINE

Cade

"YOU SMELL NICE."

I glance at my twin brother and smile. "Thanks, sweetheart, but I'm still not putting out tonight. I have plans."

He shakes his head as he pulls up behind my personal truck, clearly used to my inappropriate humor and understanding I'm joking. "All I was saying is you don't smell like ass."

I snort, reaching for the door handle. "That's because I showered. I do tend to do that nightly after I get home from work."

"Yeah, but," he starts, leaning over and inhaling, "I smell cologne."

Pushing against his shoulder, I grumble, "Quit hitting on me! I'm your brother, sicko."

He chuckles and rolls his eyes. "You're dumb. And here I thought Cam was my dumbest sibling."

I bark out a laugh. "I'm telling him you said that."

"I'm sure he'll believe you," Collin replies. "Anyway, just here picking up your truck?"

Rolling my eyes, I shake my head. "Just ask what you want to ask. Quit beatin' around the bush."

"You going up to the door?"

"Yes," I reply, glancing toward said front entrance. I know she's home. I see her Cherokee in the driveway.

"Well, have a good night, but I'll be busy with Lizzie later, so if you need another ride home, call Camden. He's a loser and probably not doing anything."

I bark out a laugh and open the passenger door. "I'm telling him you said that too."

"I won't deny it. Have a good one," Collin adds, waving as I close the door and head for the porch.

I wait until he backs away from my truck and drives off before walking up the steps and knocking. Oaklee answers the door wearing light blue scrubs and a smile. "Hi," she says, the faintest hint of a blush on her cheeks.

"Hello," I state with a beaming smile. "I know you just got home from work, but I thought we could discuss our options for dinner."

She nods and steps back, granting me entrance. As I pass, I press a light kiss to her cheek, subtly inhaling the scent of her skin and hair. "What was that for?" she asks, a bit of humor laced in her question.

"That was just a simple hello, beautiful."

Narrowing her humor-filled eyes, she asks, "You kiss all your friends hello?"

"Only the hot ones," I reply with a wink. "And I only have one in that class." I clap my hands together and give her my complete attention. "Now, let's talk about dinner. Any preferences?"

"Not really."

"Pizza?"

"Love it," she says, her eyes seeming to light up just at the suggestion.

"Well, let's go," I insist, turning to the front door. "I'll drive."

"Wait, I need to change."

I give her a once-over, committing every curve of her body to memory. "You look great."

Her brown eyes narrow. "I'm in scrubs."

"And no one wears them better than you do, Oaklee."

She rolls her eyes dramatically and shakes her head. "That was the cheesiest line I've ever heard."

"Not a line when it's the truth."

She exhales dramatically. "Still, I'm going to change. Give me five minutes."

"Whatever."

Before she disappears down the short hallway that leads to her bedroom, she sasses, "Don't touch anything."

My eyes brighten with mischief. "Because you're hiding things? Like what? Bodies? *Hustler* magazines? Men?"

That gets the result I was looking for as she rolls her eyes once more. "Yes, I'm hiding men all over the place. I keep them chained up in the closets."

"I knew it." I wave two fingers between us. "You and I…we're in sync."

A single eyebrow shoots toward the ceiling as she asks, "Because you also keep men chained up in your closets?"

"Not since the last one got away," I reply with a tsk. "Anyway, pizza. Go. Change. Or don't. I think you look beautiful just the way you are."

She spins around and continues on her way, but I don't miss the way her cheeks turn pink before she goes. I move around the living room, noting nothing has changed since I was standing here last night. There are still a few boxes needing to be unpacked, but for the most part, the living room is comfortable and homey.

Spotting a closet behind the front door, I almost open it, just to make sure she's not hiding anything—or anyone—but I don't. Everyone has secrets, and it's not my place to snoop around to try to discover hers. I have plenty of my own skeletons, that's for sure. No need to poke around in someone else's closet.

Glancing at a side table, I catch a framed photograph. I'm not sure if it was here last night, but I notice it now. Picking it up, I take in the three people smiling at the camera. The middle is clearly Oaklee, donning a white hat and white jacket and holding a small pin and rose. On either side of her is an older gentleman and woman, most likely grandparents. They seem happy, proud even, as they grin for the camera.

"Those are my grandparents. They basically raised me."

I glance over my shoulder and find Oaklee standing there, watching me. She changed into a purple top and a pair of blue jean capris, and on her feet are a basic pair of slip-on sandals. She doesn't look like she stepped off a runway or that she spent her week's salary on her outfit, but she looks…beautiful. Stunning, really. Her hair is still up in a ponytail, though she has adjusted it and brushed it out following a long day at work.

"This was the day you became a nurse?"

She nods, stepping closer until she's beside me. I catch a whiff of something fruity with a hint of jasmine. "My pinning ceremony. Honestly, I was surprised they came. I hadn't expected it, though I had secretly hoped. They both worked at that time, and I knew it wasn't going to be easy for them to get off work to attend."

"But they did."

She flashes a grateful smile. "They did." Looking up from the photo, she meets my gaze once more. "Ready?"

"For pizza? Always," I state. Placing my hand on her back, we move to the front door and step outside. "I'll drive."

"I can follow you," she offers. "This way you don't have to go out of your way to bring me home."

I just flash her an easy, charming grin. "You think bringing you back here would be a hardship? Beautiful, any chance I get to spend a few extra minutes with you is pretty good, if you ask me. Plus, this gives me a chance to try to steal a kiss at the end of the date," I state with a wink.

She stops in the middle of the sidewalk. "Is this? A date?"

"Of course," I reply, grabbing the passenger door and pulling it open. "First off, there's the fact we're going to get food. Food constitutes a date." After she climbs inside, I add, "Two, I showered. If I was just grabbing a bite or a beer with my friends, I'd jump in my truck and head straight for our destination, not caring if I smelled like a sweaty construction worker."

I shut the door and jog around the front end to the driver's door. As soon as I climb inside, I fire the truck to life and crank up the air-conditioning. Then, I turn in my seat and meet her gaze. "And finally, three, because you're beautiful, and I'd be an idiot not to take advantage of all opportunities as presented."

Again, cue the blush. It's cute as fuck.

She clears her throat. "What if I'm looking at it as just grabbing dinner with a friend?" There's a hint of humor in her eyes as she waits for my reply.

I put my truck into gear and state, "We can start there, but at the end of the night, you'll be admitting it's a date."

Her soft chuckle fills the truck cab. "And why is that?"

I glance her way and smile. "Because at the end of the night, you'll be begging me to kiss you."

"Hmm," she hums, keeping her eyes on the road in front of us. "This must be some pizza."

"The best. You'll be so appreciative of my expert second date skills, wooed by the Italian delicacy we're about to feast on, you'll be dying for a kiss."

I don't miss the way the corner of her mouth turns up in a faint smile. "Second date?"

"Tequila equals a date, beautiful."

She barks out a laugh. "I didn't know that."

I shrug. "I don't make the rules, only follow them."

She snorts and shakes her head. "Something tells me you don't follow any rules."

I toss her a wink and pull my truck away from the curb. "You may be right about that."

It doesn't take long to drive the few blocks to the main drag and pull into the lot adjacent to the pizza place. Before the doors are even open, the scent of Italian hangs in the air, enticing you with garlic and rich marinara. The moment I turn off the truck and release my seat belt, I ask, "Ready?"

"Definitely." Jumping out, I meet her around at the passenger door and close it when she exits. "I can already smell the deliciousness."

"Have you had Mario's yet?" I ask, leading her to the front entrance.

"Only their Sicilian sub sandwich. Allison and I ordered them last week for lunch."

"Mmm, those are good," I reply, my stomach already growling with hunger. "I haven't had one in a while though. I'm more of a large pizza man, myself."

She shakes her head, reaching for the door handle and pulling at the glass door. "Of course you are. You probably eat the whole thing and then run a mile afterward without so much as gaining a single ounce."

I bark out a quick laugh. Rubbing my hand over my stomach, I reply, "I'll have you know it takes two miles of running to keep this belly looking this flat. Lord knows if the beer and pizza had its way, I'd look like a forty-five-year-old soccer dad, wearing grass-stained athletic shoes and bitching about moles tearing up my yard."

She covers her mouth and giggles. "Wait, you're not forty-five, are you?"

"Thirty-two," I reply, just as Mario walks around the corner. "Cade! Welcome! And you bring a pretty lady."

"I sure did, but she's mine. Keep your pizza-making hands off my woman," I tease the man I've known most of my life.

He scoffs and offers a smile to Oaklee. "See what I deal with from this one? The disrespect." Reaching out, he takes Oaklee's hand and offers a polite shake. "Nice to meet you. I'm Mario."

"Oaklee," she replies.

"Ahh, pretty name for a pretty lady."

"Stop hitting on her," I instruct, earning a laugh from the older Italian man, just as I expected.

"So touchy. Come on, Miss Oaklee. I've got the best table in the house for my new friend," Mario announces, offering her an elbow as if he were walking her down the aisle of a church. He stops in front of the table along the back wall, tucked in the corner. It's no more private than any other table, but it feels more intimate than most. "The best table," he proclaims, pulling out Oaklee's chair and waiting for her to have a seat before helping slide it in.

"You're walking a tightrope, my friend," I mutter goodheartedly as I take the seat across from her.

Mario just laughs in my face. "So touchy." To Oaklee he says, "When you get tired of this Neanderthal, come see me." He's clearly joking, but he adds in a wink for good measure as he sets two menus down on the table. "Taylor will be over here to get your order shortly. And if this one gives you any trouble, you know where to find me."

Then, he's gone, leaving us alone at our table. "I'm never coming here again."

Oaklee giggles. "He's fun. You can tell he's fond of you."

"He loves to give me a hard time, which is exactly how I like it. Mario's a great guy."

"Good evening, I'm Taylor. Can I get you both something to drink?"

"I'll just have ice water, please, no lemon."

"Same," I order.

"Would you like to put in an order for an appetizer?" she asks.

Oaklee glances at me. "You order, since you know the menu."

I nod, turning my attention to our server. "Pepperollies and breadsticks with cheddar and marinara."

She jots it down on her order form. "Great. I'll get this put in and bring your drinks while you look over the menu."

"What do you like on your pizza?" I ask without looking at the menu. I have it memorized.

"Any veggie but green pepper, and I prefer pepperoni over sausage."

I nod, already deciding on the perfect deep-dish pizza.

"I can't believe I haven't been here yet. Do they deliver?"

"They do. I believe it's from four to eight during the week," I tell her as Taylor delivers our ice waters to the table.

"Your appetizers will be just a few minutes. Are you ready to order a pizza?"

I nod. "Large deep dish with pepperoni, onion, mushroom, and premium cheese. Oh, and tell Mario not to be a cheap bastard and skimp on the cheese."

She smiles as she jots down our order. "I'll be sure to relay the message and will have your appetizers out shortly."

"Thanks, kid," I state. The moment she walks away, I add, "One of these days, he's gonna spit in my pizza."

Oaklee makes a face. "I hope it's not today!" she bellows through a giggle.

"No, it won't be today. He likes you."

She grins proudly. "I'm very likable," she says before sipping her water.

"That you are, beautiful. So, tell me. Why nursing?"

She lifts her shoulders casually and picks at the corner of her napkin. "My mom, she was...an addict. She'd get clean but then find herself back with old friends and diving into old habits. I didn't know my dad, and I'm pretty sure she didn't either. I bounced between living with my grandparents and my mom until I was about thirteen, and then finally stayed with them.

"I remember when I was about fourteen or fifteen, I was in my room doing homework and heard a ruckus downstairs. I went to find out what was going on and found my grandpa in the bathroom, bleeding everywhere. He had cut his hand in the garage, and it was pretty deep. I grabbed a towel and applied pressure, remembering something I had read in health class about slowing the bleeding.

"I didn't have my license yet and he couldn't drive, so I ran next door to the neighbor's house and got Mr. Wilson to take us to the ER. By the time we got there, I had the bleeding all but stopped, and the doctor was so impressed, he let me watch them clean up his hand and put twelve stitches in his palm. I realized right then, I wanted to help people and nursing was a good fit."

Something crosses her features, but I can't really pinpoint what it is. It's a mixture of sadness and longing, perhaps, but that doesn't really make sense, since she set out to become and nurse and made it happen.

Any further conversation about it is halted by the arrival of our appetizers. “Here you are,” Taylor says, setting the basket of fresh, warm breadsticks with cheddar cheese dipping sauce next to a small plate of three pepperollies with marinara sauce. “Plates,” she adds, placing two small plates on the table too.

“Thanks, Taylor,” I state, preparing to dive in.

Our server nods. “Be back shortly with your pizza.”

“Oh my goodness, what are those?” Oaklee asks, pointing to the plated appetizer.

“These are pepperollies. Like a mini pepperoni pizza, rolled up and baked,” I state, placing one on each of our plates and then adding a scoop of marinara dipping sauce.

“They smell heavenly.”

“And they taste even better,” I announce, taking a huge bite. “They’re my favorite appetizer,” I add, trying to cover my mouth as I talk and chew at the same time. My mom would tan my hide if she saw me talking with my mouth full, but sometimes, hunger overrules manners.

“Oh my God,” she sings, her eyes wide as she chews. “These are… wow,” she adds, covering her mouth with her hand like I did.

“Exactly. Best date ever, huh?” I ask, offering a cheesy grin as I prepare to devour a breadstick. “Mario and his crew make these fresh.”

She takes a breadstick and dips it in cheese sauce before enjoying her first bite. “I could probably just eat these for my meal and die a very happy, overweight woman.”

I snort and smother part of a breadstick with cheese. “I hear ya.”

“Carbs make me happy,” she replies with a shrug. “My hips may not like them, but I sure do.”

My eyes drop to what I can see above the table, and even though it’s not a lot, I sure as fuck like it. Her hourglass shape is one of the first things that drew me to her the night we met, and I’ll be damned if I’m going to sit here and let her think men only want model-skinny women with no ass or tits. “I think carbs look good on you,” I tell her.

She rolls her eyes. “If you say so.”

“I do,” I reply emphatically. “And I’m always right, trust me. Both of my brothers and my sister may not agree, but they know the truth. If I say something, it's true, and you, beautiful Oaklee, are absolutely perfect the way you are. I say, eat the carbs. There are only a few true joys in life, and let's be honest, pizza and breadsticks are definitely near the top of the list."

She grins. "But not at the top?"

"Nope," I tell her, drenching the tip of my pepperollie in marinara. "That's reserved for an activity with much fewer clothes." I wink and watch as it, along with my words, trigger a blush.

"Here we are," Mario announces, interrupting our conversation. "My very best pie with all your favorite toppings." He levels me with a pointed look. "And extra premium cheese, because I'm not a cheap bastard."

I bark out a laugh and take the spatula he offers. "Thanks, Mario."

"Enjoy. Holler if you need anything else," he says before retreating to the kitchen and leaving us alone once more.

I scoop up the first slice and place it on her plate. Her eyes dance with excitement as she reaches for the Parmesan cheese and sprinkles some on the top of her slice. "I have a feeling this is about to be life-changing."

Grinning, I take my own slice before giving her my attention. "Completely agree, beautiful Oaklee. Completely agree." I can tell she knows I'm not talking about the pizza, and that makes me happy.

Feeding her makes me happy.

Being near her does the same.

I've never felt this comfortable around a woman before, but do you know what? It doesn't scare me or bother me.

In fact, it fuels my need to see her smile, and right now, that includes feeding her, so that's where my focus will lie for the time being. The last thing I'd want to do is freak her out because I'm thinking about stripping her naked, having my wicked way with her, and making her stay afterward. She just got out of a serious relationship, remember?

Leveling her with a small grin, I reach for her hand and give it a squeeze. "Bon appétit."

CHAPTER TEN

Oaklee

"I couldn't eat another bite," I insist, trying to keep from releasing the button on my capris so they're not so tight around the waist.

"Worth it, right?"

"Soooo, worth it," I agree, drawing out that first word.

"Well, how was it?" Mario asks, appearing as if summoned.

"It was the best pizza I've ever had," I tell him, earning a wide grin.

"I'm so happy to hear. I assume you're too full for dessert," he says, a little glint in his hazel eyes.

"Definitely," I say

"I could eat something," Cade states, patting his belly as if he didn't just polish off two pepperollies, the same number of breadsticks, and half a deep-dish pizza.

"Of course you can. You're like a human garbage disposal," Mario teases. "Anyway, I took the chance that my new friend here likes chocolate, so I made one of my famous cookies, still warm from the oven," he says, placing two bags on the table. "And I'm including some of our homemade ice cream you can add to the top when you're ready. It's all bagged up and ready to go."

My mouth drops open. "You make your own ice cream?"

"Of course! I'd never buy it if I was going to serve it to my customers. Everything here is fresh and made to order, including the ice cream."

Cade reaches for the bags. "Spoons?"

"Two in there, my hungry friend. Make sure the beautiful woman gets her share."

Cade's mouth drops open. "One time I ate more than my half. It's not my fault she took too long in the bathroom."

Mario barks out a laugh, making his entire belly shake. "She was pissed too, rightfully so, considering she was the one who ordered it." He levels me with humor-filled eyes and adds, "He ate the whole thing, my new friend. The. Whole. Thing."

Cade rolls his eyes. "Let's go. I don't want you subjected to any more of this man's lies."

Mario cackles hard and sets the bill down on the table. "Don't skip out on the check, buster." Then, he turns and heads toward one of the neighboring tables to say hello.

Cade grabs the check and his credit card and hands it to Taylor as she approaches. When she moves to the counter, he turns to me and says, "I know we tease each other a lot, but it's only because we really like each other. Mario's a great guy."

"Oh, so he was teasing when he said you ate your date's dessert?" I ask, knowing what's coming.

Cade winces. "In my defense, I didn't eat it *all,* as indicated."

I can't help but giggle and take the bag from his hand. "I think I'll hang on to this, thank you very much."

All he does is smile, and when Taylor brings his card and the slip back, he scribbles his name down and a healthy tip without even batting an eye. "Ready?" he asks.

"Yes." As we move through the room, Cade finally acknowledges those in the room with a wave goodbye. We step outside, the sun falling in the September sky.

I climb inside the truck, Cade right there to open and close the door for me. As I fasten my seat belt, I give him my complete attention. "Thank you for dinner."

His eyes are soft, full of delight and maybe…desire? "You're welcome. Thank you for accepting." He starts the truck and turns on the air. "Well, what do you think, Oaklee? Wanna take a little ride with me?"

"Is that code?" I ask, trying not to think about Cade getting naked, but failing miserably.

"Get your mind out of the gutter," he teases with a big smile. "I don't sleep with my gal friends."

"Right," I reply, heavy on the sarcasm.

"I don't."

My mind spins a little. He doesn't sleep with his friends? Just random women? From what I hear about him, he never falls short on finding company to warm his bed, not that it matters to me. I'm not looking for that, right?

But then Allison's suggestion comes back to me.

I'm not looking for serious right now, but maybe a little fun would do my wounded ego and pride some good, you know?

"So…you don't want to sleep with me?" I find myself asking, even though I should probably keep it to myself.

He turns to face me, leveling me with an intense look. "More than I want my next breath."

"But you just said you don't sleep with gal friends."

"I don't."

I rub the side of my head. "You're a little hard to follow sometimes."

He flashes an award-winning grin. "Actually, I'm not. If you wanted to have sex right now, I'd take you back to my place and give you more orgasms than you could count. I'm not being cocky, beautiful. That's a promise, and I always fulfil my promises. But something tells me you're not ready for that, considering you just got out of a serious relationship, so until then, I'll be your friend. Your very hot man friend, who wants to strip you naked and do wicked things to you with his tongue." He winks, and I feel my cheeks heat up and my nipples pebble against my bra. "In fact, I've already done it three times in my mind."

Warmth rushes through my veins and floods my core, causing me to wiggle a little in my seat. I've never...throbbed like this. I was with Lance for six years, and it never felt like this. This heavy sexual tension that's practically a living, breathing entity between us. Just more proof than we weren't right for each other. I was always second best, my needs lagging behind whatever his were.

The thought of being at the top of Cade's list is thrilling.

"Any more questions?"

"Umm, I don't think so."

"Well, if you come up with more, just ask. I'm an open book, Oaklee. I'll never beat around the bush or lie. You want to know something, ask me." He puts the truck in reverse. "Oh, and when you're ready for those orgasms, all you have to do is ask."

The air in the truck cab is stifling, even with the air-conditioning on high. Maybe that's just the Cade effect. He makes me hot and bothered at the most inappropriate times.

As he pulls from the parking spot and drives toward the entrance of the lot, he asks, "What do you say, beautiful? Wanna go see one of my favorite spots?"

"Yes," I reply instantly, realizing I really do want to see it. Wherever it is will give me a little more insight into the man sitting beside me.

He turns left onto the main artery through town and drives past the businesses I've come to know and patronize since I arrived in town. I pay attention to the route he takes, still learning the streets and areas of Cooper Town. We pass through a residential neighborhood and the grade school and eventually reach a wooded area on the edge of town. We turn off the road and follow the winding path that's big enough for two vehicles to pass safely. There's also walking trails and pavilion shelters of different sizes.

"This is the Cooper Town Park," he says.

I take in the large space, everything from the women walking to the kids fishing in the pond. There's a large pool with a splash pad that's unoccupied off to the left, as well as a pickleball court, and a variety of playground equipment sprinkled throughout.

We drive down the lane and turn off in to the smaller of the two parking areas. Following his lead, I unfasten my seat belt and climb from the truck. When we meet at the back of his truck, I ask, "This is one of your favorite places?"

He nods, offering a faint grin.

"Because it's a great place to pick up hot moms on the walking trails?" I tease, loving how his head falls back as he laughs.

"What? No," he replies, shaking his head. "While I know pretty much everyone who walks the trails, I don't come here to pick them up. Half the women are married, taught me in school, or work with my family. Not exactly prime pickings for companionship, if you know what I mean." He takes a deep breath and looks out at the landscape. "This is one of the places I come to decompress at the end of a long day."

I scan the same view he's taking in, and feel the tranquility and simplicity wash over me. The trees are starting to turn, golden leaves mixed with an abundance of greenery, and the birds are singing a spirited melody as the sun drops for the evening. There's no one around, as most people are gathered near the playground equipment or walking trail. Back here, it's out of the way, almost private, and I like it.

"Come on," he says, extending his hand toward me.

I take it without thinking and let him lead me toward the trees. "Should I send a text to a friend, telling her where I am?" I joke, noticing we're veering off the trail.

"Not necessary. I'm rarely up to no good out here. Too many witnesses," he states with a smile and a wink.

I look around and duck beneath a lower branch, careful not to trip over any of the limbs lying on the ground. "I don't know. Looks pretty secluded to me. Is this where you'd take the girls to make out, back in the day?"

Again, he chuckles. “I plead the Fifth on that one. But when I was younger, some buddies, my brother, and I would come back here after we'd go to the pool for a while. We used to throw rocks at beer and pop cans, or whatever else we could find. Once we even snuck some beer from our friend Wyatt's fridge and came back here to drink it. The only reason we were busted was because we had flashlights and one of the town officers showed up. Busted our asses hard. Took us all home and waited there until we told our parents what we did.”

“Oh my goodness, how much trouble were you in?”

“At fourteen? Caught drinking a beer by a guy who went to school with my dad? Yeah, we were in some pretty deep shit. Wyatt had it worse though, because it was his dad's beer. His pops took him out to the barn and made him drink another one. He only made it about halfway until he threw up. Then, he had to clean it up and shower before he could go pass out. Wyatt didn't drink for a while after that,” he says with a chuckle.

“No kidding. I hope none of you drank for a while after that.”

“Well, we were only fourteen, so we did wait a bit. But…we were also kids with a lot of time on our hands. Sometime during our senior year, I think we started sneaking it out again. Or we had another friend who'd use his brother's ID and go buy it.” He flashes a sheepish grin. “We were trouble back in the day.”

“And now?” I ask, grinning from ear to ear because I know what's coming.

“Now? We're perfect, model citizens, Oaklee.”

I bark out a laugh as we come to a stop at a clearing in the trees. There's a large stump left from a tree long cut down, wide enough for someone to sit and watch the stream of water pass by. “Wow.”

“Yeah,” he says, escorting me to the stump. “Have a seat.”

I do as instructed, and even though it's not a huge stump, there's enough room for both of us to sit. Of course, we're very close, but I don't think either of us mind. In fact, I rather enjoy having his arm and hip pressed against mine.

"Do you fish?" I find myself asking as we watch the water swirl around downed tree limbs and large rocks.

"Here? No, but I do at my buddy Wyatt's place." Something crosses his features as he looks out at the water. There's pure happiness reflecting in his eyes with just the mention of his friend's house.

"Your favorite place," I deduce, realizing he said this was *one* of his favorite places.

"Yeah. I spend a lot of time there. We four-wheel, fish, camp, and just hang out. He has acres and acres of land, including lots of farm ground and pastures, so it's not all play. We work a lot too, even if it's just keeping up with fencing and chopping down trees."

"Sounds nice." I try to picture it based on what's in front of me.

"It is," he says, his eyes moving from the stream in front of us and settling on me. "Wanna see it?"

"Now?"

"No, but we could if you really wanted to. Saturday. Wyatt's having a fish fry in the afternoon and a bonfire afterward. It's likely to last all evening. You should come."

"Oh, I don't want to impose," I say, just as a very light breeze sweeps through the trees, picking up my hair and sweeping a bit across my face.

Cade reaches over and moves it, gliding his big, rough fingertips across my flesh. A shiver rakes through me, but not because I'm cold. His touch does that to me, causes an instant reaction. One I can't explain nor have experienced before. But it's all-consuming and makes me hyperaware of how close we are.

"You wouldn't be," he insists quietly. "Wyatt is all about people. The more, the merrier. And it would give you an opportunity to meet a few more people your age in town. Plus, I'd get to show off my new gal friend." He gives me one of his big, gorgeous grins that makes my clit throb between my legs.

"I don't know," I start, but he cuts me off before I can say anything else.

"I know. It'll be fun. After the fish fry, I'll take you around the farm and show you all my favorite spots."

I watch him out of my peripheral vision, catching the flash of eagerness on his handsome face. I know I shouldn't, but what else will I be doing on Saturday afternoon? The clinic is open until noon on Saturdays, though I don't work every one. Allison and I rotate, and this weekend is mine.

I shift where I'm sitting, my hip bumping against his. I can feel the heat of his body radiating through me. "Can I let you know?"

"You have my number," he replies with a wink. He seems to do that a lot, and I can see why. He's so charismatic, like a magnet drawing me in.

We sit in silence for a few more minutes, the sun continuing to drop behind the trees, taking the temperatures with it. After another shiver hits me, Cade stands up and extends his hand. "Come on, beautiful. Time to take you home."

We make our way back to the lot where his truck is parked, stopping before we reach the back end. Our line of sight is drawn to the pond across the lot, where a father and son are wrapping up their fishing expedition. The little guy reels with everything he has, the dad giving instructions as the fish on the line reaches the surface. It pops up and the little guy hollers, jumping up and down as the dad pulls the line up and shows the fish to the boy.

"Have you ever fished?" he asks, startling me away from the scene before us.

"No."

"I'll take you fishing soon," he vows, smiling as he too watches the father and son. The dad takes out his phone and snaps a quick photo of the boy holding the line up high, proudly displaying his catch.

When the dad takes it off the line and they throw it back in the water, the little boy waves goodbye to the fish and they start to gather up their equipment.

"Come on, show's over." Cade opens the passenger door and waits for me to climb inside.

As we pull from the parking lot and continue through the park, I find myself looking around and taking it all in. "There seems to be a lot of activity here. It's safe, right?" I ask, thinking about walking through the park.

He nods. "It is. I don't think I've ever heard of an issue here." He glances over at me quickly before returning his eyes to the road. "Cooper Town is relatively safe."

"Not that Cincinnati isn't safe, but I suppose it just depends on your neighborhood. And bad things can happen anywhere."

"They can," he confirms. "Occasionally, there's some petty theft that happens or a fight breaks out and someone gets severely injured, but we don't have high crime. If you are thinking about walking though, I'd suggest doing it with someone. You're safer in pairs."

I nod in agreement, wondering if Allison would be interested in a walk or two a week. It's such a pretty area, and it wouldn't take too long to get there from my rental.

Before I know it, Cade is pulling up to my house. This time, he pulls into the driveway, stopping near the front sidewalk. He jumps out before I do, making his way around and opening the door for me. "Thanks," I tell him, climbing from the truck cab.

His hand wraps around mine as we make our way to my front door. I pull out the key and slip it in the knob, pushing open the door before turning to face Cade. "Thank you. For dinner and taking me to the park."

"You're very welcome. I had a great time," he says, moving closer. He stands directly in front of me, so close I can smell the soap on his skin and the detergent on his clothes.

I gaze up, my eyes clashing with his blue ones, and feel air lodging in my throat.

"Good night, beautiful," he murmurs, leaning forward enough to press his lips to mine.

No, not to my lips.

He kisses my cheek. Well, that spot right where my cheek and the corner of my lips meet. It's very…sensual and exciting. When he rises to his full height once more, he gives me a boyish grin. "Just a simple good night between friends, sweet Oaklee."

Then, with his hands shoved in the pockets of his blue jeans, he turns and heads away, walking down the steps and back to his truck. I stand here in the doorway, watching as he pulls from my driveway. He honks as he continues on his way, leaving me standing here long after he's gone. After a few minutes, I finally go inside and lock the door.

My heart is tapping a happy little beat in my chest as I practically run through every part of my evening with Cade. The truth is, being with him just felt…easy. Like I could be myself for what feels like the first time in a very long time. I want to get to know him. I'm completely attracted to him, more so than I ever expected, especially for a woman who just left a long-term relationship very recently.

But he makes me feel alive and wanted, and that's a damn good feeling.

I take a deep breath and pull out my cell phone. I tap on his name and let my fingers do the rest. When I reread the message and smile, I tap send and set the phone on the counter. My heart is pounding, but only because the anticipation is overwhelming.

Cade doesn't want a relationship, and that's okay, because that's not what I need. I need someone to show me a good time. To help me get over the betrayal I feel when I think about my time with Lance. To prove to me I'm worthy and more than capable of having a little fun.

And something tells me Cade is exactly the person to do that.

My phone chimes with his reply, and I glance at the screen.

Me: I'd love to go Saturday.

Cade: Here's where to meet me. Wear something you're OK getting dirty. Maybe bring a change of clothes for the bonfire.

Cade: And Oaklee? I can't wait to see you again.

I fan my face.

Yeah, I'm in big trouble with this one.

CHAPTER ELEVEN

Cade

I FINISH CUTTING UP THE ONIONS AND MUSHROOMS AS PEOPLE START to arrive. Wyatt has two fryers going over near the barn, and they're about up to temperature for cooking. Under the shade of the big oak tree, he has a few tables and chairs set up and a Bluetooth speaker pumping classic country from his phone.

"Hey, what can I help with?" my twin asks when he reaches my side.

Ignoring him, I give my full attention to the gorgeous woman at his side. "Hey, Lizard. Tired of the stiff yet? I'm available," I offer, waggling my eyebrows and giving her a big smile.

She reaches over and pats my arm. "Sorry, big guy. I'm quite fond of the stiff," she replies.

"Hey," Collin grumbles.

Lizzie moves to his side and kisses his cheek. "You're my favorite stiff though."

"Eww, don't do that around me. I'm starting to feel all warm and fuzzy," I mutter, faking a big shiver in disgust.

"Oh, don't you worry, Cade. One of these days, someone's going to knock the wind right out of your sails. It's going to be glorious," she proclaims, her green eyes sparkling with delight.

"Watch your mouth," I tell her, pointing the onion slice in my hand at her.

Lizzie rolls her eyes. "I'm going to take this taco salad over to the table," she says, most likely to my brother, and I don't miss the way his eyes follow her every move as she walks away.

"You're drooling," I mutter, placing the sliced onions into a baggie.

"Do you blame me?" my brother asks, a faint smile on his lips.

I don't fail to acknowledge the change in my twin ever since he fell hard for Lizzie. When she bought the bar earlier this year, she slowly chiseled through the brick wall he erected around his heart, knocking down the layers and helping heal the hurt he still carried. Those scowls he always wore have slowly been replaced with smiles, and for that, I'm grateful.

I glance back at Lizzie, who gives Wyatt a hug. "Nope. Not at all."

Collin gives her a full-watt smile, watching as our friend basically hits on her. Of course, Wyatt isn't actually hitting on her. He's subtly giving Collin a hard time and ruffling feathers, much like I do. My twin exhales and shakes his head. "If you'll excuse me, I have to go rescue my girlfriend from the moron."

I snort and finish my task, making sure everything's sliced up to be battered and deep fried with the fish. I say hello to more friends, all bearing food to share and coolers of drinks. Before I know it, the gathering is in full swing, and Wyatt's signaling it's time to start cooking.

Glancing toward the driveway, I realize I'm a little disappointed not to see Oaklee. She said she was coming, and even confirmed earlier this morning when we chatted on her way to work, but I haven't talked to her since. I had a rare Saturday off, but that doesn't mean I got to sleep in and relax. I got up early, went for a run, and then sent her a simple little good morning text message. That turned into a phone call while she was driving, and a promise to see me later in the afternoon.

Yet, she's not here.

Wyatt, Collin, Alex, and I get to work on preparing the food. Of course, we have a crowd gathered around, everyone chatting and watching us prepare the deep-fried goodness. Alex and I man one fryer and start with coating the onion slices in beer batter, making homemade onion rings, while Collin and Wyatt start the fish. I try to keep my attention on what I'm doing, considering I'm dealing with splattering oil and scalding hot food, which is probably why I didn't notice Oaklee join us until I was finishing up the last round of onion rings and getting ready to start the mushrooms.

Just as I'm about to deposit some of the coated mushrooms into my fryer, I hear a laugh that makes me stop. I look up and find Oaklee and Lizzie talking together, standing over near the edge of the barn. My eyes are glued to her beautiful face, the way her hair is pulled back and tied high on her head, and the fact her laughter floats through the air like a hymn.

As if feeling my gaze, she looks over and smiles. That simple gesture crashes into my chest, causing my heart to race and my palms to get a little sweaty. Not to mention what it does below my belt. My balls ache, and it takes everything I have not to grow hard standing in the middle of a big group of friends.

"Earth to Cade." Alex snaps his fingers in front of my face to get my attention.

"Sorry," I state, using the strainer basket to place fresh mushrooms in the oil.

"Ahhh, I see what's got ya so distracted. You brought a friend." He flashes a knowing smile before returning his attention to the woman across the way.

"Eyes over here," I grumble, earning a hearty laugh from my friend.

Like, he doubles over, careful not to drop the bowl he's holding, and laughs. Hard. "Never thought I'd see the day," he says, standing back up and trying to compose himself.

"The day for what?" I ask, depositing the mushrooms and making sure they're not sticking together.

"The day you fell for a woman. I knew it was coming with our boy

Collin over there, but you? Thought you'd be single and mingle for the rest of your life."

I make a face. "Who said anything about falling for a woman?" The question leaves a nasty taste on my tongue and a churn in my gut, but I ignore it.

"Well, first off, there's the fact you warned me away from looking at her. Usually you call dibs, but you've never told me not to look. Not to mention the fact you've glanced over there no less than six times since you noticed her arrival."

Realizing I'm doing exactly what he just accused me of, I peel my eyes away from Oaklee and glare at my friend. "She's hot. Excuse me for looking," I reply casually.

"Oh, she's hot, all right," he agrees, his appreciation of the view evident.

"Knock it off," I mutter, my tone turning harder than even I expected.

"See?" he states, taking a swig of his beer and pointing at me. "You like her. Admit it."

I scoff but refuse to give him what he wants. I keep my eyes where they should be, and that's on preparing some of the food.

"First round of fish is up!" Wyatt hollers, taking a pan of deep-fried goodness over to the picnic area under the tree. Alex follows behind, carrying the container of onion rings with him, and the crowd starts to move in that direction. The thing about my friends is they'll eat all day. Sure, we'll make a plate, but one of the best parts about a fish fry is the grab and go. We'll snack on this stuff far into the night.

"Hey."

I look up and smile. "Hi. Glad you found the place all right."

"How could I not? Once I got out in this direction, I just had to follow the line of trucks," she states with a chuckle.

"Yeah, when Wyatt has a party, they come out of the woodwork. Did you get a drink? I have a cooler over by the porch. I grabbed some of those fruity can things I saw in your fridge, but there's also some bottled water and Dr. Pepper."

She tries to hide a smile but fails. “Dr. Pepper?”

“Best damn soda there is,” I insist. Plus, I might have seen that in her fridge as well.

“I have to agree with you on that one.” She looks around and then down at my fryer. “What are you making?”

“I’ve got breaded mushrooms coming up.”

“Mmm, I love those,” she says.

“Good. You can try one of the first ones up,” I tell her, poking the strainer into the oil and making sure the mushrooms are separated.

Oaklee rocks back on her heels and looks around. “Do you mind if I grab a bottle of water from your cooler?”

“Of course not. That’s why I told you it was there. What’s mine is yours, beautiful,” I practically sing, then smile as I watch the grin spread across her lips.

“Do you want something?”

“Yeah, go ahead and bring me a bottle of water too.”

“No beer?” she asks.

“Not while I’m cooking, but when I finally dive into the fish, you can bet your sweet ass I’ll have a beer. It enhances the flavor.”

Her cheeks blush and she averts her gaze for a brief moment. “Of fish?”

“Yep. And of the beer in the batter. Plus, it’s a law. When you eat fish and have a bonfire, you’re required to have a beer.”

She giggles and shakes her head. “Funny, I’ve never heard of that particular law before.”

“Oh, you just wait, beautiful. I’m about to blow your mind with my extensive knowledge on all the things,” I say, reaching for a fresh pan to start scooping the ready mushrooms. “Go ahead and grab us some waters, and when you get back, these’ll be coolin’ off and about ready.”

She nods before stopping. “Which cooler?”

“The blue and white one to the left of the steps.”

I watch her walk away, noticing the way her jeans mold to her curves.

I've never really thought of myself as an ass man, but damn do I love watching hers as she walks away.

"You get drool on the food, and I'm gonna be pissed."

I turn to Wyatt and narrow my eyes. "You want something, or are you just over here to stick your nose where it's not wanted?"

He laughs, throwing his head back and drawing everyone's attention. "Oh, Cade, Cade, Cade. You're funny." He takes a drink of his beer. "That's the hot one from The Lizard, right? The one who turned you down?"

I huff, fishing the rest of the mushrooms out of the oil and preparing to add a second batch. "You're annoying."

He just grins and winks as Oaklee rejoins me. "Well, hello, I don't think we've officially met. I'm Wyatt Larimore. Welcome to my humble abode." The fucker extends his hand and brings Oaklee's to his mouth to kiss her knuckles.

"Well, thank you," she replies, smiling politely.

"You need anything, *anything* at all, you just let me know," he sings, turning on the charm to the nth degree. I've seen women practically fall at his feet when he adds in a little country boy drawl, but I don't see any of that with Oaklee.

"I appreciate the offer, but I'm good," she replies, handing me a bottle of water and giving Wyatt a big smile.

He covers his heart, like he's wounded. "Well, damn, I'm too late. This one treats you bad, you call me." He winks at Oaklee, and even though I know my friend is joking, I still want to punch him in the face. "I better get back over to the other fryer and make sure Collin doesn't fuck up my fish any more than he already has," Wyatt states, humor filling his eyes.

"You're the dumbass who left him over there, alone," I chastise.

"Lizzie! Did he fuck up my fish?" he hollers, walking away and to where my twin and his girlfriend stand.

"Ignore him. He hits on everything and everyone," I grumble, twisting off the cap of my bottle of water and taking a long swig. "Thanks for this, by the way."

"You're welcome," she replies, taking off her cap and doing the same. "And I can see why you're friends. You're both full of shit."

I bark out a laugh and shake my head. "You might be on to something there." After setting down my bottle of water, I grab one of the mushrooms and hold it out to her. "It's hot, so you'll have to blow."

Her eyebrows arch up as a mischievous smile crests her lips. Suddenly, the food and fryers aren't the only things feeling a little hot. "I'll make sure to blow," she murmurs, moving her lips closer to the mushroom and doing just that.

Blowing.

I feel it fan across my fingers, and I almost toss the mushroom on the ground, throw her over my shoulder, and cart her off to the barn to do very wicked, very dirty things to her. And yes, there would be some blowing.

She takes the mushroom as I move the food around in the oil, making sure they're cooking evenly, but watch as she takes her first bite. Her dark eyes light up as she chews. "This is delicious."

"It's all in the secret sauce," I tell her with a wink, earning a bark of laughter.

"I'm sure there's blowing involved there too," she sasses, and I can't help it, but my cock starts to get hard. The images parading through my brain are not appropriate, and there's no way to stop them. She took the lid off, and now they can't be put back in the bottle.

"Got anything to go over?" my twin asks, holding a pan of fish.

"Yep," I tell him, dumping the pile of mushrooms onto the side of the pan. "Wait," I add before he can walk away. Quickly I grab four slices of fish, making sure to grab each variety. "Thanks."

I place the fish on a clean paper towel, wishing I had thought far enough ahead to have a couple of plates over here for us, but this will do for the time being. In a bit, I'll send her over to get a plate of other food and more fish, if she wants, and then she'll have plenty of room to fill a plate.

"Here," I say, holding up the first piece. This is bluegill."

She nods and takes a slice of fish, nibbling a small bite. "Oh, that's good."

"It's one of my favorites," I tell her, shoving half of my strip of fish into my mouth and chewing.

She takes another bite of her piece as I retrieve the second batch of mushrooms from the fryer. "Sorry, I got sidetracked," Alex states when he rejoins us.

Oaklee looks over to the large group of people congregating around the food. "The blonde with her boobs hanging out?" she asks, smiling as she finishes off her first piece of fish.

Alex just grins. "See? Distracting."

He jumps in, helping me finish battering the last batch of mushrooms, and while I continue to steal glances at Oaklee, something hits me. Not too long ago, I would have zeroed in on whoever it was he was talking to. I might have even gone over there and flirted a little too, leaving him standing at the fryer to cook.

My gaze returns to the woman standing close. She's looking past the barn, the warm breeze gently moving the random hairs hanging around her ears. Suddenly, I want to finish this up and jump on my quad. I had already planned to take her for a ride around the property, and now, watching her stare out at the landscape, I want that more than anything.

More than I want to eat the delicious food over by the oak tree.

More than I want to check out the blonde with her boobs hanging out.

More than I want my next breath.

I'm ready to feel her arms wrapped around my waist and her thighs hugging me tightly, but more than that, I'm anxious to share my favorite spots with her and see them through her eyes. I want to hang out with my friends, share a few beers, and tell old stories around the fire, and I want to do it with her at my side, laughing along at the ridiculousness being shared.

Because there's a lot of ridiculousness with this group.

"Yo, Cade. You're burning the mushrooms."

I glance down and grab the strainer, quickly scooping the vegetables out of the oil. They're not burnt, but they're a bit darker than I normally cook them.

Alex dumps them in the bowl and pats them down with fresh paper towel. "I'll run these over to the masses and be sure to tell them it's your fault they were burned."

I snort. "I have no doubt you will."

"You burned them?" Oaklee asks, returning to stand beside me as I start to clean up some of the mess.

"Not burned. I was…distracted."

"By?" she asks, her lips curled slightly upward.

"You."

"Oh."

I step toward her, not touching her since I have greasy, gross hands that need to be washed, but close enough that our bodies are only a whisper apart. "You're very distracting, beautiful Oaklee."

She gazes up at me and licks her lips. I zero in on them, wanting to claim them with my own in front of God and everyone here. "I'm sorry."

"Don't apologize. It's not your fault you're completely gorgeous, and distracted me from what I was doing."

And there it is. The light blush she gets every time I compliment her. She always seems so surprised by the compliments, which just pisses me off. What kind of asshole dates this woman and doesn't tell her every chance he gets how amazing and beautiful she is?

A cheating asshole who doesn't see her worth, that's who.

I clear my throat and turn off the heat to my fryer. "Let's go make plates. Then, when we're done, I'm taking you for a ride."

Humor fills her eyes once more as she grins up at me. "A ride, huh?"

"Damn right," I reply, stepping back from the heat source, but wishing I wasn't still feeling a little hot under the collar, if you know what I mean. "Now, let's go grab some grub before the rest of the assholes eat it all. Then, you're all mine."

CHAPTER TWELVE

Oaklee

"DON'T LOOK NOW, BUT HERE COMES MY BROTHER."

I practically pull a muscle in my neck to look for Cade. My eyes clash with blue ones as he moves from the opposite side of the barn to where I'm standing with his sister, Charli. Collin and Lizzie left a few minutes ago for work, both scheduled at the bar this evening.

"Doing okay?" he asks the moment he reaches my side.

"Of course she is. She's with me. Go away so we can talk about you," Charli insists, making me smile.

"Well, you've talked about me long enough. I'm stealing her away," Cade tells his sister.

"Fine, whatever. I'll just go over to that big group of single guys and hang out there," Charli sasses, making me giggle when she flashes a wolfish grin to her brother.

"Charli," he grumbles as she saunters away, but it's no use. She continues on her way, as if he didn't say a word. "She's going to be the death of me."

"She'll be fine, Cade. None of those guys are going to fuck with her,"

I state, praying it's true. But I've been watching them all for hours, talking to a few of them, and generally getting to know the people Cade considers friends. I truly believe none of them would touch her. The respect they all have for each other is evident. Many of them are more than just friends.

They're family.

"They won't if they know what's good for them," he replies gruffly before returning his attention to me. "Anyway, are you ready?"

"For?"

His grin is wolfish. "Your ride."

Ignoring the heat in my cheeks, I toss my water bottle in a nearby trash can. "I am."

Cade takes my hand and walks me into the barn. I've already met Winnie and Rough Rider, Wyatt's horses, but they still grab my attention as we pass by. Winnie neighs, letting us know she's not happy to be passed by, so I silently promise to visit with her again when we return.

I've never been around horses. Hell, I've never been around a farm like this. Cows, pastures, and so much open space it takes your breath away. It's completely opposite of the city where I came from, and I can easily see why so many people move to these parts of the world and never leave.

We walk to a back area of the barn where four ATVs sit. I know one is Collin's, because Lizzie and I talked about it earlier, and another belongs to the man standing beside me. Wyatt owns one, and from what I've gathered, the fourth is Camden's.

Cade walks over to one parked along the wall and climbs on. It's a larger, orange machine, the word Rancher across the side by the handlebars. He fires it up, pushing the throttle button. He puts it in gear and drives forward, giving me enough space to climb on. He shifts forward on the seat, holds out his hand, and says, "Normally, we'd wear helmets, but we're just putting around the farm. Hop on."

Placing my hand inside his, I set one shoe on the footrest and swing my leg over. My sitting position is basically with my front pressed right against his back, my arms wrapped around his waist. I inhale, catching a unique mixture of woodsy soap, deep-fried food, and a touch of sweat. What's wild is how much I like it.

Does that make me a weirdo?

I'm pretty sure it does.

"Hang on, beautiful," he says, just before I feel the machine jolt forward.

My arms tighten, my chest presses firmly against his back. But I have no time to worry about it, because we're moving swiftly across the property, riding alongside a fenced-in pasture with cows, and heading away from the house. Once we turn the corner and reach a straightaway, he taps my arm. "Hold on."

I tighten around his waist moments before he guns it, and we shoot forward. A scream flies from my mouth, but it's not one of fear. It's of freedom, because that's exactly what this feels like. The wind blows my hair and burns my face. There's a rumble between my legs, vibrating up my spine. The landscape passes by so fast it barely registers.

And the man I'm holding on to for dear life is at the root of it all.

When we reach trees, he slows way down and carefully turns into the timber. We scoot around, but at a much slower pace than just a bit ago. I'm able to sit back a bit and take it all in, keeping my arms wrapped around his waist, of course.

We move through the trees on well-worn paths. I watch squirrels chase each other, see downed trees that have been cut up and appear to be ready to be moved, and a slice of water rushes by the banks of a shallow creek. It's a beautiful piece of land, and the more I see, the more I feel content and comfortable.

He slows and eventually parks beside the waterway. "Well, what do you think?"

"Of the scenery or the ride?" I ask, finally letting go of his waist and sitting back just a bit.

"Both."

"Well, for my first ride, it was fun. A little faster than I expected at first, but I felt safe with you. And then when we got here and the beauty is almost overwhelming," I tell him, just as a fish jumps from the water with a splash.

He gives me one of his sexy little grins. "I gunned it from the start on purpose. Partly because I wanted you to experience the thrill of a ride, but mostly because I just wanted to feel your arms tighten around me." There's no apology in his eyes as they dance with humor and honesty.

"Oh, well, that was sneaky."

He snorts and turns his attention to the water. "It was smart, not sneaky." He takes a deep breath and lets it out slowly. "And this? This is my favorite spot."

I take it all in with fresh eyes, spotting a few dead trees in the water and what appears to be a small log jam at the bend. "I can see why you love it."

"I come back here alone, usually when I need to think through an issue or process a long day. Wyatt knows when I'm here, just leave me be."

"Why did you bring me?" I find myself asking, especially in light of the fact he just said he always comes alone.

He exhales before placing his warm hand on the top of my thigh. "Because I like you, and I enjoy spending time with you. You're new here, and I can understand what that feels like. Even when you're surrounded by people, it can feel isolating and lonely. When I was in the military, I was always with someone, usually a group, but I could still feel as if I was the only person there. I missed my family a lot. We've always been close, so being away from them was a big adjustment for me. I missed the hell out of my brother, Collin. We went from being together twenty-four seven to enlisting in two different branches of the military and moving to different parts of the country."

He stares at the water in deep thought, and even though I'm sitting behind him, I get a good look at his profile. "This won't necessarily be your favorite spot, but until you find one of your own, I thought I'd share mine with you."

My heart just...soars. It beats with the intensity of a thousand drums. His thoughtfulness and kindness mixed with the sincerity of his statement is something I'll never forget. There's a thickness in my throat as I whisper, "Thank you for sharing it with me."

He nods, and for the next twenty or so minutes, we just sit here. I rest my chin on the back of his shoulder, making sure not to apply too much pressure so it doesn't hurt him, but needing to feel anchored to him somehow anyway.

Finally, he asks, "You ready for the last of our ride?"

"Sure."

Cade fires up the machine and backs away from the creek. We mosey around the timber, making our way to the other end of it. When we get close, I spot a handful of tents all erected between the trees. And just outside, in a large space of pasture, is a mountain of logs and limbs ready to be lit on fire.

He stops his quad near a tent off to the far left. "This one's mine."

"You're camping here?" I find myself asking, taking in the medium-sized dome tent that could easily sleep four or six people.

"Yeah, a group of us usually do when we have a fire and drink. It's just safer that way," he informs me, and I can see his point. No one is driving after drinking, and someone is here to make sure things don't get out of control.

"Smart," I reply, taking in the campground area. There are five tents of all different sizes and shapes, but nothing elaborate.

"It took us a few nights of sleeping on the ground around the fire before we realized we were idiots. We started pitching tents, which most of us had anyway from our regular four-wheeling trips we take to Indiana. Plus, it keeps us from getting too out of hand, like throwing Alex's prescription glasses into the fire."

I crane my neck to look at him. "You threw his glasses in the fire?"

"Well, not intentionally, but they were wrapped in a sweatshirt, and everyone was teasing him about needing the extra layer of warmer clothes to sleep in, especially since no one else brought more clothes, so the sweatshirt got chucked into the fire. We didn't realize they were in there until about five minutes later, when it finally hit Alex."

"Oops."

"Yeah, so now the rule is anything in the tents is off-limits."

"Throwing things in the fire is a normal occurrence?"

He shrugs. "I'd love to say no, but unfortunately, we're an immature, rowdy bunch, and so I plead the Fifth." He points to the big pile of logs and limbs, as well as a small, more strategically wood pile. "Right there is where we'll have the fire. It gets pretty big and hot, so we make sure it's a ways out from the trees."

I nod, my eyes returning to his tent. Something niggles at the back of my mind, and I do everything I can to push it away. The last thing I want to know is if he has women who share his tent with him, but now that I've seen the place he'll be sleeping later, I can't stop the thoughts from peppering my brain. I mean, since the moment I got here, everyone has confirmed he's a known bachelor and is never short on the company of ladies. I'm sure there's been plenty who have slept in that tent, and the fact I feel jealous of them is pretty astonishing to me.

"You okay?"

"Oh. Yeah." My chuckle is awkward at best. "I was just lost in thought for a minute. All good now."

He sits up straight and places his hands on both of my legs. The heat pours through the denim as he splays his big paws out across the material. "No one."

His words confuse me, because I didn't ask him a question. "What do you mean?"

"I've never had anyone in my tent besides my sister, Charli. This place, it's magical, and as much as I like women, with them comes a whole slew of drama. No offense."

I bark out a laugh. "None taken."

"Anyway, when I'm here, it's not to pick up women. I'm here with my friends and family and just having a good time. I want to relax after a long week, laugh with the people I'm closest to, and not have to think for a while."

I lean forward, resting my cheek against the back of his shoulder. "I like that."

After a beat, he asks, "What did you think of your first four-wheel ride?"

"I'd definitely go again," I respond, then instantly regret it. I don't want him to think I'm seeking another invite.

"Good, because I definitely want to take you again."

I smile against his shirt, subtly inhaling the scent of his detergent mixed with a little dirt. I'm like a lunatic, leaning in and sniffing a sexy man every chance I get, and from this position, that's pretty frequent.

"Come on, beautiful. Let's get back to the house. It won't be long, and we'll move back here. We'll bring some of the food to the fire so we can snack, but we get the rest of the mess cleaned up tonight so it doesn't attract critters."

He fires up his machine, but before we continue on our way, I ask, "Cade?"

"Yeah?"

"I'm having a great time."

He turns as much as he can, snaking his arm around my waist. "Next time, we'll go fishing, and it'll be just us."

"I'd like that," I answer, referring to the fishing and the fact we'd be the only two there.

"Good. We'll plan for a Sunday coming up." Then, he bends down and presses his lips to my cheek, very close to the corner of my mouth. I almost shift, to move just a fraction to the left so our lips actually meet, but then I think about his comment about me having to make the first move. To be honest, as much as I want that, I'm not sure this is the right time or place.

"We should get back. I wouldn't put it past Wyatt to send a search party, just to be ornery."

I grin, knowing he's right. I may not know Wyatt as well as the rest of those attending, but he seems like the type to tease and maybe harass his friends a bit, as much as possible. They all do. Even after hanging around them the last few hours, I can clearly tell, and I love it. Not only are they entertaining, but you can feel their friendship as if it were a tangible thing.

We make our way back to the house, where the party is in full swing. It looks as if more people have arrived since we left for our ride around the farm. I'm anxious to visit with Charli more, as well as get to know some of the other residents of Cooper Town.

After everything that happened last weekend with Lance, I wasn't one-hundred-percent sure I'd stay. I mean, I was planning on it, considering I just started a new job and signed a one-year lease on a rental. But there was always an option to leave. It would have cost a ton of extra cash, breaking leases and relocating yet again, but now. . .well, now I know I made the right choice to stay.

This place is quickly becoming home. One I'm building for myself. And considering my childhood was a bit messy, having a place of my own has always been at the top of my list. I love my grandparents dearly and appreciate what they did for me during my time of need, but there was always a slight disconnect. I always felt like they didn't want to have to raise me, but did so out of duty.

We park his four-wheeler by the barn, but he doesn't pull it inside. Something tells me it'll be used again soon. Maybe that's how we all get back there, although I saw plenty of vehicle tracks too.

I can almost picture the scene. A dozen pickup trucks parked around the bonfire, tailgates down and full of friends. Maybe a bottle of moonshine passed around, with cows and horses off in the distance, and country music playing through a speaker just loud enough to hear but not so loud you can't talk to someone next to you. The entire scene makes me smile, and to be honest, it reads like a country song or something out of a Kelly Elliott novel. She writes delicious cowboys, and even though these guys aren't particularly cowboys, it still fits.

Cade climbs off first and extends his hand. "Come on, beautiful. Let's have some fun."

CHAPTER THIRTEEN

Cade

I CAN'T STOP STARING.

From across the fire, I watch Oaklee as she sits on my tailgate and laughs at something my sister or her friend, Sommer, said. The three of them were engaged in an animated conversation, punctuated by the swigs from beer bottles or cans of fruity seltzers.

I'm not just keeping an eye on her because she's beautiful, however. Ever since we moved back here and lit the bonfire, she started drinking and really letting her hair down. She's met just about everyone, and she appears as calm and polite as possible.

But now that the sun has gone down and the booze is flowing, I'm seeing a whole different side of Oaklee. She's fun. Her laughter fills the air, and the flames dance in her eyes. She seems so carefree and happy, and in the moment, I'd do anything to see this side of her over and over again.

Watching her isn't a hardship.

She spots me—or feels my gaze—and says something to my sister before hopping off the tailgate and making her way toward me. There's a slight sway to her gait, and even though she doesn't appear to be drunk, she's most definitely a little tipsy.

"Hey, you," she says, stepping to my side and facing the warmth of the fire.

"Having a good time?" I ask.

"I am. Your sister and Sommer are fun," she replies, taking a drink of her seltzer.

I just smile, especially since those two have probably told every embarrassing story they could think of, as long as it starred yours truly.

"So, I have a bit of a problem," she says, leaning toward me.

I bend down slightly, her body brushing against mine as she gets nice and close. "What's that?"

"Well, I've been drinking. I said I'd only have one so I could drive home, but then one turned to two, and now I'm feeling all warm and tingly and I know I shouldn't drive home."

"Definitely not," I confirm, already knowing where this is going—or at least, where she's gonna end up. "I do have a solution for your dilemma."

"You do?" she asks, turning to face me. Her chest presses against my arm, and it takes all the strength I possess not to just pull her into my embrace, ensuring her entire body is pressed firmly against mine.

"I do." I reach for her hip and rest a light hand against her. "I happen to have a tent."

"I saw," she sings, dark eyes darting to where I told her my tent is positioned.

"And I might have a big blanket in there. Big enough for two," I confirm, doing all I can not to move my hand or flex my fingers, even though they itch to slide beneath her shirt and touch her soft skin.

"Do you have a pillow?" she asks, her question laced with humor.

I tsk and mumble, "Only one. We'd have to share."

"Hmm," she says, twisting lightly from side to side. Not enough to dislodge my hand but enough for me to notice her movements. "Do you hog the covers?"

"Oh, I'm a blanket hog for sure," I state, unable to fight the grin.

"I bet you are, but if I bunk with you, you'll have to share the blanket and the pillow. That means we might be closer than normal. I mean, we won't be able to put a buffer of pillows between us to keep from touching."

"No, we won't," I agree, feigning disappointment.

"I think we can do it though."

My eyebrows raise as a wolfish grin spreads across my face at her unknowing innuendo. "Are we still talking about keeping our hands to ourselves...or *not* keeping them to ourselves."

One of her adorable blushes creeps up her neck and stains her cheeks pink. "Well, I guess we'll find out, won't we."

I lift my arm and sling it around her shoulders. She sags against my side, her own arm wrapping around my waist. "Oh, beautiful, you are definitely trouble."

She sighs and rests her head against the side of my pec. "I could say the same about you, slugger."

I don't know how long we stand here, my arm slung over her shoulder and hers on my waist, but it's quite a while. Alex comes over and chats for a while, even going as far as to go to my cooler and grabbing Oaklee and me each another drink. I might bake him a cake tomorrow as a thank you, because letting go of her wasn't something I wanted to do.

When my sister and Sommer come over, Alex slips away to throw a little more wood on the fire. "You two look cozy," Charli sings, waggling her eyebrows.

"He's warm and strong and holds me up so I don't face-plant onto the ground," Oaklee states with a drunk little giggle.

"Well, come on. It's potty time," Sommer says.

"I can run you up on the Mule," I suggest.

"You will do no such thing. We're perfectly capable of walking up to the barn, thank you very much," Charli sasses, pointing her finger at me. "Besides, now that she has some liquor in her, we can get her to talk about what happened when you two went for that ride and were gone for a good forty-five minutes."

"A lot can happen in forty-five minutes," Sommer adds with a giggle.

"All right, friends, let's go pee," Oaklee states, reaching for Charli's hand. The three of them link arms and head off into the darkness, the sounds of their giggles barely heard over the music and talking.

It's not a long walk to the barn, maybe a hundred yards are so, but I wish they'd have let me take them on the Mule. Wyatt brings it down here for that very purpose, to easily transport people from the barn and the bonfire, but some of the women do walk.

Once they fall farther than the glow of the fire, I almost go after them. What if one of them trips and falls? What if a wild critter attacks them? What if they get lost?

I'm being completely ridiculous, and I know it.

Nothing is going to get close to the ladies, not with the size of the fire. And if one of them fell and needed help, they'd call. And getting lost?

Fuck, I've lost my mind.

I chug half the beer I'm holding just to give myself something to do. I'm drinking a lot slower tonight than I usually do, and I'm not going to lie to myself about the reason why. It's Oaklee. I'm constantly making sure she's all right and having fun, making sure her drink is full, and no one is bothering her. I've paid more attention to her in the last few hours than I ever have for a woman—maybe even all of them combined.

"You all right? You look like you're about to run off into the night and slay dragons."

I glance at my youngest brother, Camden, and raise an eyebrow. "Slay dragons?"

"Yeah, you have this don't fuck with her look on your face or you'll stab someone with a damn sword," he states.

I snort. "I don't have a sword. At least not a metal one," I joke.

My brother shakes his head. "Definitely not what I was talking about."

I glance toward the barn, catching sight of the trio of giggling women as they reach the building. There's enough light outside to see as they slip inside the wide-open doors and disappear. When Wyatt bought the property from his parents, he remodeled the old studio apartment in the hayloft, as well as updated the bathroom. The old one had a tiny shower stall, a pedestal sink, and an avocado green toilet. Since he didn't need the apartment for a farmhand, he opted to make the bathroom bigger and take out the wall between the kitchenette and living and bedroom space. It wasn't very functional anyway, and now he uses it for these kinds of gatherings. The extra fridge space comes in handy, as does the old couch and recliner. There have been plenty of times one of us would crash up there, so we didn't have to drive home at the end of a long night of either working or playing or both.

After a few seconds, I ask, "Having fun?"

"Yeah. You?"

"Sure," I state, watching as Wyatt pulls out his guitar. I can't help but smile. "Things are about to get musical."

Camden chuckles and takes a drink of his beer, finishing it off. "Want another?" he asks, but I shake my head.

"I'm good." I don't mention the fact I've been nursing this one for a bit now, trying to make sure I have my wits about me. "You driving?"

"Nope," he replies, twisting the top off a beer and taking a drink. I recognize the brand instantly as the one Lizzie's dad and uncles own. "My tent's up."

"Good," I reply.

"Oaklee staying with you? Or did you throw a tent up for Charli and Sommer, and she's staying with them?" he asks.

I'm barely able to bite back my groan. Shit. Charli and Sommer. I usually let my sister and her friend crash with me. My tent could easily fit all four of us, but to be honest, four's a crowd. The last thing I want is my sister and her friend lying right next to me and Oaklee while I'm holding her in my arms for the very first time.

My asshole brother snickers. "They can crash with me and Q."

That makes me smile. Charli hates Q for whatever reason or at least loves to give him shit. Maybe hate isn't the right word, but he definitely gets under her skin regularly. He's like the annoying little brother who knows exactly which buttons to push and does it as often as humanly possible.

"I bet Charli's gonna love that."

Cam laughs. "For sure, but my tent is a little bigger than yours, so it'll be easier to fit four in there."

"I've got an extra blanket in mine, or we can run up to the barn and grab a few from the apartment." I know Wyatt keeps some up there for times like this.

"No, it's good."

"Thanks, man," I say as the music from the speakers is killed and Wyatt starts strumming his guitar strings.

He plays around for a few minutes, warming up his fingers and playing small chords of music. I know it won't be long now before the singing starts, and I'll be asked to join in. I usually don't mind though. I love to sing. In fact, I'm pretty damn good at it. But tonight is about spending time with Oaklee, and I can't do that if I'm standing next to my best friend and singing along to whatever country song he decides to play.

"Hey." Oaklee slips her arm back around my waist, and I reflexively drape mine around her shoulders. My sister and her friend walk over to their cooler and then toward a group of women from town. "Wyatt plays guitar?" she asks, her eyes wide with anticipation.

"He does. Learned when he was a little shit of about seven. His grandpa played all sorts of instruments and taught him."

"He even plays the piano, but don't tell him I told you," Cam adds.

"Why not?" she asks, turning her attention to my younger brother.

"Because he says it's not cool enough," I reply with a chuckle.

"I think it's very cool," Oaklee says. "Do you play an instrument?"

"Nope," I answer. "You?"

"Oh, no. I thought about joining band in junior high like all my friends, but we couldn't afford an instrument."

"I'm sorry," I find myself saying, feeling terrible for the little girl with a shitty homelife.

"Nothing for you to be sorry about," she states with a shrug. "It is what it is." She takes a deep breath before adding, "I'm sure my grandparents would have done what they could to rent me an instrument, but I could tell it wouldn't have been easy. Their finances were already stretched pretty thin, with adding a third mouth to feed and care for. They did what they could, and I'll always appreciate that."

I reach down and take her hand, giving it a gentle squeeze.

"Cade, get your ass over here!" Wyatt hollers from the log he's using as a bench.

"Ready for this?" I ask, glancing down at her.

"Ready for what?"

"Singing."

Her eyes widen. "I don't sing either."

"Cade!"

I exhale and shake my head. "Well, unfortunately for me, I do. Come on, let's go over with the rest of them."

Leading her to the group, we walk around the perimeter of the circle until we're behind Wyatt. "'Bout damn time," he mutters. Then, he glances up at Oaklee and flashes a blinding smile. "Hey, Oaklee. Did you know our boy here can sing?"

"I've heard recently," she replies, squeezing my hand now in support.

"Well, he sounds a little like George Strait, only he's uglier."

Everyone laughs at my expense, but I don't give a shit. I could be the butt of every joke told for the rest of the night, and I'd still be having one of the best nights of my life. Having Oaklee here—showing and sharing with her my favorite spot—has been pretty damn remarkable.

Wyatt strums a chord, the song already taking shape. He starts singing "That Summer" by Garth Brooks, and a few hum along. Wanting to keep Oaklee close to the fire, I move behind her and rest my arms over her shoulders. She leans back, her head pressed into my chest. It feels so fucking good.

So right.

We sway to the music, both of us listening to the song, which quickly turns into a second, and then a third. They're all ones I've heard before, but listening to my friend sing and play guitar never gets old.

Eventually, he glances back, and I know what's coming. All eyes seem to be on Oaklee and me as I release my hold on her and move around to sit next to my friend. "All right, boys and girls, how about a little Kenny Chesney?"

He starts playing the opening chord to "She Thinks My Tractor's Sexy," and I belt out the words like I do any other time. Only this time, I feel Oaklee's presence behind me, feel her eyes boring into my head.

By the time the song is about done, several of the guys are singing along and a couple of the ladies are dancing. In fact, I'm pretty sure I know who is dancing. It's my sister and Sommer, twirling each other around as if they're on the dance floor at a wedding reception.

We play and sing a few more songs before I get up and return to where Oaklee stands. She snakes her arms around my waist and yawns. "Ready to crash?" I ask, my heart thumping a little harder in my chest at the idea of getting her into my tent and in my arms.

"Yeah, I think I'm tapping out," she says, giving me a sheepish grin with gazed-over eyes.

"All right, let's go," I say, taking her hand and walking away from the crowd.

"Cade, where the hell are you going? We have one more song!" Wyatt bellows.

"You can do this one without me," I holler, not stopping until I reach my tent.

It's far enough away from the fire that we no longer feel any of the heat, but it's a little quieter. Not that anywhere would be quiet right now, not with all the singing and carrying on happening.

I bend down and lift the zipper, stepping aside to allow her to enter first. The windows are open now, but I know I'll be closing them soon. It may be September, but the nights still get cool. However, it's perfect sleeping weather, outside in the tent in the fresh air with a blanket.

It's pretty damn close to heaven.

I flip on a battery-operated lantern and catch Oaklee's eyes zeroed in on my bedroll. It's not as comfortable as an air mattress, but it sure beats the hell out of sleeping on the hard ground.

Since she doesn't have anything to change into, and frankly, I never really bring anything to sleep in, I point to the bed. "Have at it."

She toes off her athletic shoes and slowly climbs beneath the blanket, making sure to only take a corner of the pillow. I pull my flannel off, tossing it in the corner of the tent and zip up the door and windows, leaving only a sliver open to ensure we get a little fresh air. "I can close that all the way if you get too cold," I tell her before bending down and unlacing my boots.

Finally, I turn off the lantern, crawl onto the bedroll, and lay my head on the pillow. She wiggles toward me, shifting to her side, so I do the same. "I had the best time today."

"I'm glad," I reply as the opening notes of "Friends in Low Places" comes to life.

"You have a beautiful voice," she murmurs, listening to the chaos erupt that usually ensues with the song.

"Thanks. I like to sing."

"You can do it anytime you want," she tells me with a smile.

My grin matches hers. "Just say the word."

We lie there for several seconds, humming along to the song until it finally ends.

"Cade?" she asks after a minute of silence.

"Yeah, beautiful?" I whisper, letting the heat of her body soothe my soul. I never knew lying beside a woman like this could be so damn comforting.

"Remember when you told me you'd kiss me when I was ready?"

My heart starts to beat harder, my breathing lodging firmly in my throat. "Yeah, I remember."

"Well," she starts, placing her hand on my arm and sliding it up to my shoulder. "I'm ready."

"For a kiss?"

She nods. "Yes."

We're already close, but I go ahead and lean toward her a bit more until our mouths are aligned. My brain shuts off and the alcohol swims through my veins, mixing with lust and anticipation. I suddenly feel drunk, but I know it's not from the beer. It's Oaklee. That's the effect she has on me.

I focus on her lips, on the way they part as her breathing picks up. Her tongue darts out, licking at the plump bottom lip in preparation.

She wants this.

She asked for me to kiss her.

"It would be my pleasure."

CHAPTER FOURTEEN

Oaklee

THE MOMENT HIS MOUTH MEETS MINE, THE FOGGINESS IN MY brain clears and my body fires to life. Warmth spreads through me, and I'm not certain if it's from the alcohol or the way his hand is sliding down my side. It's a heady feeling, one I've never had from a kiss.

How sad is that?

All those years I spent with Lance, and we were basically just going through the motions. No, it wasn't always bad, but it became stale at some point in time and neither of us rectified the situation properly. Six years together was too long. I know that now. But it was comfortable and familiar and everything I lacked growing up. He didn't always treat me like crap, just a distant second to whatever it was he wanted or needed.

Okay, fine.

He treated me like crap.

But now isn't the time to dwell on past mistakes, because there's an incredibly gorgeous man kissing me, making me feel alive for the first time in a very long time. Something told me kissing him would be life-changing, and after only a few seconds, I'm proved correct.

I place my palm against his chest and can feel the rapid beating of his heart beneath my palm. I'm sure it mirrors my own. His body is hard, a testament to the work he does and what I assume is also a workout regimen. I know he runs, but it's clear weights are involved too. No man I've ever touched has been this muscular, and while a strong physique isn't top of my priority list when looking for a man, now that I've felt Cade's chest, it appears to be inching closer to the top.

His mouth moves, his tongue slips between the seam of my lips and delves inside. He tastes faintly like beer, but it doesn't bother me. All I want is to experience more, because if the kissing is this good, the rest has to be on a whole new level.

I'm not sure how long we lie here, kissing, but it feels like a lifetime. Yet, only a few seconds all the same. Our hands stay where they are, not moving to cop a feel in any way. It's hard, even when I want to explore his body like Magellan, but this isn't the right time. Not when we're surrounded by people and inside a small tent.

Finally, he pulls back and sighs. His warm breath fans across my face, and when I open my eyes, I spot the faint smile on his lips.

"Cade?" I whisper as he presses a gentle kiss to the corner of my mouth.

"Yes?"

"I'm not kissing you because I'm a little tipsy."

I feel his lips turn into a full-blown smile as he brushes them across my jaw. "And I'm not kissing you because you're a little tipsy."

I exhale and turn into his neck. I can smell the burnt wood on his skin. I never thought the scent of a bonfire could be so damn sexy, but it is. Smelling it on him might be one of my favorite scents ever.

"Sleep, beautiful," he murmurs softly, slipping his arm beneath my neck and drawing me close.

"I had the best time today." I know I've said it before, but it needs to be said again. Today was…amazing.

"Me too," he agrees, placing a gentle kiss to my forehead.

I feel myself starting to drift, even as I replay the entire day's worth of activities through my head. It's the distant sound of laughter outside the tent and his slow breathing that lulls me to sleep.

"Time to wake up."

I feel lips press against my forehead as I slowly open my eyes.

"Here," Cade says, looking every bit as bright-eyed and bushy-tailed as I've ever seen. He's definitely an early riser. Not that I'm not, but usually after a night of drinking, I prefer to sleep in and relax the day away.

Unfortunately, that's not in the cards for me. First off, I slept in a tent last night on someone else's property. I don't have the luxury of sleeping in until I get hungry or need a little caffeine jolt.

But then something hits my nose…

"What's this?" I ask, slowly sitting up and taking the drink offered.

"Just a simple good morning." He flashes an easy, wide grin, as if he didn't just run out and order coffee from the shop in town for me.

I take a sip, and of course, it's something I would order. "Thank you."

I look at him through my lashes, taking in his appearance. He's freshly showered and changed, his teeth are brushed, and he shows no signs of drinking the night before or sleeping outside. I, on the other hand, am the exact opposite. I slept on the ground, in yesterday's clothes, and my breath smells like something died in my mouth. I'm wearing yesterday's makeup all over my eyes, no doubt making me a winner in a racoon impersonation contest.

I sip my sweet coffee, wishing more than anything I had a toothbrush right now, but thankful I do have something to help rinse away some of the grossness. "You ran out and got this for me?" I ask, running my hand across my forehead and pushing my hair back.

He shrugs. "I know how much you like them."

"I do. Thank you," I repeat, grateful for the caffeine. Glancing around, I ask, "What time is it?"

"About eight. Everyone else is still sleeping, I think," he says. "It's been quiet since I woke up at five."

My eyes widen a little. "You've been up since five?"

He just casually lifts a shoulder. "Five is sleeping in."

"You're nuts," I tell him with a chuckle.

"A little, yeah," he replies with a laugh. "So, big plans today?"

I shake my head before taking another sip of the soothing cup of Joe. "I need to mow," I tell him.

"Want some help?"

An eyebrow shoots toward my hairline. "You want to help me mow? Like walk beside me and help me push?"

He flashes me one of his charming little grins. "If that's what you want to do."

"That's silly," I confirm, shaking my head at the ridiculous picture.

"Probably, but I'd still do it if you wanted."

I shake my head. "What about lunch instead?"

"Deal. Ever shoot pool?"

I nod. "A little. I'm not any good though."

"Well, I'm practically a professional, and I'd be happy to show you a few tricks I've picked up over the years," he suggests.

"You want to show me how to use your stick?" I watch him over the top of my coffee and almost laugh out loud when my words hit him.

He barks out a laugh and shakes his head. "My stick is your stick, beautiful. Anytime you want to use it, it's yours." He winks before turning his attention to the tent. "I know it's early, but Wyatt's already out there, stoking the fire. We usually make breakfast for everyone before we start tearing down the tents."

"What's for breakfast?"

"A little bit of everything. We use a big cast iron pan and make a mixture of eggs, bacon, sausage, and cheese. And Wyatt also makes campfire French toast."

My stomach growls at the mention of such delicious food, making me blush. "Sounds good. Can I help?"

“Nope, but you can sit in the chair beside me and watch the magic happen,” he replies, reaching down and grabbing a bag. “It’ll probably swim on you, but I grabbed some clothes so you didn’t feel like you were stuck in yesterday’s stuff. After we eat, you can head home and get ready.”

“I’ll help tear down the tent,” I insist, wanting to be part of it for some reason. Despite needing a shower and a toothbrush, I can’t help but feel like one of the group when I’m with them.

He watches me for a few seconds before nodding. “All right. Go ahead and throw on the clothes and then come out to the fire. I’ll have your chair ready to go.”

I watch as he slips out of the tent, zipping it closed behind him and leaving me alone. I can hear movement outside and the murmur of voices, letting me know Cade isn’t the only one up. I’m sure Wyatt is out there too, and they’re preparing to make breakfast for those who are still here this morning.

Retrieving the small duffel bag he set beside me, I open the zipper and glance inside. There’s a gray crewneck sweatshirt on top, and as I pull it from the bag, I can’t help but bring it to my face and inhale. It smells like him, despite the scent of detergent on the material. There’s a faint scent of Cade clinging to the fabric, and it brings a smile to my face.

I replace yesterday’s shirt with the sweatshirt Cade brought me and also find a pair of joggers in the bag. They’re black and will no doubt swim on me, but the thought of getting out of my jeans is very enticing. So, I go ahead and shimmy out of them and slip on Cade’s. As expected, they’re huge, but since they have a drawstring in the waist, I’m able to cinch them closed as best I can.

The last thing in the bag is a ball cap. It’s black with a black leather emblem on the front of the Marines emblem. It looks worn, but in good shape. It also smells of Cade. Wishing I had a brush or comb to work through the tangles in my hair, I end up pulling it back, adjust the strap on the hat, and slip the hat on my head. Once it’s in place, I push the hair through the hole in the back and let it hang down.

I'm sure I look completely ridiculous in his oversized clothes, but I've never felt so comfortable.

I shove the clothes I took off into his duffel. I find my cell phone and turn on the camera, horrified at what I see. I don't wear a lot of makeup, but what I do wear is exactly as I expected. It's smudged beneath my eyes, and without a make-up wipe or water, there's no way for me to remove it. I try, however, retrieving the sleeve of my shirt and gently rubbing beneath my eyes to eliminate as much as I can. It's not perfect, but it's better than it was before, which'll have to do for now.

Then, I grab my coffee and exit the tent.

It's much cooler outside, and I'm certainly grateful to have the sweatshirt. Wyatt, Cade, and Alex are standing at a table, working, and a handful of bag chairs are set up around the fire. Camden is sitting in one of the chairs, tapping away on his phone, and his friend Quinn is walking from the house, making his way to the fire with a carafe of what I assume is coffee.

"Morning, sunshine," Wyatt greets, wearing a big smile as he scrambles eggs in a large bowl. We're talking three cartons of eggs sitting there, and he's expertly cracking each one and adding it to the bowl.

"Hi," I reply shyly, taking a seat beside Camden and crossing my legs in the chair.

"Sleep well?" Camden asks, putting his phone down and giving me his complete attention.

"I did," I answer, knowing that's because of the man I snuggled against. It didn't even bother me to sleep on a bedroll, which is basically a glorified piece of padding. I still slept like a baby.

"Charli and Sommer should be up soon. They'll be cranky until they get coffee and breakfast, just to warn you. They were up half the night, sitting around the fire and telling lies about everyone." The way he grins lets me know they weren't lies at all. They were probably sharing embarrassing or wild stories, which seems to be a common occurrence with this bunch.

"Is the princess up yet? I brought her coffee," Quinn says when he reaches the spot we're all at.

"Not yet. I'll let you do the honors and wake the bear," Camden states with a grin.

Quinn pours coffee into two Styrofoam cups before moving to the cooler by the table and retrieving a bottle of creamer. He pours some into both cups, a little extra into the one on the right, as if he knows exactly how they take their coffee. I suppose, if they do this often, he most likely does. Then, he takes off toward Camden's tent to wake up the ladies.

"This'll be fun," Camden says, getting up to pour himself a cup of coffee. He doesn't add any of the fancy creamer to his though.

About thirty-seconds later, noise erupts from the tent. The voice is loud, and clearly a woman. It's just far enough away I can't hear what they're saying, but a man's voice joins in quickly before Quinn stomps out of the tent, rubbing his head.

"That went well," Camden deduces, smiling over the rim of his coffee.

"Charli hit me."

I can't help but grin, though I do try to hide it.

"The claws came out before I was even all the way inside the tent. She whacked me, causing me to spill some of the coffee on my hand before I could hand it to either one of them. She's a menace."

Camden barks out a laugh. "That she is."

"I heard that!" erupts from the tent moments before Charli and Sommer come staggering out. "Why are we up so early?"

"It's after eight," Cade replies, having moved to the fire to begin cooking the French toast.

"Too damn early," she grumbles before walking over to the chair beside me and plopping down in it. That's when she notices my coffee. "Hey! Who brought you that?"

I feel my cheeks blush. "Umm, your brother?" I answer sheepishly.

"What the fuck? You didn't think to bring me some? All I got was this cheap shit Quinn brought me."

Cade smiles, flipping his first batch of French toast in the large cast iron pan. "She's way prettier than you. You were hatched on a fence post, remember?"

Charli flips her brother off, sipping her coffee as she throws daggers at him.

A bubble of jealousy sweeps through me. Not at them, per se, but at the close relationship they all clearly have. I didn't have siblings, so this type of teasing is foreign to me, and even though they're joking and harassing each other, you can tell it's done with love. That's where my jealousy stems from. I've never had that type of bond, nor will I ever.

"Good morning," she finally says, turning to face me. "You look… well rested." She waggles her eyebrows.

I shrug. "I've never slept in a tent before. It was actually pretty comfortable."

Charli nods. "I do agree, except when you're rooming with your brother and his dumb best friend."

"You could have slept outside," Quinn mutters.

"It would have been quieter. At least out here I wouldn't have had to listen to the freight train snoring all damn night," Charli sasses.

He grins. "That wasn't me snoring, sweetheart. That was you waking yourself up."

She gapes at him, clearly getting worked up even more. "You're an ass."

He barks out a laugh. "You keep reminding me of that."

She rolls her eyes and turns to face me. "Anyway, I'm completely jealous of your coffee and would probably do some pretty sketchy stuff to get it from you, but I'm overall happy you're here."

"Well, thanks?"

She laughs. After she sips her coffee, she leans her head back against the chair and sighs. "This is the life, isn't it?"

I look around, at the trees with the tents scattered between them, and the people I'm sharing this moment with. It feels amazing, honestly. Right. Content.

And then my eyes zero in on the man starting his second batch of French toast for the group of people. He's compassionate to those he holds dear and wants to make sure they're taken care of. I noticed it last night, but this morning it's more evident. Not only did he run out and grab me my favorite drink, but he's preparing breakfast for the dozen or so of us still here after a night of fun.

He's pretty special, if you ask me.

As if sensing my eyes on him, he looks up and smiles. It reaches his eyes, making them appear even brighter and more vibrant than ever before. Something about this man makes my heart race and my knees weak. He's Kryptonite in one tall, gorgeous package.

He gives me a wink, like he can read my thoughts. I watch as he flips the next batch and then places them in a roaster with the first set. Wyatt is finishing up a massive pot of scrambled eggs with all the fixings inside, including a handful of shredded cheese. By the time he's taking it off the fire, it smells so delicious I can't wait to dive in.

Cade places his pan off to the side, out of the way so no one can get burned, and turns his full attention to me. He extends his hand, helping me stand from the chair I'm sitting in. Warmth zings through my veins, rendering me speechless. All I can think about is returning to the tent and maybe doing a little more kissing.

Of course, preferably after I've brushed my teeth.

"Come on, beautiful. Let's eat."

CHAPTER FIFTEEN

Cade

"YOU SEEM...HAPPY."

I look up at my twin and narrow my eyes. "I'm always happy."

He snorts and shakes his head. "If you say so."

I take my cue stick and walk around the table before lining up my shot. After I tap the cue ball, sending it into the four, it sinks into the corner pocket.

"Everything went all right last night?" he asks from her perch on a stool as he waits his turn to shoot.

"Yep. No one lit their ass on fire, if that's what you're asking," I say, trying to figure out my next shot. I don't have a clear angle on the seven ball, and the two is being blocked by one of Collin's.

"Always a good thing," he agrees, taking a drink of his Coke.

A cackle of laughter pulls my attention to the bar, where Oaklee is chatting with Lizzie and a few of the regulars. The football game is on the TV, but no one is paying any attention to it. Burt and Larry are both listening to Oaklee's story, hanging on every word, and laughing like it's the funniest thing they've ever heard.

"I rest my case."

I turn to my brother, who is giving a rare, wide smile. "What are you talking about?"

"You're happy, and I think a blind elephant can see why. I rest my case."

I pick the lesser of two evils when it comes to my shooting options and line it up. The ball bounces off the rail, not anywhere close to what I was trying to do. Standing up, I rest my hands on my stick and ask, "A blind elephant?"

He shrugs. "I don't know, but I made my point."

"You really didn't. What you said makes no sense."

"I speak the truth. Now, I heard she spent the night in your tent."

I roll my eyes. "Camden or Charli?"

"Does it matter?" he asks, lining up his shot and easily sinking the thirteen.

"Yes. Camden I can pummel the next time I see him," I say, watching as he moves into position for his next shot.

He chuckles before settling in and moving the stick with a fluid forward motion. "Make sure I'm there when you do. I'll bring the popcorn."

I flip him off and get comfortable, since he seems to be on a roll. We finish out the game, and even though it would be Oaklee's turn to play the winner—Collin—we both set our sticks down on the table and head to the bar. My twin leads the way, clearly heading straight to his girlfriend behind the bar. Since he also works here, no one teases him about being back there. What they do tease him about is the kiss he plants on her lips in front of her customers and God.

"Gross! Lizzie, you just let any ol' slob go back there and kiss you?" I belt out.

Collin doesn't break stride on his kiss. He just lifts a finger, flipping me off. "I can't believe you're doing this in front of your customers," I state.

They finally pull apart, and Lizzie looks a little shocked. Her eyes are glazed over and her mouth is hanging open. Something tells me, if they have it their way, she'll need "help" with something in the storage room for about ten minutes and come back out looking awfully satisfied. I mean, that's what I'd do if the woman I loved was giving me the fuck me eyes right here in the middle of her business.

Patrons be damned.

"I got this, if you need a few minutes alone," I state, indicating behind the bar and causing her to blush.

Lizzie quickly spins around and retrieves a fresh beer for Burt, even though he didn't order one. "We're good, Cade, thanks." She opens the can and sets it in front of the customer.

"All right, the offer stands. You two need a minute in the back, I'm your guy." And because I'm an asshole to my twin, I point at him and add, "I'm aware this guy only needs a minute, tops. We did used to share a room in high school."

Again, he flips me off, making the regulars laugh.

I walk over to where Oaklee is sitting at the bar and take the empty seat to her left. "How're you doing?"

"Good," she replies, taking a few pieces of popcorn from the bowl in front of her and popping them into her mouth. "This place is pretty great," she adds, speaking of the bar.

"It is. She's made a lot of positive changes since she bought it earlier this year, and in turn has seen an increase in customers." As if to punctuate my point, the door opens and a group of five guys comes in and heads for the bar. I recognize them all immediately.

They take a table in the middle, chairs facing one of the TVs to watch the game. Blake, a guy two years older than me in school, comes up to the front to order two buckets of beers. "Hey, Cade. How ya doing?"

"Not too bad, Blake. Work going well?" I ask, even though I don't care. The guy's a douche.

"Going great. You out at Wyatt's last night?"

"Yep," I say, my hand on the back of Oaklee's chair and my eyes on the TV.

I see his eyes on us in my peripheral vision, and I know he's zeroed in on Oaklee. I can practically feel the wheels in his head spinning, trying to figure out who she is. It usually doesn't take too long before the gossip gets around and any new person is identified. He's probably heard about her, but if he's smart, he'll keep his mouth shut and move about his business.

"Hey, I'm Blake."

Obviously, that's not going to happen.

Oaklee turns and gives him a polite smile. "Oaklee Daniels."

"Ahhh, the new nurse in town. I heard they had a pretty one working at the clinic," he replies, giving her a big smile. I feel the pressure on my teeth as my jaw tightens. The last thing I want is this asshole hitting on Oaklee right in front of me. He's liable to lose those pearly whites of his.

I'd gladly knock them out for him.

"Yep, I work at the clinic," she confirms politely.

"Here ya go," Lizzie states, setting the two buckets on the counter. "Want to start a tab?"

"Please," Blake confirms, pulling his card from his wallet and handing it to Lizzie. He turns to me and asks, "Gone are the days where you just trust everyone, right?"

Clearly he's referring to the fact the old owner used to just write down the tab on a piece of paper and total it at the end. Now, Lizzie has a computer system that keeps track of those things, but she uses a card to hold it, so if someone slips out without paying, it'll automatically charge the card on file.

Honestly, it's a good thing, especially in light of the increase in business. Chuck's Place wasn't nearly as busy as The Tipsy Lizard, thanks to all the positive updates Lizzie's made since she purchased the old bar. Now, she doesn't have to worry about someone stiffing her when her back is turned.

Lizzie returns with his credit card. "All set. Let me know if you need anything else."

I see the way his eyes light up, and he's probably two seconds away from saying something inappropriate that'll get his ass beat. Collin walks over, behind the bar, and casually steps up beside Lizzie. He doesn't touch her or throw his arm over her shoulder, like he's marking his territory, but just the sight of him standing there must be enough for Blake to keep his trap shut.

"Hey, Collin." He nods his head in greeting and grabs the two buckets. He turns toward Oaklee and adds, "Welcome to Cooper Town, Oaklee. I'm sure I'll see you around."

Then, he takes his beers and walks over to the table behind us. "Fucker," I mutter to myself, but I know they all hear me.

"He's an asshole," my brother adds.

Lizzie turns and gives him a smile. "I can handle assholes," she says and goes up on her tiptoes and places a tender kiss to his cheek.

"I know you can, but that guy just...pisses me off. He's entitled and thinks he's better than everyone else," Collin mutters.

"I briefly thought of asking about him for Allison, but he's definitely full of himself," Oaklee adds.

"Yeah, he's single for a reason," my brother states.

I take a drink from my cup and turn to Oaklee. "Wanna play another game?"

"Sure," she replies, already spinning around on her stool.

I don't say anything to my brother, even if it's his turn to play. He won't care. In fact, just a quick glance lets me know he has no intention of walking away from Lizzie right now. He wants to be where she is, and that jealousy slices through my chest once more.

I push that emotion aside and take Oaklee's hand, walking with her toward the back wall where the pool table is located. In doing so, I pass Blake and his friends, and it takes everything I have in me not to aim a smug grin that way. Instead, I do a chin lift to the group and keep on walking.

I slide the quarters into the mechanism and release the balls. "I'll rack," she says, hip-checking me out of the way.

"My balls are yours," I joke, heavy on the innuendo.

She giggles and places all fifteen balls in the rack. Once they're arranged properly, she moves it to the point on the table and carefully removes the wooden triangle. "Have at it."

I chalk the tip of my cue and take aim. When I hit the cue ball, it careens into the fifteen other balls on the table, sending them flying. One of each falls into a pocket, giving me the option to choose what I want to play. Since my next shot is an easy five ball in the side pocket, I settle on low numbers and take aim. It falls easily, but I miss the next shot.

"Aww, poor baby," Oaklee goads, making me smile.

I lean against the wall, enjoying the view of her playing. She walks around, surveying the table, and settles on an easy shot. When it falls, she does this little shimmy that makes my balls ache.

The ones between my legs, not on the table.

She's positively the most spectacular woman I've ever laid eyes on.

She's a vision.

"Oh yeah," she sings, moving around the table for her next shot.

"Lucky shot," I tease.

"Maybe, but five bucks says I still beat you." She gives me a pointed look and waits for me to reply.

"Five bucks, huh? How about we make it more interesting, and we each get to pick our winnings."

Her lips crack a smile. "Hmm, I get to pick what I win?"

Nodding, I reply, "And I get to pick mine."

She thinks for a few seconds. "Well, part of me would love for another coffee to show up Monday morning at work, but I know you have work yourself. So, how about this… If I win, you have to mow my backyard like you offered. But you have to do it without your shirt on."

I bark out a laugh.

Oaklee shrugs, her cheeks turning darker than I've ever witnessed. "I mean, if I'm going to sit on my back porch, sipping lemonade while you do manual labor, I might as well get a show."

"Deal," I agree readily. "Now, if I win," I start, leveling her with a serious look of contemplation. "If I win, I get to mow your yard, *shirtless*, and at the end, you have to give me a kiss."

She looks completely unamused. "If you win, you want to mow my yard?"

"Yep. I actually enjoy it, and if you think walking around your backyard without a shirt on so a gorgeous woman can gawk at me is a hardship, you would be completely wrong."

"That's dumb," she retorts.

"It's brilliant, because after I win, I'll mow your yard *and* get a kiss as a thanks."

Her eyes narrow a bit and she fights her smile. "You don't think you would have gotten a kiss regardless?"

"Well, I didn't want to assume. This way, when I win, it's guaranteed."

Shaking her head, she sighs. "Fine. If you win, you mow my yard shirtless, *and* I'll give you a kiss. You have a deal." Oaklee steps forward and extends her hand for me to shake.

"Deal."

We play the game, shot for shot, and providing a little extra back-and-forth banter. She distracts me by shaking her ass and dancing around. I'll admit, she easily achieves her goal, because I can't keep my eyes off her. But in the end, with one ball left on the table for each of us, I sink my last one and the eight ball.

I win.

"You cheated," she declares, setting her pool stick down on the table.

I bark out a laugh. "How so? Because I wasn't the one trying to completely distract the other one with boob shots when I bent over."

She gasps and blushes. "I did no such thing!"

Crossing my arms over my chest, I raise an eyebrow. "You literally squeezed your boobs together when you were bent over the pool table and looked up at me."

She giggles. "I was dancing to that song."

Now it's my turn to giggle. "Whatever, temptress. The fact remains; I won. Therefore, I shall be collecting my winnings shortly."

She rolls her eyes. "I'm not really sure this can be considered a loss for me though."

I give her a wink and move to where she stands. My hand wraps around her hip as I gently move her closer to me. "I told you; it's a win-win."

"Come on, let's go up and say goodbye to Lizzie and Collin. I want to make sure I'm mowing in the heat of the day, so I get nice and sweaty while you're ogling me shirtless."

I love the chuckle that comes from her lips as we make our way back up to the bar. The crowd cheers as the Bengals score six on a touchdown run, and even though I'd usually be front and center in front of the TV, watching the game, all I want to do is be near Oaklee. Even if that means mowing her yard.

"We're taking off," I say to my brother, who is now sitting at the end of the bar, off by himself where he can watch the TV and Lizzie at the same time.

"All right," he replies, allowing me to pull him into a hug. I'm a hell of a lot more touchy-feely than he is, which is something he's had to just deal with over the years.

"You go on shift tomorrow morning, right?"

"Yep."

"Well, be careful. I'll see ya when you get home Wednesday," I say. My twin is a full-time firefighter and works forty-eight-hour shifts. It can be long, grueling work, sleeping when you can in a bunk with a bunch of other firefighters, but he loves it. It's been his calling ever since he enlisted in the Air Force.

I throw Lizzie a wave as Oaklee runs behind the bar and gives her a hug, and then we head out together. Since we ate a late lunch at the diner down the block, my truck is parked right out front. I help her climb inside the cab and a minute later, we're headed back to her house.

So I can mow her yard.

Shirtless.

And collect my winning kiss.

I'm the first person to use her new electric mower, and I admit, it's a nice little machine. It covered the ground in her backyard easily, the battery still having life left in it by the time I'm done.

When I stop the machine, I can't help but glance up to her small back porch. She's sitting in one of her kitchen chairs, since she doesn't have anything back here yet, and smiling, sipping her lemonade. She's definitely enjoying the show.

I put the mower back in the garage, removing the battery so it can charge, and head back out to where she's seated. As I approach, she hands me a second glass of lemonade. "Nicely done, Mr. Miller."

I chug half the contents of the glass, not because I'm thirsty, but simply for the fact she's eyeing me like a piece of steak, and she's starving. "I'm glad you like it."

She grins over the rim of her glass. "The view is definitely... appreciated."

I chuckle a gravelly sound and shake my head. "I'm happy to be of ogling service. Anytime you need some eye candy, just give me a call."

"Will do."

Glancing at my watch, I realize it's pushing six and I need to head out. The last thing I want to do is overstay my welcome, even if I was invited. I'm trying to take this whole thing at her pace, and that means not rushing or pushing the boundaries. She may have consented to some kisses, but we haven't talked about anything more. Right now, I need to just leave her with a little tease and the thought of more.

"I should head back home. I have a few things I need to do to prep for work tomorrow. You know, another long day of women objectifying me."

She shakes her head. "So, you operate your big machine without a shirt on too?"

I step forward, hold her gaze, and lower my voice. "Honey, I do my best work with my big machine without my shirt on." By the time I wink, she's already starting to blush.

Taking a single step back, I prepare to head out to my truck.

"Wait, where are you going?" she hollers before I can retreat down the steps.

"Home."

"But...what about the rest of your winnings?"

I smile, my hands shoved in the pockets of my jeans. "Only if it's still on the table. I don't want to push."

She sets down her glass of lemonade and approaches, holding my gaze with every step she takes. "It's still on the table."

Then, she goes up on her tiptoes, places her hands on my chest, and presses her lips to mine. It's a chaste kiss, but one of the best I've ever had. I'm fully prepared to let it be just that when her left hand moves up to my jaw and slides along the roughness on my cheek. Her mouth opens and her tongue slips out, dancing against my lips. I open immediately, letting her taste wash over me.

She slows her movements and pulls back. Her eyes twinkle as she gazes up at me, a faint smile on her freshly kissed lips. "Thank you, Cade."

"I'd come mow every single day if I needed to. I'd even do it with scissors."

She chuckles and shakes her head. "That won't be necessary."

"Have a good day at work tomorrow," I tell her.

"You too. Be safe."

"Always." And with that, I turn and walk down her steps and follow the sidewalk to the driveway. There's a smug smile on my face the entire way.

Best. Bet. Ever.

CHAPTER SIXTEEN

Oaklee

"GOOD MORNING," I SING AS I ENTER THE CLINIC AND HEAD FOR the nurses' station.

Allison arrived minutes before me and spins around. "You're awfully happy. I heard you had an exciting weekend out at the farm," she suggests, waggling her eyebrows.

"Oh, stop it," I tell her, slipping my purse into the cabinet for personal belongings. "Nothing happened."

"Nothing?" she asks, tracking my movements with her eyes.

"Well, nothing but a little kissing."

She gasps. "I knew it! Tell me everything!"

I shake my head, setting my coffee down on the desk beside the computer I use. "I don't kiss and tell," I tease.

"Of course you do!" she proclaims, grabbing her own coffee and spinning her chair to give me her undivided attention. "Spill."

"Well, he invited me to come out to the fish fry and bonfire at Wyatt's place. He knew I had never been on a four-wheeler, so he took me for a little trip around the property. I had a really good time. Met a lot of people who I'll recognize moving forward but won't remember their names," I tell her with a chuckle. I've always been good with faces.

"Then..."

"Then, I had a few drinks around the bonfire. It was a good time, honestly. I've never laughed that hard in my life. Cade and his friends are something else."

She nods. "Their antics are legendary," she agrees. "Anyone could give you stories for days. Did he sing?"

I feel my cheeks heat up as I remember the sound of his voice. It was pure honey and sex, that's for sure. "He did."

"He's good, isn't he? I've heard him sing before, but usually somewhere when he just belts out a song," she says with a laugh.

I can totally see it. Cade has that type of personality.

She sips her coffee and asks, "So, are you ready for today?"

Switching gears to talk about work, I start my computer and prepare to log in. "As ready as I can be."

"I was told the physicians' schedule is here. Apparently, there are three physicians going to be filling in for Doc. One Monday and Wednesday, another on Thursday and Saturday, and a third for Tuesday and Friday."

"I nod. "Makes sense. I'm glad it's a set schedule and we don't find out who the doc is until they show up," I say, going through my log in process. When the system is on my screen, I check today's schedule over. The first appointments should be arriving any minute to truly get our day started.

When our phone buzzes, Allison grabs it first. "Yes?" She listens for a moment and adds, "We'll be right up." As soon as she replaces the phone on the receiver, she says, "Fiona would like us to come up front for a moment."

I nod, grabbing my coffee and following Allison up to the office. Becky is at the front desk, checking in a patient, as we head to Fiona's desk near the back. "Good morning," she greets with a pleasant smile.

"Morning," I reply.

"Okay, I'll make this quick. Dina is on her way in and will work from here today. She has finalized the schedule for specialty services that we will begin utilizing here at the clinic. We're starting with Podiatry services on Fridays, both morning and afternoon appointments, and also a combination of gastroenterology on Tuesday mornings and orthopedic on Thursday afternoons."

"Wow, that's great," Allison says.

Fiona nods. "It really is. Dina and I talked, and on those days, Allison will take the specialty services patients, while Oaklee, you'll handle the regular clinic patients."

"Understood," I reply.

"Apparently, they started scheduling appointments last week for these services, and we already have several patients scheduled for this week."

My eyes widen.

"This week?" Allison asks.

"Yes. The podiatry services have been in the works for a while, while the other two services are fairly new in discussion. However, when they started calling patients who are on a waitlist at other clinics, they found it fairly easy to start filling a schedule."

"Wow, that's great. I thought it would take longer to get those started," Allison adds.

"Honestly, me too, but once the ball started rolling that way, it just all fell into place. The physicians had clinic availability, so working out an updated schedule and whatnot seemed painless." She pulls out two sheets of paper and hands one to each of us.

"This is the schedule for the rest of the month. It's also been updated in the system, so you can check there when needed. But I wanted to show you the physicians who are coming to us until Doc comes back. Mondays and Wednesdays will be Dr. Rhenna Barnland, Tuesdays and Fridays will be Dr. Lance Williams, and Thursday and Saturday morning will be Dr. Beverly Clawton."

A swishing fills my ears as I register her words. I scan the paper, searching for a name and praying I misheard somehow.

But there it is.

Dr. Lance Williams.

And I'll be his nurse on Tuesdays and Fridays directly.

"Oaklee? Is something wrong?"

I glance up, my eyes wide. "What?"

"You just gasped."

"Oh," I reply with an awkward chuckle, clearing my throat. I'm suddenly parched, so I take a quick drink of my iced coffee. "Uhhh..."

"Dr. Williams is her ex," Allison announces, clearly picking up on my lack of ability to speak all of a sudden.

"Oh, no. I didn't realize that," Fiona says, shuffling a few papers. "I can ask Dina if we can do some finagling."

"No," I blurt out. Even though I'd rather have a root canal with no numbing medicine, I won't ask for my new bosses to switch things around. I refuse to be a high-maintenance employee, even though I really want to. If they were to ask me to be the RN for specialty services, then great, but I refuse to ask for a change.

Even if I really, *really* want to.

"It's fine," I state with an awkward chuckle. "Really. We parted on decent terms. I can handle working with him for a few hours."

"Well, it would be more than a few hours," Fiona says. "I mean, it's two days a week."

"I don't mind switching," Allison interjects, trying to help.

"I appreciate that, really, but it's fine. I know Allison is the better fit for specialty services. She's filled in for some of them at other clinics, so she knows the routine," I state.

Fiona nods. "That is true, which is why we chose her over you. She's already cross-trained in their procedures."

"I'll be fine, promise," I say, trying to sound lighter than I feel.

"All right, but if there's any issues, I want you to tell me ASAP. I mean it."

I nod a few times and take another drink. "Will do, Fiona."

Just then, the door opens and Dina walks in. "Morning, all," she says breezily as she passes through the front office and heads for the corner desk she uses when she works from this office.

"Hi, Dina," Allison says.

"Hi," I add, feeling a bit numb still.

"We're gonna get ready for the first patients," Allison says, practically dragging me out of the front office area. The moment we get back to the nurses' station, she asks, "Are you okay?"

"Yeah."

"I can't believe Lance is going to be one of the doctors covering for Dr. Houston."

"Me either," I mutter, wishing what I heard wasn't true.

"Well, if he gives you problems, let me know. I'll gladly switch with you and make his life a living hell," she vows, making me laugh.

"I don't think that's necessary, but I do appreciate the offer."

"All right, let's get to work. I'll take the first patient back to Room 1, and you take room 2."

"On it," I tell her, taking the chart she hands over and following her to the front waiting area.

Time to get to work.

I've tried not to think about Lance or the fact I'll be working with him two days a week, but it's been increasingly difficult as the day continues. I'm worried I won't be able to remain professional, when all I'll want to do is punch him in the junk every time he opens his mouth.

"You okay?" Allison asks as we pass each other in the doorway of the nurses' station.

"Yeah, of course. Why?"

"Well, you've been standing there, glaring at the wall for the last thirty seconds."

Exhaling, I shake my head. "I'm just…thinking."

"Yeah, I bet. Maybe a little one-on-one time with a sexy construction worker will help improve your mood later," she suggests, waggling her eyebrows.

"Stop."

"No way. I think you should pursue something with him. He's obviously into you, and a few orgasms does a woman good after a breakup with a shitty boyfriend. Believe me, I know."

My own eyebrows shoot heavenward. "Know how?"

She shrugs and leans in close. "There was a guy. He wasn't the best to look at, but he was packing and knew how to use it. He helped me get over Zack in under a month."

I snort a laugh and shake my head. "You're bad."

She shrugs. "A girl's gotta do what a girl's gotta do. Remember that." She moves to the hallway, chart tucked under her arm. "I'm certain Cade would help you forget all about the douche, and since he's not looking for anything serious, you wouldn't have to worry about that. Just have some fun, Oaklee."

I open my mouth to respond when Becky pokes her head around the corner. "Hey, Oaklee. You just received another delivery."

"Mmhmm, a delivery," Allison mutters as I pass her, heading toward the front office.

Sitting on the counter is a small plastic bag with a white container inside. I grab the bag, feeling three sets of eyes on me. Without answering the questions they don't have a chance to ask, I return to my workstation and pull the Styrofoam container out. Written on the top is a note.

Thought you'd appreciate something sweet to get you through your afternoon. ~C

The handwriting is too pretty to be his, which tells me he made another call and placed an order for delivery. When I open the lid, I find a large slice of cheesecake with chocolate slivers and a drizzle of fudge over the top.

"Oh my God, that looks delicious," Allison says, entering the room behind me.

"Doesn't it?"

"From the diner. They delivered?"

"Apparently," I reply, replacing the lid and setting it aside.

"Eat it."

"I will," I tell her, grabbing my next chart. "Let me get Mr. Fredrickson into his room and then I'll share."

She grins widely and turns her attention to Dr. Barnland, who is stepping out of Dr. Houston's office. "We've got a physical for employment in Room 1, and there's a sixteen-year-old with an abdominal rash in Room 2."

The older woman with gray hair and a friendly smile nods. "Sounds good, thank you."

"I'll go get Mr. Fredrickson," I state, following behind Dr. Barnland and slipping past as she knocks on the door for Room 1.

I say his name into the open waiting room, but already pick out who he is, considering there's only one older man in the room at this moment. "Mr. Fredrickson?"

"That's me," the gentleman says, standing up and walking to where I stand.

"How are you today, Mr. Fredrickson?"

"Fine as frog hair," he replies with a cheesy grin, making me smile.

"Well, that's good. We'll stop at the scale and then head into exam Room 3."

"One hundred seventy-two."

I look at the older gentleman curiously. "What's that?"

"My weight. One hundred seventy-two," he states with a decisive nod. "And my blood pressure is one twenty over seventy."

"Sounds like you keep good track," I state, watching as he steps onto the scale.

One seventy-two.

I note that on his chart and point to the open door in the hallway. "Let's step inside the room."

I take his vitals, smiling when they're exactly as he stated.

"Betcher wonderin' how I knew all those numbers, huh?"

"Well, I can assume you take your health very seriously and regularly take your own vitals."

He nods. "My wife. She was a nurse for forty-seven years. When we first got married, it started as a way for her to practice her trade. Then, over the years, it became a habit. It's how she keeps her talons in me," he states with a barky laugh. "I'm kiddin', but she does enjoy utilizing her skills, even after she's retired."

"I bet she does," I agree, writing the rest of his vitals in the chart. "Looks like you're here for your annual blood work. Is there anything you specifically want to talk to Dr. Barnland about?"

"Yeah, I got something going on with my left foot. I was hoping she could take a look."

"Can you take off your shoe and sock and let me see?" I ask.

"You don't get grossed out easily, do you, girly?"

I smile. "No, sir."

He does as requested and slowly takes off his shoe. The moment he removes the sock, I can see what the problem is. "What did your wife say about this?" I ask, slipping my hands into a pair of gloves.

"Oh, she had me cleaning it with peroxide, but figured an antibiotic would help."

"I would agree," I say, gently moving the red, swollen skin around his ingrown toenail. "I'm sure Dr. Barnland would be able to help. And the good news is, we have a podiatrist starting this week. Once you've had a round of antibiotics and gotten it cleaned up, we can get you in with them and have the ingrown part removed."

"Yeah, I figured. I used to wear work boots back in the day for my job. My feet weren't in the best of shape after fourteen hour days of being stuffed in a sweaty boot."

"I bet not," I reply with a little grin, writing everything down. "Leave the sock off. I'll let the doctor know you're here, and we can get that toe looked at. Then, I'll do your labs and send you on your way."

"Sounds fair. I'll just wait here," he says, grabbing one of the *Men's Health* magazines from the wall rack and getting comfortable in the chair.

"It shouldn't be too long," I tell him before leaving the room and closing the door.

By the time I chat with the doctor and she goes into Mr. Fredrickson's room, I barely have time to use the restroom, let alone eat my cheesecake. So, I place it in the small fridge kept in the nurses' station and continue with my day. I draw Mr. Fredrickson's labs and send his prescription to the pharmacy, and before I know it, the rest of the afternoon flies by.

As we're finishing up for the day, I remember my afternoon dessert and retrieve it from the fridge. "Have you thanked him yet?"

I glance over to Allison and shake my head. "He's busy working."

"Well, I know one way you can thank him," she jokes, and there's no denying what she's suggesting.

I crack up and shake my head. "You're incorrigible."

"Maybe I am, maybe I'm not. But you know he'd be very receptive to any form of thank you offers."

Grabbing my stuff, I wave goodbye to the rest of the staff, who are all preparing to head out themselves. Allison and I walk out the back door and head for our respective vehicles. "Have sex tonight. Then, you won't care what your douche of an ex says or does tomorrow. You'll still be flying from the orgasmic high."

Honestly, her suggestion has merit...

"We'll see," I say, opening my Jeep door and climbing inside. "See you tomorrow."

"Bye," she hollers before climbing into her own vehicle and pulling away.

While my air-conditioning cools off, I pull out my phone and send a text.

> Me: Thank you for the sweet treat. You didn't have to do that.

His reply is almost instant.

> Cade: Just a simple hello.

> Me: Well, it was very thoughtful. I can't wait to dive in.

> Cade: You haven't eaten it yet?

> Me: We got busy and I put it in the fridge. But now

I'm headed home. I might even just have dessert for supper.

Cade: Want some company?

I don't even have to think about my reply.

Me: I'll grab two forks.

CHAPTER SEVENTEEN

Cade

When she opens the door, I hold up the bag of sandwiches from the deli. "I wasn't sure what you'd like, so I took a chance and got two options."

She smiles widely, sending my heart racing like it usually does when she does that, and steps back. "I'm not too picky."

"Well, I got a chicken salad sandwich and a ham and cheese," I say, kicking off the flip-flops I slipped on my feet after running home and taking a shower.

"Either," she replies, making me stop in my tracks.

"Pick."

She looks up at me with a question mixed with shock. "Umm, the chicken salad."

I flash a grin and lean in, pressing my lips against her forehead. "See? That wasn't so hard, was it?"

She shakes her head and moves into the kitchen. "I guess I've never really had someone ask me that," she says, pulling two glasses out of the cabinet. "What do you want to drink?"

"Water's fine," I reply, pulling the two containers out of the bag and placing the chicken salad sandwich in front of the seat she used last time we shared a meal. When she sets the glasses down on the table, I ask, "What do you mean no one asked?"

She shrugs and takes her seat. "If my ex would have brought over two sandwiches, he would have chosen what he wanted first and left me with the second option, whether I liked it or not."

I sigh, hating how this douchebag has treated her in the past. "What a dick."

She grins easily. "That he is," she confirms, opening the container and finding the sandwich she requested as well as a bag of chips inside. "Thank you for this."

"Well, I can't let you have just cheesecake for dinner," I tell her breezily. "You need something to soak up the sugar."

She grins and picks up half her sandwich. "This is perfect, thank you."

"Of course," I reply, opening my bag of chips and shoving a few into my mouth.

"Umm, I do have something I wanted to talk to you about." She suddenly seems a little nervous, which I don't like, but I do my best to keep myself casual.

"What's up?"

"We found out who is filling in for Doc Houston until he returns," she starts, shifting in her seat. "Lance is one of them."

"Your ex, Lance?"

"Unfortunately," she mutters. "Apparently, he's going to be the physician coming to our clinic Tuesdays and Fridays."

"Damn."

"Yeah," Oaklee agrees. "And I'll be working directly with him because the new specialty physicians will be starting then, and Allison will be working with them."

"Can you switch?" I ask, trying to come up with any way to get her away from the asshole who strung her along for years.

"I mean, yes, but it's not that simple. Allison has filled in for a lot of those types of clinics when they're down a nurse, so she's trained in their procedures. And I'm the newbie, and the last thing I want to do is ruffle feathers."

"But that's not really ruffling feathers if you once dated the doctor and he's a complete asshole."

She giggles. "True. But this is personal. I need to keep personal and professional separate, you know?"

"I do," I agree between bites. "I get that completely, but in this case, the two are firmly entwined."

"Yes, but it's only for a few weeks. A month, actually, and then Doc will be back and all will be right with the world again."

I'm not sure I agree with her, but it's not my decision to make. Having her work beside her ex, even just two days a week, isn't something I'm a fan of. Not because she can't stand up for herself, but simply for the fact she shouldn't have to subject herself to spending time with the man who treated her like garbage. And Oaklee is so far above him, he doesn't deserve to be anywhere near her goodness.

All I know is if I had a woman like Oaklee, I'd do everything I could to make it work.

An unwelcome sadness washes over me. It's not something I'm accustomed to, but it's not exactly foreign either. I look at my parents—and more recently, my twin brother—and see the happiness they have. I'm not naïve enough to know it's not always sunshine and roses, but with them, the good seems to outweigh the bad. It's like their main goal in life is to see the smile on the other person's face, and that's what I've always wanted.

However, I knew it wasn't going to be easy, and hurt is always right around the corner. I watched my brother go through deep pain when Whitney cheated on him. Hell, he ran from it—all the way to the other side of the world. But it was still there, and that's a risk I've never wanted to take. So I've quietly sat back, lived my life, and had fun, all while hoping someday I'd find that person who made me want the "more" I'd witnessed.

Is Oaklee that person?

Hell if I know, but the fact I'm even thinking about "more" says something.

I guess time will tell, which is why I'm fine with not rushing whatever in the hell this is.

"Promise me something," I say after chewing a bite of my ham and cheese.

"What's that?"

"If he gives you trouble, you'll tell someone. Your boss, the clinic manager, someone."

She stares at me with those dark eyes, and I can see her appreciation. She's grateful I have her back, but also that I'm not insisting she refuse to work with him. I can't do that, even if my gut tells me to. We're not in a relationship, even though it feels like something is there. However, even at this stage of whatever it is you'd call this thing between us, I won't be anything close to the asshole we're talking about. She deserves better, and she's going to get that from me.

"I will," she agrees.

"Good. Now, finish your sandwich. That cheesecake is staring at me, and if you don't hurry, I'm about to grab a fork and dive in without you," I state, returning right back to easy and fun.

Her beautiful eyes narrow. "You wouldn't dare."

"Oh, I would," I confirm, dumping half the contents of my bag of chips in my mouth and chewing loudly. When I've swallowed, I add, "You underestimate my ability to keep my cool when something as delicious as that is dangled in front of me. One thing you should know about me is I have a massive sweet tooth. When I see something decadent, all I want to do is devour it."

She blushes, just as I had hoped. I also don't miss the way she wiggles in her seat, leaving me half-hard and with a huge desire to *devour*. "Noted."

We finish our sandwiches, and when I get up to throw the containers in the trash, she retrieves the cheesecake and two forks. "Come on. Let's take this to the couch."

I follow suit, placing my empty glass next to the sink and walking to the living room. She sets the dessert down on the coffee table and grabs the remote. She pulls up her streaming service and finds a show she's watching. "Is this okay?"

"I'm gonna be watching you, beautiful, so pick whatever you want," I tell her, getting comfortable on her couch.

She sets the remote down and grabs the plate. Handing me a fork, I wait for her to take the first bite, which she does. Seeing her lips wrap around the fork and hearing her moan of pleasure has my cock hard. I'm held in complete rapture as I watch the scene. Her little tongue snakes out and slides along the tine, licking off the smudge of cheesecake.

"Stop it," I grumble, shifting in my seat to help alleviate the sudden tightness in my pants.

Her eyebrows shoot up, a sassy little grin spreads across her lips. "Stop what?"

"Don't play coy, vixen. You know exactly what you're doing," I insist, narrowing my eyes.

She holds my gaze and licks her fork a second time. "So good," she sings, swirling her tongue around the tip.

"Fuck," I mutter, running my hand down my face as I watch her seduce me with a fucking fork.

A giggle slips out of her mouth, sounding sexier than any noise I've ever heard. "Sorry, I couldn't help myself."

Slowly, I reach for her fork and gently remove it from her hand, placing it on the small plate with the cheesecake, and returning it all to the coffee table. With slow movements, I angle myself toward her and prepare. Reaching forward, I slide the tips of my fingers down her right arm, reveling in the sensation of her shivering and responding. Her eyes turn into dark pools, almost like she's a little drunk.

"Oaklee?" I whisper, leaning in and running my nose along her jaw.

"Yes?" She's breathless and right where I want her.

Then, I pounce.

Before she even realizes what's happening, we're lying back on the couch, me covering her body with my own, as I tickle her. "Oh my God, Cade!" she barks out through her fit of laughter. "Stop!"

"Sorry, can't. You have to learn not to tease me," I insist, moving my fingers in her side and making her squirm.

Maybe I didn't think this through.

She's thrashing and laughing, trying to get away from me. The problem is I'm lying on top of her, and unless I get up, she's not going anywhere.

"Uncle!" she hollers, making me pause my fingers.

"You've had enough?"

"I have," she declares, panting as she tries to catch her breath.

"And you won't tease me anymore with your fork and the cheesecake?"

She grins devilishly at me. "Not with the fork and cheesecake."

My dick jumps in my pants, and I'm certain she can feel it, considering our positions. I narrow my eyes and stare at her, catching her wording. "But you're not opposed to teasing with other means, I take it."

Her smile is pure innocence, and I don't buy it for a second. "I would never."

"Mmhmm," I mumble, moving my hand so it's resting on her side. "I hope you've learned your lesson."

She bats her eyelashes innocently. "I have."

"Good."

Neither one of us moves. Our eyes stay locked, and I commit the feel of her against me to memory. I'll use it later when I'm alone and home and jacking off, because being this close, our bodies pressed together, is definitely sticking with me for a while.

Probably for the rest of my life.

"Cade?"

"Yes?"

She opens her mouth but doesn't say a word. Instead, she lifts her head and presses her lips to mine. Her hands wrap around my neck, pulling me down to cover her completely. I go willingly, taking over the kiss.

My tongue slides against hers as she shimmies her legs out from under me and wraps them around my waist. My hips automatically move, even though I don't mean for it to happen. A whimper slips from her mouth as she rocks her own hips.

"Fuck," I grumble, trying to deepen the kiss, catch my breath, and not blow my load all at the exact same time.

"Maybe, if you play your cards right," she quips, nipping at my bottom lip.

My head starts to swim as the lust reaches into my pants and strokes my balls.

No, wait.

That's Oaklee.

Her hand is somehow between our bodies and she's cupping my balls through my jeans. Swallowing over the sudden intense dryness in my throat, I ask, "What are you doing?"

She chuckles. "If I have to explain it to you, I'm not sure I'm with the right guy."

An easy growl slips from my lips as I roll us to our sides, careful I don't fall off the couch in the process. "You're with the right guy, beautiful. I promise."

She holds my gaze, her fingers applying the perfect amount of pressure as she rubs. "Is this okay?"

"More than," I assure her, my teeth a little gritted. My left hand slides along her hip to her ass, lifting her leg and placing it over my hip. "You know, if you're touching me, maybe I should touch you. Turnabout *is* fair play, Miss Daniels."

Making sure there's room between our bodies for both our hands, I slowly start to move toward her pussy. When I graze my hand over her scrubs, right where the apex of her legs is, I feel the heat of her excitement. I can almost feel the wetness through her pants. It's enticing, mesmerizing, consuming.

She rocks her hips and gasps. Her mouth is open, her eyes are wide, and the pressure she applies on my balls grows a little more intense. "I have an idea," she offers, kissing across my chin.

"I'm all ears."

"I'm wearing stretchy waistband pants. There's more than enough room for your hand."

"Hmm," I mumble, placing my hand against her stomach and slowly lowering it. With my fingertips inside her waistband, I ask, "Are you sure?"

"I am. But I can't help but wonder if maybe I could do the same," she says, her cheeks already dark pink.

"I don't have stretchy pants."

"No, but they do have a button and zipper."

"They do," I confirm.

Without waiting for me to say anything else, she reaches down and releases the button and lowers the zipper. Then, her hand is there, shimmying between the material of my blue jeans and boxers. Feeling the heat of her flesh through the thin cotton boxers, my balls tighten, almost painfully. Precum is seeping through the boxers.

My own hand finishes its trek down her body, meeting the soft, wet material of her panties. The moment I brush across her clit, she whimpers and squeezes her hand. I thrust forward, mimicking what I'd be doing to her if we were both naked and I was between her sweet thighs.

I keep rubbing her clit, sensing she's getting close. Her body is starting to shake, her hand on my balls getting more frantic. She moves slightly, sliding her hand up and down my shaft. Leaning forward, I claim her lips, letting our tongues dance as we both get closer to coming.

"I can feel it, beautiful. I know your pussy is about to soak my fingers through these panties. Let go."

Oaklee cries out as she comes, and I'm in pure heaven. Watching her come is by far the most spectacular thing I've ever witnessed. I ignore my own need for release as long as I can, soaking up every moment I possible.

When the faintest smile crests her lips and her eyes crack open, she wraps her hand around my dick as best she can and pumps. My fingers are coated in her wetness, brushing against her clit, and I can feel my own release building fast. My spine starts to tingle as she moves her hand. When she brushes her fingertip across the sensitive spot at the head of my cock, I explode.

Taking her lips with mine, I come hard, hot semen filling my boxers. With my eyes closed, I concentrate on the sensations of her hand rubbing me and her mouth against mine. It feels like my orgasm lasts forever, but when it finally subsides enough for me to draw in a ragged breath, my body starts to shake.

"You okay?" she asks, humor in her question.

"I'm better than okay. You?"

"I'm…yeah." Her eyes are closed and there's a big smile on her lips. "I'm good."

"Just good? I'll have to do a little better next time," I insist, pressing my lips to the corner of her mouth.

"Hmm, I think I'm very much looking forward to that," she whispers coyly.

I pull my hand out of her pants, and she does the same, but we lie here for several more minutes, kissing. Finally, I pull back and say, "I should head home so you can get cleaned up and off to sleep."

"What about you?"

"I'll clean up at home," I tell her, even though the thought of driving home with pants full of cum doesn't sound like any fun.

I climb from her couch and make a face, feeling it squish between my skin and my underwear and slide down my legs. But I ignore the discomfort. I head over to my flip-flops and slip them on my feet. Then, I turn my attention to Oaklee, who approaches with a touch of hesitation in her dark eyes.

"Come here," I direct, pulling her into my arms and kissing her lips.

"Thank you for dinner."

"You're very welcome," I reply, releasing my hold on her and moving to the door. If I don't go now, I never will.

"Sorry we didn't get to share dessert."

I wink at her. "Oh, beautiful, we did. Lock up behind me."

"Good night, Cade," she whispers, offering a smile as I go.

"Night, Oaklee."

It's uncomfortable to walk, but there's still a little extra spring in my step as I head to my truck and climb behind the wheel. Backing out of her driveway, I take off for home.

Home to shower.

Home to replay every moment I shared with her tonight.

Home to dream about the most stunning woman in the world and what it felt like to witness her come against my fingers.

And what a great fucking dream that'll be.

CHAPTER EIGHTEEN

Oaklee

I TAKE A DEEP, CALMING BREATH AND ENTER MY CODE INTO THE back entrance of the clinic. I'm here before Allison, which is surprising, but I'm arriving a few extra minutes earlier than normal. I've been up since before the sun, my mind already dreading my workday.

I let the door close loudly behind me and note the light already on in the front office. I'm sure Fiona is already here, usually beginning her day at seven thirty. The light is also on in Dr. Houston's office. Normally, that wouldn't strike me as odd, but since Allison isn't here yet, not a physician, it catches my attention.

Setting my coffee down on my workstation and placing my purse in the cabinet, I turn around to see if a light was left on and yelp. "Jesus," I practically holler, covering my heart with my hand.

"Didn't mean to scare you," Lance replies, a knowing smirk on his smug face.

"Oaklee, are you all right?"

I turn to the voice and smile. "Yeah, sorry, Fiona. Dr. Williams startled me, that's all."

She looks back and forth between us and nods. "Okay. Let me know if you need anything."

"I will, thanks. And good morning," I reply, pasting a big fake smile on my face.

"Good morning to you," she says before disappearing back into the office to continue her work.

"May I speak with you?" Lance asks.

"About work?" I inquire, turning my attention to my computer and pressing the on button.

"Sure."

I sigh, knowing it's not about work at all. Grabbing my iced coffee, I spin around, leaving plenty of space between us. He takes a step closer, but I hold up my hand. "That's close enough. We are working together on a professional basis. That's it."

His eyebrows shoot up and a smirk falls across his lips. His hands move to his starch-pressed white lab coat. "You think I want something from you? Awfully full of yourself, aren't we?"

"No, but I know your game, Lance. You may be the physician two days a week at the clinic where I work, but that's it. We're not friends. We're not anything."

He steps closer, his eyes softening as he approaches. "We used to be a lot of things, Oaklee."

"Used to be is the key phrase there. Not anymore."

He opens his mouth to say something, but we're interrupted by the back entrance door opening. "Good morning," I hear Allison say as she enters the building.

Lance takes a small step back but is still blocking the doorway. Allison steps around the corner, entering the nurses' station and stops dead in her tracks. "Hi." Her eyes move from Lance to me, a look of worry crossing her features.

"Good morning, Allison. This is Dr. Williams," I say politely, hoping to keep any tightness out of my voice.

"Ahh, Dr. Williams," Allison says, extending her hand. "I've heard a lot about you."

I have to bite my bottom lip to keep from smiling.

"All positive, I'm sure," he replies with a warm smile as he shakes her hand.

Allison chuckles. That's her only reply.

"Well, I'll let you two get your day started. I came in early to learn the layout of the facility and meet the staff. I'm happy to be able to help in Dr. Houston's absence," he says, returning to his usual, charming self.

I don't reply, but Allison does.

"Listen, Dr. Williams, I know it might be a bit uncomfortable working here, given your previous relationship status with Oaklee, but I'm sure everyone can keep it professional, right?"

"Of course." There's a tightness around his mouth I notice immediately. He definitely doesn't appreciate being called out by Allison.

"I thought so, but I wanted to say something regardless," she adds with a warm smile that's too big and clearly fake.

"I can understand your concern, but I have no intention of causing Oaklee or anyone here any extra stress. I want this to be a comfortable working environment." He flashes his own fake smile, making me want to roll my eyes.

"Excellent," she replies, pushing past him and entering our space. "If you need anything, let me know. I'll be right here," she adds, leaving a heaviness hanging in her statement. She's telling him she's watching him without saying the words.

Man, I love this woman.

"Nice to meet you, Allison," he replies before turning and exiting our small work area.

When we know he's across the hall, she turns her attention to me. "I hate him," she murmurs softly as to not be overheard.

I can't help but smile. "Something else we have in common."

She snorts. "What did the parasite say?"

"Nothing, really, but I'm sure if you hadn't walked in, he would have. We had only just started talking."

"Well, the offer still stands, if he gives you problems, let Fiona know and I'll trade you. Specialty services aren't much different than our regular clinic procedures. I'm certain you can pick it up quickly."

I exhale and take a sip of my iced coffee. "Thank you for the offer, but I'm sure we'll be fine. Lance is a lot of things, but when it comes to his career, he's always been one-hundred-percent dedicated. That was part of our problem," I say, recalling all the times he put himself, his career, and schooling above everything else, including me.

"If you say so." Shoving her purse in the cabinet, she turns to me and adds, "I'll still junk-punch him if you want."

I grin. "Not necessary, but thank you for the offer."

Nodding, she moves over to her computer and turns it on. "Anything happen with you-know-who since we last spoke?" She glances at me, sipping her own iced drink.

I feel my face heat. "Maybe…"

Her eyes widen. "Tell me everything," she whisper-yells.

"Nothing much to tell, but he came over again after work and brought sandwiches from the deli."

"He's such a sweetheart. Did he bring you anything else?" she asks.

When I don't reply, she spins in her chair and gasps. "Did he bring… the D?" she asks quietly.

"No! I mean, well, no, but kinda."

She looks concerned as she tries to understand. "Honey, usually there isn't any question about whether he brought it or not, especially if he's using it right."

I shake my head and chuckle. "We didn't…you know, but we did fool around a little."

"Yeah? And?"

"And…it was…"

"The blush says it all, honey. Good for you."

We don't talk about Cade or what happened last night again, mostly because the moment the clinic opens, we're being pulled in every which direction. Dr. Liu, the gastroenterologist, arrives and from the first moment I met her, I can tell she's a delight. She's young and energetic, and even though I'm not her nurse directly, I can tell her patients connect and respect her.

I remain in complete professional mode the entire morning, speaking politely to Lance, but refusing to engage any further than what is deemed necessary. When he steps in a little too closely in the hallway, I do my best to sidestep away, always keeping as much distance as possible. He realizes his nearness is a problem for me, I'm sure of it, because he always wears a faint smirk on his smug-ass face. It makes me want to punch it off him.

Or let Allison kick him in the balls.

Just before noon, Allison catches me at the nurses' station while I'm sending in a prescription. "Everything going okay?"

"Yep," I reply, eyes on my screen while I complete the refill request.

"I'm ordering a sandwich from Mario's. Do you want anything?"

I instantly recall the deliciousness Cade and I had when he took me to the pizza joint, and my stomach growls. "I'd love something from there," I tell her.

She slides a notepad to me. "Write down your order and I'll call it in. I have to stop by the pharmacy and grab something, so I'll pick them all up."

"Sounds good," I reply, reaching for the notepad and scratching down what I want. I opt for a personal pan pizza with veggies and a side salad, even though I would much rather have Mario's freshly baked breadsticks. I skip a drink, knowing I have a few cans of something caffeinated, as well as some bottled water, in the mini fridge behind me.

"Oaklee, you have a delivery," Becky says from the doorway, catching my attention.

There's a little extra spring in my step as I head to the front office to see what Cade sent. Because, if I know anything, it's that whatever has arrived is from the man I've been spending my free time with.

When I reach the office, I spot a vase sitting on the counter with a single flower inside. It's a gorgeous pink lily that smells amazing and draws a smile to my lips. Collecting the vase, I return to my workstation quickly without asking any questions once more, despite the fact Becky was staring at me, waiting on me to comment.

Setting the vase by my computer, I grab the card wrapped around the vase.

Just a simple hello. Hope your day is as beautiful as you. ~C

Warmth spreads through my body, landing firmly between my legs. I've replayed everything that happened last night over and over again, remembering what it felt like to have his fingers rubbing against my clit. Even through my panties, it felt better than almost every other sexual encounter I've ever had. It makes me wonder how amazing it would be without all the clothing barriers. What if we were both naked? What if he was hovering above me, slowly sliding that big cock of his inside me for the first time? My nipples tingle with desire, and I can practically feel his thumb rubbing across each hard bud.

"Oaklee?"

I spin toward the entryway, startled by the sudden appearance of Lance. "What?"

He glances at the flower first before slowly meeting my gaze. "Delivery?"

Clearing my throat, I nod. "Yes."

He doesn't say anything for a few seconds, making those seconds feel much longer than they are. "Are you seeing someone?" he finally asks, crossing his arms over his chest and taking a defensive stance.

"That's none of your business," I reply, standing up and preparing to finish up my final patient for the morning.

"Actually, it is…if you were seeing someone before we ended our relationship." His tone is snarky and accusing, and it immediately puts me on edge.

"I'd never do that," I state pointedly. "I'm not *you*."

He tsks. "Don't play the victim, Oaklee. You were just as much a problem in our relationship."

"You're right, I was. I kept going back to you, and I gave up valuable time in my life to be with you. Fortunately, that's something I don't have to ever worry about again."

He opens his mouth and takes a step forward, prepared to say something that will most likely be insulting or degrading. It wouldn't be the first time. He plays dirty and fights to win before eventually switching gears and turning on the charm in apology.

"You are finished with the patient in Room 3, correct? I'm sure she's more than ready to leave. Do you have any orders for me?" I ask, biting back the hatred I feel for this man.

He lifts his chin defiantly, hating that I'm calling him out in regards to our positions. In his eyes, I'm the nurse and supposed to take the orders, while he—the almighty doctor—gives them. "I'd like Mrs. Vargas to make an appointment with a cardiologist. We can send over a referral to the heart center at the hospital, but she also requested a written referral."

I nod, turning my attention to my computer, essentially dismissing him.

At my computer, I pull up the document I need and fill in her personal information. I do it quickly, considering the older woman has been waiting patiently in her exam room for longer than I prefer. I sense Lance's presence behind me, but I refuse to acknowledge him. Instead, I keep my focus on what's in front of me, and the moment I have the referral filled out and sent, I print a copy and prepare to go to the exam room.

Lance is still there, blocking the exit.

"Excuse me," I state with a touch of condescension in my tone.

Okay, so not so much a touch as a full-blown attitude.

"Of course, *nurse*." He most definitely uses my title as an insult, the slimy fucker.

Instead of dropping him where he stands and risking my license, I move quickly past and hurry to the room. I knock rapidly and open the door, apologizing for the wait. Once I've wrapped up the appointment, I walk Mrs. Vargas to the front and tell her to call our office if she has any issues with her referral.

"Thank you, dear," she replies, making the last few steps herself to the counter to check out.

I turn around, making sure to keep my gaze directly in front of me as I slip inside the exam room and prepare it for the next patient. Just as I'm finished wiping down the bed with a disinfectant wipe, I spin to leave and stop in my tracks.

There stands Lance.

Again.

"You need to move," I tell him, stepping forward and preparing to leave.

"You need to stop this little game."

"What?" I ask, my jaw practically dropping to the ground. "You're unbelievable."

"I know you're still mad about what you saw when you stopped over at my apartment, but—"

"I'm not still mad," I blurt out, interrupting his statement. "I realized really quick I wasn't mad. I was done. I was tired of being your afterthought, Lance. I won't do it again. We have to remain professional, but if you can't do that, I'll have to go to Fiona and request one of us be moved."

His smile is cocky, the arrogance ebbing from his pores. "And who do you think they'll move, huh? You, the little nurse, or me the medical doctor?"

"I honestly don't care. They can move me to wherever necessary, but something tells me you'd crawl out of whatever little rathole you come from every day and show up anyway. I can do this, but not if you're unwilling to cooperate. This is your last chance. You don't talk to me at all, except for what information I need to do my job. If you can't abide by these ground rules, then I'll have to go to Dina and changes will be made."

He narrows his eyes, hands on his hips. "You think you're so smart."

"I'm *just a nurse*, trying to do my job, Dr. Williams."

"As you wish, Oaklee," he states, turning on his heel and exiting the room.

I stand here for a few minutes, trying to calm my racing heart. I wish

I knew what I ever saw in that dickweasel. I guess I'm just as stupid as he suggests, considering how many times I went back to him when he apologized. I'm the idiot here, that's for sure.

The back entrance door opens, and I hear voices. Once the room is cleaned and ready, I leave the space and head to the nurses' station to finish charting. I don't even look into Dr. Houston's office, where I hear Lance and Dr. Liu engaging in a friendly discussion. Allison is standing at the cabinet, putting her purse away.

"Hey. Mario said he'd deliver down to us as soon as our orders are ready," she says, grabbing a bottle of water from the fridge and popping off the lid. "Want one?"

"Give me one of those Mountain Dews," I request.

Her eyes widen before she reaches for the can. "Really? That bad of a day?"

I shrug, popping the tab and taking a long drink. "It's fine. Nothing I can't handle."

Allison sighs. "I wish you'd let me just go to Dina and switch with you."

"No," I insist, shaking my head. "I will not be a problem child."

"You're hardly a problem child when your ex-boyfriend is being an insufferable wanker."

I snort at her comment and smile. "That he is, isn't he?" I don't even care that he can probably hear me across the hall.

Fuck him.

"I'm serious," she maintains.

"I know you are, and I appreciate it. Truly. But I'm fine. I will get through this, one day at a time. It won't be long, and his time here will be over and done."

"You know that's not really how it works, right?" she asks.

"Of course, but that's what I'm gonna tell myself for now. In the meantime, I'm going to keep my head in the game and my eye on the prize."

Allison glances at the flower and smiles. "Let me guess, the prize just so happens to be a tall, muscular construction worker who knows how to use his tongue *and* what's between his legs?"

I shrug, unable to fight my grin. "Sounds like a nice prize to me."

"Oh, I agree one-thousand-percent. I hope you take full advantage of that *prize*."

I turn my attention to my computer and make the notes needed in the last chart. Dr. Liu stops by to say goodbye, heading to the next clinic she will be seeing patients at. Thankfully, Lance stays in Doc's office, and I'm relieved to get a short reprieve from the all-knowing, watchful eyes of my ex.

Glancing up, I spot the pink lily in the vase and smile. It's gorgeous, on the verge of its full bloom splendor. I'm actually quite grateful he didn't send a rose. The asshole across the hall used to send them when he'd fuck up—which, looking back now, seemed to be a lot. What Cade sent was unique and special, just like him.

I grab my phone and prepare to type out a thank you text. However, as my fingers hover over the screen, a different idea forms. Not an impersonal message sent through the phone, but something else. Something to really catch his attention and show him how much I appreciate his thoughtful little gifts.

Cade Miller isn't going to know what hit him.

I smile to myself as my plan is made.

"Pizza's here!"

CHAPTER NINETEEN

Cade

I JUST SLIDE ON A PAIR OF RUNNING SHORTS WHEN I HEAR A KNOCK at the door. Grabbing the T-shirt from my bed, I slip it over my head as I make my way to the living room, shaking out my wet hair.

I can't help but wonder who's here. Any of my family or friends would use the back door near the garage, which means this is most likely a solicitor. I should just go back to my room and finish getting ready, leaving whoever's here to think I'm not home.

When I reach the door, I glance at the driveway, surprised to see a Jeep Cherokee sitting there. Worry hits me square in the gut as I release the deadbolt and turn the lock on the knob. "Oaklee," I say before the door's completely open.

There she stands, wearing dark blue scrubs and holding a pink lily. "Hi." She appears a little nervous.

I hold open the door and step back. "Is everything all right?"

"Yes. No. I don't know," she mutters, glancing around before returning her attention to me. "I'm sorry for just dropping by. I hope it's okay I asked Allison where you lived. I realized this afternoon I didn't know, and I feel bad about that. I'm a terrible friend."

I give her an easy smile. "You're not. It's never come up, and I've always just dropped by your place, sometimes unexpected. So this is a nice surprise." Noticing she's still standing by the door, I wave my hand toward the couch and add, "Wanna come in?"

But she doesn't move. Her eyes do, as she looks at the couch I indicated, but her feet remain rooted in place. "Oaklee?"

She swallows hard and levels me with a look so intense it almost knocks me back on my ass. "I wanted to come over and say thank you. For this," she says, holding up the flower. "And for everything else. Your little surprises are…nice. And welcome. And make me feel valued. No one," she says, clearing her throat, "has made me feel like that."

Her words are rushed, like she's trying to get them all out as quick as she possibly can. Glancing down, she brings the lily to her nose and gently inhales. As she does, a soft smile plays on her lips, making me do the same. "I'm glad you like it."

And it pisses me off completely that she feels that way. Not the appreciation part, but the fact no one has ever made her feel like that before.

Fuck him.

"How was work? I know you had to work with—" My statement is cut off as she steps forward and places her finger against my lips, essentially shushing me.

Her dark eyes burn with an intensity I've never witnessed before. "I don't want to talk about him. I'm not here because of him."

My throat feels thick and my heart pounds in my chest. "Why are you here?" I ask, needing her voice now more than ever.

She steps even closer, brushing her chest against mine as she lifts her arms and wraps them around my neck. My hands automatically go to her lower back, holding her in place. "Because I haven't been able to stop thinking about you."

My athletic shorts would be pitching a tent if she wasn't pressed against me. In an instant, my cock is hard and ready. Usually, the sound of her husky voice or the feel of her pressed against me is enough to cause that reaction. And while both definitely hit the mark tonight, it's her words that have me ready to throw her over my shoulder, take her to my bedroom, and bury myself so deep inside her body I never want to come out.

Her words mean everything.

"You don't say." I run my finger down the side of her face, watching as she shivers from the contact.

"All day, Cade, and the closer the clock got to five, the achier I would get."

I almost groan, picturing her sitting at her little work desk, wiggling in her chair as she tries to find some sort of relief. "Where do you ache?"

She pulls back just a bit, and using the flower, drags it from her neck to her chest. "Here," she indicates, circling the lily over the mounds of her tits. "Here too," she adds, gliding the bud down her abdomen and stopping it over her pussy.

"Hmm, sounds like a problem," I deduce, dropping my voice low and husky. "But you came to the right place, beautiful. I'm an expert at digging until I find the problem." Sliding my hand down her stomach, I let my fingertips brush the top of her panties.

She snickers, bringing the hand not holding the flower up to her mouth and covering it. "Oh my God, that was kinda cheesy," she bellows through her giggles, making me smile.

"Did you expect anything less from me?"

She lifts a shoulder and places her hand on my chest. We stand there, staring at each other. I'm pretty decent at reading people, and I have an idea of what she's thinking, but to be honest, I don't want to be wrong, so she needs to spell it out for me.

"Tell me what you're thinking."

"I'm thinking we're both wearing too much clothing," she states boldly.

My fingers flex against her lower back and dance across her panty line once more. "You sure?"

Instead of speaking, she goes up on her tiptoes and presses her lips to mine. I move fast, wrapping both arms around her and lifting. Her legs snake around my waist, caging my cock between our bodies and driving me absolutely wild.

The kiss turns ravenous instantly. Her hands dive into my hair, her nails score across my scalp. I thrust my groin into her pussy, wishing there were no longer any clothing barriers between us. All I want is to feel her hot, wet body wrapping around me like a glove. It's what dreams are made of, and it appears all my dreams are about to come true.

"Oaklee," I murmur, using the back of the door as leverage to hold her in place. "You're killing me."

"Same, Cade," she whispers, kissing against my jaw. "All I've been able to think about is your fingers against my clit last night, and I need more."

My hands knead the globes of her ass. "Are you sure?"

"Of course I am. Now, are you gonna keep talking or are you gonna start stripping?"

I grin against her mouth and press a small kiss to her lips. "Oh, I'm definitely gonna strip, but first, you."

I set her down, and the moment her feet hit the ground, she's toeing off her slip-on shoes. Reaching for her top, I gently start to lift it. She immediately extends her arms over her head, allowing the material to be removed. Once I toss it to the side, I take in the absolute beautiful sight before me. She's stunning, that's for damn sure. A vision in a light blue bra. I can't wait to see the rest of her.

She slips her fingers inside her elastic waistband and shimmies her bottoms down her legs. I'm entranced with every beautiful inch she exposes of her body, taking in the shape of her legs, the swell of her hips, the wet scrap of light blue between her thighs. It's all so damn hypnotic, so erotic, like a wet dream I'm living in real time.

"You're wearing a lot of clothes still," she says, reaching for the T-shirt I had just slipped on my head moments before I opened the door.

"I am," I confirm.

Oaklee grabs my shirt and lifts it up, exposing my abs and chest. Before I can help remove the shirt completely, her hands zero in on my body and she abandons my shirt in favor of touching my skin. My chest tightens as her fingertips glide, first along my abs and then up to my pecs. "My God, you're like a work of art."

"I'm not, sweetheart. It takes a lot of running and gym work to combat the beer and pizza I consume."

She grins, her attention riveted to watching her hands dance across my skin. I go ahead and lift my shirt the rest of the way off and toss it to the side. Then, I hold completely still as her hands slide down my abs. Her fingers tap against the waistband of my athletic shorts, and I've never been so glad to have slipped those on than ever before. It makes it damn easy for her nimble fingers to maneuver beneath the waistband, hitting pay dirt the moment they wrap around my cock.

"Fuck," I mutter, closing my eyes and letting the euphoric sensation of her soft hand around me send shockwaves of bliss through my nervous system.

"Yes. Let's," she murmurs, using her other hand to push my shorts down to my ankles.

I reach behind her and release the clasp of her bra, almost coming where I stand when I get my first up-close and personal view of her glorious tits. They're the perfect size for my big hands, which is exactly what I do. I pinch her right nipple, rolling it between my fingers while holding them firmly in my palms. Then, my mouth descends. I'm desperate to taste, to lick, to suck.

Oaklee leans back against the door, her right hand still wrapped around my cock. I tease her nipples, committing the feel and taste to memory, while her hand slowly works up and down my cock. When the pleasure becomes too much, I release my hold on her and take a step back. "Don't move, beautiful," I insist, turning and hightailing it to my bedroom.

I dig a condom from my bedside drawer and hurry back to the nearly naked woman I get to fuck. When I round the corner, she's exactly where I left her, leaning against the front door. She's wearing just the panties, those dark orbs eye-fucking me as I approach.

I'll tell you what, this woman is definitely good for my ego.

I rip open the condom and slide it on my dick. Then, I turn my attention to the scrap of blue covering the Promised Land. She shakes her hips as I glide them down her legs, my lips pressing kisses across the front of her thighs. I can smell her arousal; she is glistening on her pussy. If I wasn't in such a damn hurry to feel her, I'd take my time and taste it, but unfortunately, that's going to have to wait for next time.

Reaching around, I pull her flush against my body and claim her lips with mine. Her arms wrap around me as she rises to her tiptoes. "You sure, beautiful?" I ask, almost without breaking the kiss.

"Very sure, Cade. Hurry. Please." Her words are a plea, thick with desperation, and I'm too weak to deny her anything.

"Hang on," I say, right before grabbing her under the ass and lifting.

She squeals as her legs wrap around my waist; my cock nestled perfectly between us. "I'm gonna break you," she insists, locking her ankles behind my back.

"I got you. Don't you worry about me," I tell her, pulling back just a bit. "Now, put me where you want me."

She reaches between us and wraps her fingers around my cock. I can feel the precum leaking into the condom as she shifts her position enough to move me to her entrance. When I feel the head of my cock slide into her body, I meet her eyes and slowly push forward.

It's pure fucking heaven.

The best feeling in the entire world.

When I'm fully seated inside her, I stop, letting her adjust to my invasion and for me to try to catch my bearings. She's so fucking tight, and even though the caveman in me wants to move, to claim her in every way possible, I refuse to give in.

I brush my lips against hers softly. "Cade," she moans as she tries to wiggle.

"Relax, beautiful. I got you," I encourage, feeling her internal muscles let go a little as I deepen the kiss. "That's it. I don't want to hurt you."

"I won't break," she insists, her arms tightening around my neck.

"I know you won't, but I need to give you a few seconds to adjust."

I run my lips across her jaw and down her neck, feeling her pussy ripple around me. She's sensitive there, something I make mental note on for later.

Finally, I start to move. My pace is slow at first, my cock pulling out to the head before pushing all the way back in, but as the minutes pass, things start to pick up. My body starts to move on its own, fueled by the sweet noises she makes and the way she grinds against me.

My legs and arms are starting to burn, but I ignore the discomfort. My entire focus is on this woman, on making her come. My hips start to thrust harder, driving into her as we both chase our release. Her muscles start to tighten, and I can tell she's close. "You wanna come, beautiful?"

My question causes her internal muscles to spasm. "Oh God," she replies, her eyes closed as she just…feels.

"I can tell you're almost there. Your pussy is squeezing my cock. It's gonna feel so fucking good when you explode. Do you want to come, Oaklee?"

A whimper falls from her lips.

I thrust up and roll my hips, letting my pubis rub against her clit. She cries out as her nails dig into my shoulders. She's so tight and pulsing, it's almost hard to move, but I manage. I pull out and thrust again, doing the same roll of my hips to rub against her clit.

The third time is the charm.

Oaklee comes hard, her muscles gripping me so tight it triggers my own release. I rock forward, unable to open my eyes as I fill the condom. My body just moves on its own, reveling in the rightness of our joint release. I spasm and jerk until I'm boneless and sated.

I lean forward, pinning her body against the wall. "You all right?" I ask, running my lips down the column of her neck.

"I'm better than all right," she whispers, a smile stretched across her mouth. When she slowly opens her eyes, she asks, "When can we do that again?"

A bark of laughter erupts from my mouth, and I slide my lips across hers. "I'm gonna need a few minutes to recoup from that."

She grins, kissing me back. "Maybe we should grab some food. You know, build our strength back up?"

I slowly start to lower her feet to the ground and pull myself out of her body. When she's standing, I return to the kiss. It's lazy, yet erotic, as we both come down from the high of release. The truth is, I could kiss this woman every minute of every day and still want more.

Finally, I pry my mouth from hers. "Food is definitely on the table."

"What else is on the table?" she asks, her coy little smirk making my cock jump.

"Well, if I have my way, you will be…after I feed you."

A blush spreads up her neck and stains her cheeks. "Hmm, I like the sound of that," she states, grinning from ear to ear.

"Come on, beautiful. Let's get cleaned up and figure out what's for dinner," I tell her, grabbing the pile of clothes on the floor and taking her hand, leading her to my bedroom. Pointing to the open door, I say, "Bathroom. Take all the time you need."

She grabs her clothes from the pile and heads inside, closing the door behind her. I remove the condom and toss it in the trash can, grabbing my T-shirt to clean myself off. Then, I slip back on my athletic shorts and retrieve a fresh shirt from my closet.

Just as I'm pulling it over my head, the bathroom door opens and Oaklee emerges. "All yours."

My feet carry me that way, but not to the bathroom. I stop in front of her and pull her into my arms once more and kiss her lips. "So, dinner first, and then I'll eat you for dessert. Then what?"

She watches me for a moment before answering, "Then I think I'll head home." I open my mouth to comment, but she cuts me off. "I want to keep this what it is, okay? Fun. Two consenting adults enjoying each other's company however they want, but at the end of the day, I go home or you go home."

My throat is suddenly thick, because even though I was going to suggest bending her over the couch, to hear her say the words I've always said to women is a little unsettling. The image pops into my head of her in my bed, of her curled at my side as I drift off to sleep, and I'll be damned if I don't like it more than I should. I never let anyone spend the night here, nor do I stay at their place. We just…move on. That's always the plan and I make it well known before we even move it toward physical.

This is exactly what she said.

Fun.

Two people enjoying each other's time and company for a bit and then going their separate ways.

The only problem with that thought is I kinda like hanging out with her, more so than any other woman before her.

That fact alone seems to complicate things a little in my mind.

But I won't get into that now.

Now, I need to focus on feeding her.

"Deal," I tell her, taking her hand. "Come on, beautiful. Let's eat."

CHAPTER TWENTY

Oaklee

I SHOVE MY FEET INTO OLD SLIP-ONS AND CHECK MY APPEARANCE in the mirror. It's a beautiful Sunday afternoon, but the weather is definitely starting to turn cooler since it's now early October. I'm wearing a pair of old jeans, a T-shirt, and a crewneck sweatshirt, compliments of Cade. It's the one I wore last weekend when we went camping and never returned. I like it too much, and possession is nine-tenths of the law, right?

It doesn't smell like him, since I've washed it the two times I've worn it, but it feels like an extension of his warmth. Like a hug. He's even seen me wear it earlier in the week when we were hanging out but didn't ask for it back or comment about me stealing it. He just smiled and moved on. I can't help but wonder if maybe he likes seeing me in it.

Warmth spreads through my chest at the thought.

I ignore it.

The loud knock has me spinning around and exiting the room. I grab my bag off the couch and meet Cade at the door. "Hi," I greet, stepping out into the early afternoon sunlight.

"Hey," he replies, his eyes dropping down to take in his sweatshirt. He grins, but doesn't say a word. "Ready?"

"Yes." Glancing down at my outfit, I ask, "Is this okay?"

He takes his time, perusing my body as if assessing my appearance. When his blue eyes return to mine, he nods. "First off, you could be wearing a potato sack, and you'd still be the most stunning woman in the world. But I know that's not what you meant. You were asking about your attire in regard to our little fishing adventure, and that answer would be yes. As long as you're fine getting a little dirty."

My cheeks heat up, because in that moment, I'm replaying the last time I got a little dirty. Friday night, after an exceptionally long day of dealing with Lance at the clinic, we met at my place to watch a movie and unwind. No movie was actually watched, but I had two orgasms right there on my couch.

I slept like a baby that night.

"Knock it off, dirty girl. You're supposed to be learning the art of fishing today, not thinking about the different things you'd do to my pole."

Shaking my head, I let a little giggle fly as we walk to his truck. Once I'm inside, on the passenger's seat, I glance behind me after catching the scent of something sweet. There's an insulated bag sitting there, and even though I can't see what's inside, I have an idea.

When Cade climbs behind the wheel, I ask, "What's in the bag?"

He grins mischievously. "It's a surprise."

"Is it cookies? It smells like cookies. Chocolate chip ones. And brownies," I insist, watching as the smile falls from his lips.

"How did you know that?"

I want to keep playing the ruse but am unable. I start to giggle, covering my lips with my hand.

"You peeked, didn't you!" he blurts out, glancing back to see if the bag is open.

Shaking my head, I claim, "I didn't, I swear. There wasn't enough time for me to peek."

His blue eyes narrow. "Then, how did you know?"

Smiling sweetly, I shrug my shoulders. "A woman never reveals her sources."

Exhaling, he throws the truck in reverse and backs from my driveway. "Lizzie," he finally states, shaking his head. "Mom took some to Collin this morning too."

"I heard they're delicious."

"They are," I agree as I head toward Wyatt's place. "Almost everything Mom makes is top-notch, with the exception of Salsbury steak. She ever makes that, and we're skipping the dinner invite."

I can't help but laugh. "My grandma used to make tuna cakes, and I'd want to vomit the moment the scent permeated the air."

"Tuna cakes?" he asks, making a horrified face.

"Like crab cakes, but with tuna. Way cheaper to make, and to be honest, completely disgusting. That smell would linger for days, Cade. Days!"

He chuckles. "No tuna cakes, good to know, but what about crab cakes?"

"Those I like. This nice little gourmet restaurant not too far from where I lived back home had them for special every Friday night. I'd order them with a side salad often. They were delicious," I recall, wishing I were back there for a night, if only to order the crab cakes.

"I'm not sure we have anywhere in Cooper Town that makes crab cakes, but I'm sure they do in North Ridge. I'll do some checking and see if I can find a place. We can go for dinner one night."

"You don't have to do that."

"I know I don't have to, but I want to."

Warmth moves through me, spreading from my chest through my extremities. Any time he says something sweet like that I want to swoon. He's definitely a charmer, and often puts my wants and needs before his, but when he says things like that I start to entertain ideas I shouldn't. He's not a relationship kind of guy. I've known that from the beginning. So I need to keep those thoughts out of my head. We'll never be anything more than just friends with benefits, if that's what you want to call this, so the sooner I get that through my thick skull, the better off I'll be.

We ride in silence out to Wyatt's farm, both of us humming along to the song on the radio. Turning into the driveway, I find the barn open with Wyatt's big truck parked in front. "We aren't interrupting his day, are we?" I ask, releasing my seat belt as he turns off his truck.

"Don't care," he replies with an ornery gleam in his ocean-blue eyes. "No, I texted him and let him know we're coming. He's out in one of the pastures mowing and knows we're headed back to my spot."

I nod and catch sight of the side-by-side sitting next to where we parked. Cade starts unloading the gear from the bed of the truck, while I grab the bags from the back seat. Of course, while I do, I pop open the bag and sneak one of the soft chocolate chip cookies. I pop it in my mouth and take a bite, savoring the gooey goodness that's practically melting on my tongue.

"What are you doing?"

I spin around, guilt written all over my face, I'm sure. "Nothing," I mutter, my mouth still full of the cookie.

He shakes his head and slowly moves toward me. His motions are calculated and smooth, like an animal stalking its prey, and all I can think about is the time he tickled me on the couch. "I think you're lying to me."

I chew fast and swallow, hiding the fact I still have half a cookie in my hand. "I would never."

The corner of his mouth ticks. "No? So you're not hiding something behind your back right now?" he asks, reaching for my hand.

"Of course not."

Why do I sound so breathless?

Probably because I secretly want him to find the cookie and punish me like the bad woman I am.

My cheeks burn hot.

When his hands wrap around my wrist, he slowly brings the evidence into light, revealing the fact I am a liar. "Hmm, as I thought."

With the cookie still gripped in my hand, he brings it up to his face to inspect it. Then, catching me completely off guard, he bends down and wraps his mouth around it—and my fingers. He bites at the treat and smiles when he stands up to his full height and chews.

The Cookie Monster has nothing on Cade Miller.

Also, my panties are soaked.

"That was mine," I mutter, not really sure what to say.

"And you stole it. Therefore, you'll have to ask me very nicely if you want another one."

I already know which *nice* way I'll be asking him, but I refuse to state that now. However, judging by the smirk on his face, he knows exactly what my plan is and that it'll involve my hand, tongue, and his erection.

"Later, beautiful," he whispers, popping the last bit of cookie in his mouth. He bends down and kisses me, the taste of chocolate chip cookie heavy on his tongue.

Just as we break apart, his phone chimes with a notification in my pocket. He pulls out the device, taps the screen, and laughs. He holds the phone out so I can read it.

Wyatt: Quit fucking making out in front of my camera! I don't need to see that shit!!

I giggle, turning around to where the camera is attached to the corner of the barn, just beneath the overhang, and wave.

A second later, the phone chimes again.

Wyatt: Hi, Oaklee.

Wyatt: Now, remember, I have other cameras out on my property. Like I tell Collin every time he takes Lizzie back there, if I see something inappropriate, I'm gonna share it with everyone. Nothing is safe.

Cade: And I'd gut you like a fish.

He's smiling as he sends the message, clearly just tossing his good friend a threat he doesn't mean.

Wyatt: Well, then keep your bare ass covered up, my friend.

Cade: *insert middle finger emoji*

He slips his phone into his pocket and double checks the bed of his truck. "All right, beautiful. Let's go."

I climb into the cab of the side-by-side and watch as he starts it up. He drives us back to the timber, snaking through the trees as we head for our destination. I look around, remembering last weekend when we camped out here. The memories are fresh, and even though the weather is already changing, I can't wait until I have the opportunity to do it again.

We reach the creek at the back of the property and stop. "Ready?" he asks.

"I am."

"All right, let me get everything set up and then we can bait some hooks."

I climb out of the cab and look around. "Give me something to do."

He looks in the bed of the vehicle and pulls out a pair of small chairs. "Go ahead and pick our spot by the water."

I nod, taking the chairs and moving in the direction of where we'll be sitting. I glance around the space, finding the perfect spot in a clearing in the trees. There's a log in the water upstream a bit, but we should be far enough back to avoid getting tangled in it. "How about here?" I ask, turning around to where Cade is setting a tackle box and two poles.

"Perfect." He returns to his side-by-side and grabs the rest of the gear, including the two bags from the back seat. "The cookies stay by me," he adds, setting my bag down in front of one of the chairs.

After a few minutes of getting everything situated, he starts to prep the fishing poles. "All right, beautiful, let's bait the hooks."

When he pulls a little white container of worms from the cooler, I make a face. "I'll let you do that part."

He chuckles and nods. "It's not bad, let me show you."

I move closer as he sits down, the pole lying across his lap. He pulls a worm out of the container and holds it up. "You just sort of thread it on, like this," he says, moving the worm onto the hook with ease.

"That's it? Well, I can do that," I insist.

"Well, you can do the next one, how about that?"

"Fine," I state. I'm a nurse, for God's sake. I can put a worm on a hook.

When it's all set, he stands up. "Come 'ere, and I'll show you how to cast."

I step over to him and let him position me in front of his body. "Take the pole, like so," he instructs, demonstrating what I need to do. "Push in this button and angle the tip behind you. Make sure you're clear of people, trees, and everything else you can get caught on, and then throw, releasing the button as you do it."

He shows me a few times, and I watch every step he takes.

Nodding, I take the pole and get into the same position he was in, even with him standing directly behind me. I move my arm a few times, just like he did and get a feel for the motion. Then, I push the button in and take a deep breath. I bring the end of the pole forward and release the button, as instructed, and watch the worm fly through the air. It lands with a plop in the water.

"Damn, that was good for your first time. Reel your line until you hear the click, letting you know you have it set."

Again, I do as instructed, hearing the distinct sound of the click. "That's it?"

He nods. "That's it. Now, you wait."

He opens his tackle box and pulls out a little forked post. He easily slides it into the ground and then takes my pole from my hand, placing it between the teeth. "There. Now you can bait my hook," he says with a wink.

Cade gets the hook ready while I stare down at the little container of worms. They're moving around and looking a little nasty, covered in slime and thick dirt. I reach in and grip the closest squiggly worm and pull it out. Exhaling, I mutter, "You can do this."

"You got this, Oaklee."

I move it to the hook and stick the hook into the end. "I'm a nurse. I touch gross stuff all the time."

He snickers, reaching over to help guide me. "Yes, but this is different than what you do on a daily basis."

When the task is complete, I exhale dramatically. "I did it," I whisper, looking up at Cade.

He's grinning from ear to ear. "You sure did. You're a total badass."

I bark out a laugh. "I wouldn't go that far."

"No, you are. Most people won't do that."

Just then, I glance over to watch my pole move. "Did you see that?" I murmur.

Cade sets his pole down on the ground and takes the seat beside me. "Very slowly, lift the pole from the stand. Try not to jostle it."

I do as instructed, carefully lifting the pole. When it's firmly in my hand, I feel the bounce. "I think it's on there."

"We're gonna set the hook and reel it in, all right? You're gonna give it a little jerk up and start reeling. Not too far," he coaches. "When you feel it jerk, give it a tug and reel."

I nod, my eyes wide as I watch the tip of my pole for movement, despite being able to feel it. Just then, I feel the now-familiar yank and lurch the pole up. The end of the pole bends down hard as I try to reel in the fish.

"Keep it steady. Pull your pole up and then reel as you bring it back down, like this," he says, reaching over and demonstrating what he's saying.

I do that a few times, and gasp when I hear the splash and see the fish pop up from the water. "Oh my God! It's huge," I holler.

"That's what she said!" Cade bellows, reaching for a net and moving to the edge of the water. "Slowly reel it in, and I'm gonna grab it with the net."

He does, scooping up the fish and carrying it toward me. I'm standing, trying to hold the pole up as he reaches into the net and grabs the fish. Glancing at me, he asks, "Wanna take the hook out?"

I shake my head, making him chuckle.

"Wait, are you gonna hold it?"

My eyebrows draw together. "Are we still talking about the fish?"

He laughs. "For now, yes. We need a picture to document your first time fishing and first catch. So, do you want to hold the pole and line or the fish."

I think about my options, not really liking the idea of grabbing the fish directly. That's why I choose the other. "The pole and line."

He nods and moves to the side. "Come stand here." He hands over the pole and line.

"It's heavier than I expected."

"It's a good-sized fish," he replies, grabbing his phone from his pocket. "Smile."

I do, proudly holding my catch as he snaps a few pics.

Cade drops his phone on the chair and takes the fish from me. I watch as he maneuvers the hook out and carefully sets the pole aside. With the fish in his bare hand, he holds it up and asks, "Wanna give it a kiss before we set it free?"

"We're not keeping it?"

"Not this time. If we were fishing for the freezer, it would be a keeper, but since we're just having fun, drowning worms, we'll let this guy go."

"Okay. And no, I don't want to kiss him."

Cade moves to the edge and lowers the fish before giving him a gentle toss into the water. He swims away, making me smile. My fishing partner drops down to the water and dips his hands in to clean them off. Then, he heads to his tackle box and grabs a container of wipes. Finally, he turns his attention to me and smiles. "Not bad, Miss Fisherwoman. Probably about a three-pound channel cat."

"Only three pounds? It felt like fifteen," I grumble, recalling how it felt so heavy pulling against me while I reeled.

He crouches down in front of me and flashes a grin. "Wanna bait your hook and do it again?"

I nod eagerly.

This time, baiting the hook goes a little smoother, as does the cast, and we spend the next hour sitting in his favorite spot, watching the water, and feeling the light breeze on our faces. It's, without a doubt, one of the best days I've ever had.

And it all started with a fish.

CHAPTER TWENTY-ONE

Cade

I NEVER THOUGHT TAKING A WOMAN FISHING WOULD BE SO DAMN fun. Sure, I've been fishing with women before, but not one-on-one like this and never enjoying it as much as I am. We've been sitting here for almost an hour and have caught three fish. Each time one is reeled in, I see the internal struggle in Oaklee's eyes. Just when I think she's about to agree to take the fish off the hook, she chickens out and backs away.

It's so fucking adorable.

"So, tell me about the military. I mean, you might not want to talk about it, and I'd totally respect that, but I was just curious about it. A few people I went to high school with went in after graduation, but no one I was close with."

"I don't mind," I tell her, glancing down at my pole to make sure all is still. "I chose to enlist in the Marines, even though Collin had already settled on the Air Force. He knew he wanted to be in their firefighting program, which is the best in the world. I wasn't as into that as he was and after talking to a recruiter, was drawn toward combat engineer."

"What is that?" she asks, turning slightly in her seat to face me.

"Well, it's a boots on the ground group who work ahead of the troops to clear the path. It can include moving obstacles, like cars or rubble, and even buildings."

Her eyes widen. "You took down buildings?"

I nod. "At times, yes."

"That's kinda cool, actually."

"It was a very interesting job, that's for sure, and I enjoyed it. I was enlisted for six years. When I got back home and was trying to decide what I wanted to do with my life, I knew I was good with heavy equipment and machinery, so I checked into joining the union. I started as an apprentice and quickly moved through the program, landing at the company I still work for to this day."

"I know I said this before but thank you for your service. I'm sure it wasn't always fun and not always easy. It takes the right individuals to do what members of our armed services do on a daily basis."

"What about you? You went to nursing school. What was that like?"

I notice her fidget a little, but she jumps right in to telling me about her past, so I'm not sure why the little uneasiness. "Well, I was living with my grandparents, working as much as I could as a server at a little restaurant a few miles from their place. I was able to get some scholarships to help cover the cost, but with their limited means, I was kind of on my own for college. So, I worked as much as I could, usually five or six nights a week, depending on when they needed me."

"While you went to school during the day?"

She shrugs and nods in confirmation. "I knew it was temporary, so I did what I had to do to be able to pay for my education and help them as much as possible."

"RN is two or four years?" I ask, wishing I knew more about the profession.

"I went through the four-year program. They do offer two-year RN degrees, but I…uh, felt the four-year option was best for my future."

There it is again. The fidget. Something about this conversation makes her a little anxious.

"Anyway, right before the start of my third year, I was able to move into a little apartment with a friend. She was working full time, having just completed an associate's degree in radiology and was working at the local hospital. She also knew Allison, who was in school with me, so we all hung out when we could, which for me, wasn't that much. I still worked as much as possible at the restaurant. I basically went to school, worked, and ate and slept when I could."

"I bet that was tough."

She lifts her shoulders, as if it was no big deal. "Like I said, I knew it was temporary and was willing to put in the work."

"Working toward the dream. I get it."

"Anyway, after school, I got a job at a clinic, working with a few GP doctors. That's where I met Lance."

Just the mention of his name makes me want to throw something. That guy's the biggest douche I've ever heard about, and I don't even know him personally. And considering I was in the military with some of the biggest egos on the planet, that's saying something.

"He worked there?" I find myself asking, needing to hear the whole story.

"No, he did an internship through there. He was in med school, and we just sort of hit it off. Started hanging out after work when he wasn't busy, and before I knew it, we were in a relationship." She looks out at the water. "It wasn't always bad, but it wasn't always great either. He was always busy, as anyone going through a program like that is, so we didn't spend as much time together as we both would have liked. Or at least, as much as I wanted.

"So, we'd break up and then get back together a while later. It was an exhausting cycle, but I felt like it would be worth it in the end. But the cycle just kept repeating and repeating.

"He got his residency at North Ridge, and I was going to break up with him. His schedule was insane, as we knew it would be, but then, he asked me to move here. Not with him, mind you, but *near* him."

I sit up in my seat and give her my full attention. "What? After, what, six years?"

She nods. "He said he wanted me here, but he was in one of those tiny studio apartments used by the hospital, and he couldn't add anyone to the agreement. At first, I thought…this was it. He's actually taking the steps to move our relationship forward. I came here for an interview, thanks to a tip from Allison, and well, you know the rest."

"That was the weekend we first met," I say, unable to hide my smile.

She chuckles. "Yeah. The night some guy hit on me in a bar."

"But you turned him down."

"I did. I was seeing someone."

I reach over and take her hand, threading her fingers with mine. It's the first time we've done that, and I can't help but notice the warmth spreading through my veins. "But you're not now."

She looks over and meets my gaze. "Nope. I'm not now."

The air is charged around us as we continue to watch each other. I'm not certain what she's thinking, but if it's anywhere close to what's going through my mind, it's positive. Hopeful. And maybe with a touch of naughty mixed in.

"I didn't mean to word-vomit all our relationship details to you."

"I'm glad you did," I reply honestly, glad to know the details. "Can I ask you something?" One of the things she mentioned jumps out at me, and I can't help but circle back around to it. "When you said you wanted to do the four-year program instead of the two, what did you mean by that? Was there something more you wanted to do?"

Her entire body goes rigid, and her eyes take on a flash of panic, even though she covers it up quickly by glancing away. I hit the nail on the head with my observation, and even though I won't push her, I hope she feels comfortable enough with me to share whatever it was.

She clears her throat and continues to watch the fishing line slowly move in the water.

That's when it hits me.

Getting up, I retrieve the bag containing my mom's sweet treats and pull the baggy of cookies and the container of brownies from within. I pop open the brownies and hand them toward her.

She grins, taking one of the brownies and enjoying a small bite. "Wow, these are as good as the cookies."

"You mean, the chocolate chip cookie you stole?" I tease, hoping to make her smile again.

"I did no such thing," she counters before enjoying a second bite. "And if memory serves correctly, you did a little stealing yourself."

I gape at her, grabbing both a cookie and a brownie. "I thought we were sharing. I just took my half."

"You almost ate my fingers," she counters.

Taking my seat, I enjoy a big bite of my cookie first before glancing her way. "It's not your *fingers* I enjoy eating, beautiful."

There.

My comment triggers the blush, which makes my balls heavy and achy.

God, I love it when I say something dirty and she blushes.

"Anyway, we don't have to talk about your schooling if you don't want to. I wasn't trying to pry."

Out of the corner of my eye, I see her take another bite of her brownie before slowly getting up from her seat. When she stops in front of me, I look up and meet her gaze. She moves, straddling my legs and sitting on my lap. My cock is already hard in my jeans, and I'm certain she can already tell, considering she's sitting on it.

Slowly, she grabs my left hand and takes a bite of my cookie. My cock jumps, making her wiggle against me. If I had a free hand, I'd place it on her hip to try to halt her movements. Unfortunately, since both of my hands are occupied, she has free rein to wiggle and move, gyrating against me and driving me absolutely wild.

Holding my gaze, she says, "I wanted to continue schooling."

My heart is pounding in my chest as I wait for whatever else she wants to say.

"I wanted to be a midwife."

"Yeah? That's awesome, Oaklee," I say, a sense of pride in this woman adding extra pressure to my chest.

She nods solemnly. "I thought so too, but it just wasn't meant to be."

I'm a little confused by her statement. I mean, we haven't talked specifically about age, but she can't be thirty yet. There's still plenty of time for her to achieve the degree and credentials she's always dreamed of.

"When I was dating Lance, he was in med school. It was expensive and time-consuming. When I told him of my dream, he suggested I wait. It would be too hard on us if we were both in the midst of high-demand, high-stress schooling."

"He asked you not to continue your schooling?" I ask, feeling the venom of my words seep through my veins and burn my soul. It fucking hurts to think about.

She shrugs, as if if's no big deal, but to me, it's a huge fucking deal.

Douche isn't even the right term for that asshole.

"I agreed to it, and then, as time passed, it became less and less of an option for me. Eventually, it felt like the entire opportunity had passed me by."

"Fuck that," I blurt out. "If you want to go to school and become a midwife, then that's what you do." She gives me a smile. "I'm serious, Oaklee. Your happiness was just as important as his. Your dreams mattered too. Only a real asshole would ask you to put yours on hold so he could achieve his."

"Yes, he was a complete asshole," she says, rocking her hips against my groin. "If there's one thing I've learned through all of this, it's I've always been second to him. Everything he wanted or needed came first. What I wanted never mattered as much."

"Fuck that, beautiful. God, he pisses me off so much." I'm telling you, if the guy was standing in front of me right now, his face would have my fist imprinted in it.

"Me too," she says, reaching over and setting what's left of her brownie down on her chair. After wiping her fingers off on her jeans, she places them against my chest and leans forward. "Do you know why I've been gravitating toward you lately?"

The conversation and moment feel heavy, which is why I try to lighten it just a bit. "My sparkling personality and massive cock?"

She giggles and takes the brownie and cookie from my hand. "Well, of course that," she says, tossing them on the chair with hers and bringing her lips to hover over mine. "Because you've made me feel special. I know that wasn't your intent, since this is casual and all, but you've made me feel like what I want matters."

My throat is thick, and my heart is pounding in my chest. "Because it does."

"And more than anything, I appreciate you showing me that." She rolls her hips, grinding against my cock. "Do you know what else I'd like you to show me?"

"I'm all ears, beautiful," I say, gripping on to her ass with both hands.

"How good sex while fishing can be."

My brain short-circuits. Any thought I had flies straight out the window. I'm left sitting here, a gorgeous woman straddling me and asking for sex.

Not just any woman though.

Oaklee.

I'd give her anything she asked for, including sex in a chair in the back of my buddy's property.

Cameras be damned.

"Stand up," I tell her, pointing to her pants. "Off."

I do the same after reaching down and unlacing my boots and sliding them off my feet. By the time I stand to remove my jeans, she's there before me, completely naked from the waist down. "Fuck," I mutter, moving a little quicker.

Before I push my pants down, I retrieve one of the condoms I carry in my wallet. I always have one in there, but ever since this thing with her started, I added a few extras. I never want to be without one, not where she's concerned.

I don't even have time to pull off my jeans before she's practically pushing me into the chair. With my pants around my ankles, I sit down and sheathe my dick in protection. Then, she's there, straddling my lap and sitting on top of me. She slides down, taking me to the root in one long motion.

Our collective moans echo off the trees, but she takes no time to adjust to the invasion. Oaklee sets the pace, and it's fast. She lifts herself up and practically slams back down, repeating it over and over again. I can barely breathe as I watch her take complete control.

My hands are on her hips, helping guide her movements. She lifts up and sits back down, rolling her hips and grinding her clit against me. Her nails dig through my T-shirt, and even though I wish she weren't covering up her gorgeous tits right now, the fact she's wearing my sweatshirt is almost better than seeing her bare.

She's mine.

My balls start to tighten as I watch her move. She's wild, bucking against me and taking what she wants, and it's sexy as hell. "Cade," she mutters as I start to feel her pussy squeeze.

"Come, beautiful. Let me feel you," I say, thrusting up and rolling my own hips.

She cries out and closes her eyes as her release grabs hold. I keep moving, drawing out the pleasure as long as possible. She grips me tight as she comes, triggering my own release. I pause, loving the way she pulses around me as I empty myself in the condom, and only when I feel her starting to sag against me do I move.

When she falls forward, I take her in my arms and hold her tightly to my chest. "I think I like fishing. A lot."

I snort and press my lips to her neck. "Me too, beautiful. Me too."

After a couple of minutes of us both catching our breath, she sits up. "Thank you."

"For what?" I ask, lifting her hand and pressing a kiss to her knuckles.

"For that. For listening. For making me feel...good."

I pull her against me and kiss her lips. "Always, Oaklee. I'll always do my best to make you feel good."

That's not what I want to say, but that's what she needs to hear. She needs to be put first for a while, to be shown not all guys are selfish assholes.

To be treated like the queen she is.

My God, I can see myself falling for this woman.

Hell.

I might already be in trouble.

CHAPTER TWENTY-TWO

Oaklee

SPENDING TIME WITH CADE ISN'T EXACTLY A HARDSHIP.

That's why I've been doing it as much as I can over the last couple of weeks. We've gone fishing again, though we kept our clothes on that time, and we've watched a few movies at both his place and mine. We've shared meals and hung out with friends. We've spent nights apart, but admittedly, I don't like those evenings as much as the ones where Cade is there.

My phone vibrates in my pocket, so I quickly pull it out to check my message while I wait to call back my next patient.

Grandma: Good afternoon. Grandpa went to the doc for his follow-up. The wound healed nicely.

Me: I'm happy to hear. I'd love to come for a visit soon. I know you told me not to come when Grandpa wasn't well, but I'm hoping I can come for an afternoon soon.

I don't know how quickly she'll respond, so I'm pleasantly surprised when I spot the bubbles, indicating she's typing.

Grandma: We just started playing Euchre on Sundays with a group at the lodge. I'm not sure when we'll be available. I'll keep you posted.

I sigh and shake my head.

Me: Sounds good. Enjoy your afternoon.

Grandma: You too.

I replace my phone and shake my head. I wish things were different between us, that we had a little more of a relationship. Maybe that's my fault for not trying hard enough, but maybe not. I wasn't enough to make my mom stop the lifestyle she was living, and I refuse to beg anyone for their time. I know they love me, and if their idea of how to show love and mine are different, then it is what it is.

I'm okay.

I reach for my drink and find it empty. Exhaling, I turn around and open the fridge, only to find it about empty too. I remember drinking the last bottled water yesterday, but wasn't there a few cans of something else in there? God, I can't believe we let the fridge run empty and didn't restock it. Yes, I'm sure I can run up to the fridge in the office, used by the front-end staff, but I don't want to take something that belongs to one of them, even if I was going to replace it first chance I get.

"Oaklee," Becky practically sings as she rounds the corner to the nurses' station and deposits a bag and a cup on the counter. "You have another delivery," she adds with a smirk.

First thing I notice is the cup of something icy. It's as if he somehow knew I needed a drink this afternoon.

"Are you and Cade, like, dating?" she asks.

"Umm, no. We're just friends."

She smiles. "Small towns, Oaklee. Everyone is talking."

My eyebrows draw together in confusion as I stare at her. "Really? Why?"

"Because Cade doesn't date, and as far as anyone is concerned, he's never sent little treats to someone a couple days a week," she informs me, leaning against the doorway.

"Oh, well, it's…nothing."

She shakes her head and pins me with a look. "It has to be *something*."

I don't give her anything, because to be honest, I'm not sure what this is either. I like Becky, she's a great co-worker and I do consider her someone I can talk to, but when it comes to Cade, I'm keeping those conversations close to the vest.

"Where did this come from?" I ask, opening the white paper bag and finding a straw along with a brownie covered in powdered sugar.

"The diner. That's Mabel's famous sweet tea, and since it's a little pink, I'm guessing she added a flavor, like raspberry. It's seriously addictive," Becky says.

Popping the straw in the cup, I take a sip and smile. "Oh, that's so good."

"It is," Becky agrees. "Makes me want to run down to the diner and grab one."

"I'm sure Fiona would watch the front counter for you for a couple of minutes," I say.

"Oh, I'm sure she will, if I bring her back one," she replies with a chuckle.

"Then it's a win-win."

Becky nods and glances down the hall. "I better use the restroom quickly and get back up there." She leans forward and whispers, "Dr. Ex is on his way back here." Then, she's gone, offering a polite, "Hi," to Lance as they pass in the hallway.

"Oaklee, the patient in Room 2 needs labs, and I want to see her again in a week," he says, somewhat briskly as he continues to the office across the hall.

I get up and walk toward the hall, grabbing the chart from the door to check the notes. When I see what exactly he's ordering, I step inside and ask the patient to follow me. We walk to the small room we use for labs and testing. I verify patient information and set up the system to print the stickers. Fortunately, the woman is an easy stick, and I have what is needed drawn within a few minutes.

"All right, we're going to head back over to Room 2, and Dr. Williams will be back in shortly to finish up."

She nods and steps inside the room, while I return to the lab and make sure everything is set for the pickup later today. The hospital has a transport for testing, and the service picks up labs both morning and afternoon. Results are usually back same-day, but in some instances, can take up to twenty-four hours. Since I've worked here, that hasn't happened, but I'm told it can from time to time.

I pop my head inside Doc's office to tell Lance his patient is waiting, but I don't see him. He's probably in the private bathroom, so I turn to go across the hall to the nurses' station to wait. That's when I see him standing at my workstation. I can't tell exactly what he's doing until I step inside the room and move past him. That's when I see the white bag.

And he's reading the message written on the side.

"What are you doing?" I ask, stepping forward and snatching the brownie bag from his hand.

He slowly lifts his gaze to mine, his eyes narrowed into little slits. "Is this from the same man who sent you the flower?"

"None of your business, Lance. We've been over this," I reply, setting the bag on the counter. That's when I see the note Cade had written on the bag. It must have been backward when Becky dropped it off, and I didn't notice it before.

Saying hello to you is the best part of my day. ~C

I didn't even realize I was smiling until the jackass practically snarls.

"This is completely unprofessional," he retorts.

"You know, just when I think you can't be any more of an asshole, you prove me wrong," I whisper, rubbing my hand over my forehead where a headache is already starting to form. "Lance, this doesn't concern you, and the fact you're imposing yourself into something personal makes *you* the one who's unprofessional."

"Hey, Oaklee," Allison says, coming around the corner and practically slamming into Lance. "Oh, shoot, Dr. Williams. I didn't know you were in here. Is there something I can help you with?" she asks sweetly.

"No," he responds, turning and exiting the room.

We watch him go before she turns to me. "Why must he slither out of his hole?"

"Because even snakes need sunlight every now and again," I reply, making her laugh.

Allison spots my treats, her grin growing. "I see your special delivery arrived."

"It did," I reply, sitting down and pulling up a chart, making notes. Dr. Murphy, one of the specialists, pops his head in the room and talks to Allison about a patient. She makes notes and they discuss treatment plans for a fungal infection.

To be honest, I'm kinda glad I didn't have to work directly with the specialists. Podiatry is the one field I don't think I could do every day. Feet don't necessarily bother me, but some of the stuff I've heard come through here in the last few weeks is a little nauseating.

When Dr. Murphy walks away, I glance over at Allison. "Did you need something?"

"Hmm?" she asks.

"When you came around the corner, you hollered my name."

"Oh. Oh! Shoot! I was up front and heard we have a workman's comp injury coming in."

"Okay," I reply, grabbing the chart for my next patient.

"It's Cade."

My eyes widen as I give her my complete attention. "What? Are you serious?"

She nods, not really seeming too concerned. "Apparently, he cut his leg on something on the jobsite, and they're sending him in to have it looked at and get stitched up."

"Okay, that doesn't sound too serious," I reply, my brain starting to spin.

"Nope. His boss called and said he insisted on driving himself," Allison announces with a snort.

"Of course he did," I mutter, standing up and running my hand down the pant leg of my scrubs. "Okay, I'll go ahead and take the next patient back to the room but prep the triage room."

And then it hits me.

The triage room is being used by the specialists.

"Jeez, what is wrong with me?" I ask myself, feeling the slight tremble in my hands.

Allison reaches over and squeezes my arm. "It's because it's someone you care about."

The weight of her words gets lodged in my throat.

How did this happen, and in such a short amount of time? I haven't known him for long at all, and here I am getting all up in my feels at the thought of him being hurt.

Because he's a friend.

A close friend I've had sex with multiple times, but we don't necessarily have to dissect that detail. I'd be this worked up over Allison or Charli getting hurt, right? I'm sure I would.

Right?

I take a deep breath and shake my head, dislodging all personal thoughts from my brain. "All right, I'll run and get the patient into his room. Lance should be done with Room 2 by now, so I'll put Cade in there when he arrives."

Allison nods. "That's what I'd do." I turn to walk away when she says, "Hey, Oaklee? Maybe don't leave Cade and Dr. Williams in the room together alone for too long, huh?"

Oh fuck.

This has trainwreck written all over it.

"Good idea," I reply with an awkward chuckle.

"If you need me, holler. I can referee," she states with a grin and a wink before stepping in close. "Oh, and for the record, my money's on Cade, one thousand times over."

I bark a laugh. "Mine too."

Numbly, I walk up front to get the next patient. "Liam," I say, waiting for the sick child to come back with his parent. Mom stands up and takes the seven-year-old's hand, guiding him to where I wait. "Hi, Liam," I say, noting his glassy eyes and red cheeks.

"Hi," he whispers before barking out a cough.

"Let's stop by the scale first and then we'll get you into a room. Dr. Williams is here today, and he's going to get you checked out and on the mend as soon as possible."

I run through taking vitals for the little guy before asking about his symptoms.

"The cough started yesterday with a low-grade fever, but this afternoon, it started to really sound deep. His fever has gone up too, and I've been alternating Motrin and Tylenol every four hours," she says, the unmistakable look of worry on her face as she continues to tell me about his symptoms.

"Okay, shirt off, big guy. Dr. Williams will be in shortly, okay?"

The little guy nods and starts to remove his sweatshirt. I slip out the door and place the chart in the holder before moving to the available room and getting it all cleaned up for the next patient.

Becky pops her head around the corner and says, "Cade is here."

I nod, taking a few calming deep breaths before I exit the room and make my way up front. As soon as I open the door, I see Cade standing there in front of the big window. "Cade?"

He spins toward me and smiles. When I wave him on, he walks, each step with his left leg a bit gingerly. "Hi."

I glance down and shake my head. "What's that?"

He follows my line of sight. "Duct tape."

I close my eyes and shake my head. "You put duct tape on your wound?"

"Well, first I rubbed dirt in it, and then I covered it with the tape." He flashes a big, cheesy grin, making me giggle.

"Come on," I say, pointing to the available room.

Just before we step over the threshold, Allison steps out of the room she's in and laughs. "Nice tape job, Slick."

He grins easily. "Thanks."

Once inside the exam room, I close the door and point to the table. "Have a seat."

"Not until I do this," he says right before pressing his lips to mine. It's a chaste kiss, only lasting about three seconds, but still sends butterflies soaring in my stomach and my breathing becomes labored. "That's better."

The moment his lips press to mine, the flustered sense I felt only moments ago fades. Clearing my throat, I mutter a quick, "Let's get you checked out."

"Sure," he agrees, stepping back and giving me a long look-over. "You want me to take off my pants?"

I can't help but laugh. "Not yet, cowboy."

He tsks. "Shame. If you need them gone, you just say the word and they're gone." With a wink he finally moves over to the table and has a seat.

I set the papers for his workman's comp claim on the counter and slip on a pair of latex gloves. "Let's take a look at the cut."

Cade starts to remove the duct tape wrapped around his pant leg. When he gets it off, I help roll up the material, exposing the wound. "Not terrible," I say, examining the injury. "Tell me what happened."

He exhales. "I got off my machine as we were wrapping up for the day. I got too close to a stack of rebar and caught my pant leg on it, slicing me. Stupid rookie mistake."

I nod, grabbing what I need out of the cabinet to get around the wound cleaned up. "I'll do a little cleaning, and then Dr. Williams will come in and take a look."

"Dr. Williams, huh?" he asks casually, but there's no missing the way his jaw ticks in irritation.

"Afraid so." After I do a little cleaning, I ask, "Are you going to be nice?"

He's watching my every move. "I'll be nice, until it's time not to be anymore."

Well, I suppose that's all I can ask, right?

I finish cleaning around the wound. "Well, the bleeding has pretty much stopped. It's not terrible, but I think you need stitches."

"I figured."

"Dr. Williams will come in and check it out. He might want to irrigate it for any debris that might be in the wound. How up-to-date are you on your tetanus shot?"

He shrugs. "I'm sure I'm past due."

"Okay. I'll look in your chart, and we'll go from there. Sit tight," I tell him, tossing all the used wound care items in the trash and removing my gloves.

I write a few things down in my notes and leave the workman's comp paperwork on the counter. Lance will have to fill the majority of it out, but I go ahead and input what I can. When it's complete, I turn and find him watching me. "You okay?"

"I'm perfect," he informs me, a soft smile on his lips. "I got out of work early and get to see you."

I can't help but laugh at his weird logic. "Personally, I'd prefer if you weren't hurt to make that happen."

He shrugs and extends his hand. I place mine inside his immediately and let him draw me closer. Without bumping his leg, I stand between them and place my other hand on his thigh. "It doesn't hurt, and besides, chicks dig scars."

"I suppose they do," I confess, pressing my lips to his. "I'll be right back."

"Don't be long, dear," he replies with a cheeky grin.

I step outside and come face-to-face with Lance. His expression is full of skepticism, as he stares. "You ready for me?" he asks.

"Yes. I was just coming to give you an update," I state, stepping to the side so we're not standing so close.

"Well, what are we waiting for? Let's step inside the exam room, and you can give me the update there."

Tension fills my entire body, but the only reaction I give is a polite nod.

Something tells me Cade and Lance in the same small space together won't have a good outcome.

And I'll be right there, in the middle.

CHAPTER TWENTY-THREE

Cade

A KNOCK SOUNDS ON THE DOOR, AND THE MOMENT LANCE WALKS in, I want to punch him. There's something in his smug demeanor that instantly rattles me. Just laying my eyes on him for a second has my hands balled into fists and red-hot anger washing through me. I'm sure if I didn't know about his past with Oaklee, I wouldn't quite feel this harshly about him, but I'm certain I would have pegged him for an asshole regardless.

"Mr. Miller, I'm Dr. Williams. Nice to meet you," he says politely, yet I don't get any of warm fuzzies from this guy. I also can't help but notice how he emphasizes his title, like him being a doctor immediately makes him superior to everyone else.

Fucker.

"Call me Cade," I reply, leaving off the part about it being nice to meet him too.

It's not.

He pulls out the tray beneath my legs, extending them forward. "Can you tell me what happened?" he asks, looking at my cut.

I run through the details, keeping them basic and to the point.

"So," he starts, walking over and washing his hands in the little sink before placing gloves on his hands. "You're a construction worker, huh?" His eyes hold a touch of humor, like he finds the fact I'm in that line of work to be far beneath him.

"I am," I reply proudly. I won't degrade what I do, not to him and not to anyone else. My job is hard, challenging, and rewarding. Not to mention I work outside in the heat of summer and, at times, the cold of winter, often as vehicles and semis race past me on the interstate.

He moves the flesh around the wound to get a look inside. I'll admit, it doesn't feel the best, but there's no way in hell I'm going to show any sign of weakness where this guy is concerned.

"Nurse, let's get a suture kit and lidocaine. It looks like five or six stitches are needed to close the wound properly."

I don't know if he's trying to sound professional or what, but referring to Oaklee by her title instead of her name pisses me off even more.

"Of course," she responds politely, excusing herself to exit the room.

He examines my injury a bit more, the silence in the room almost deafening before he says without looking up at me, "So, I hear we have some common interests."

"Yeah? What's that? You like fishing and camping too?" I ask, knowing full well that's not what he means, but I'll be damned if I'm going to make this easy on him.

He makes a face of annoyance. "No, I don't have time for things like that. Being a doctor is very time-consuming."

"I'm sure it is," I reply, hoping he gets to his point soon.

"I hear you're friends with Oaklee."

"You seem to hear a lot," I reply, crossing my arms over my chest.

"This small-town thing is foreign to me. Everyone talks," he states, finally scooting back on his little stool and meeting my gaze.

I just stare back at him, refusing to acknowledge his statement.

He sighs and crosses his arms. "Look, *Cade,* I understand your attraction to her. She's hot. But Oaklee can be...difficult."

I raise an eyebrow. "Difficult? Yeah, I suppose finding your boyfriend having an affair and breaking up with him would be cause for being labeled problematic."

"You know nothing of our relationship," he retorts.

"I know you don't have a relationship," I reply, feeling a bit proud of myself for the comeback and the irritation that washes over his face.

"Maybe not at this moment, but she's always come back to me."

"Not this time, *Dr.* Williams," I state smugly and don't even try to hide it.

He opens his mouth to counter, but there's a quick rap at the door, followed by Oaklee entering the room. "I have everything we need. I apologize for it not being available in the room," she says, setting everything down on the counter before turning her gaze to me and adding, "the room we usually use for these types of procedures is being utilized by a specialist at the moment."

"No worries," I reply softly. "The good doc and I were just getting acquainted a bit."

Something that resembles panic flashes through her features. "Oh?" she asks, somewhat hoarsely.

"Yep. He was just informing me how different a small town is to the city lifestyle he's used to. You know, all the gossip and busybodies," I say. "Nothing is secret in a place like Cooper Town. Everyone talks about everything. You know, who broke up, who's cheating on who…" I leave the statement hanging, the weight of my words heavy.

Lance clears his throat. "Nurse, I want to irrigate this wound. Since he was working outside, and I'm sure the jobsite is dirty, anything could have gotten in here. Let's get him numbed up."

He turns his attention to the lidocaine and preps the syringe. I glance at Oaklee, and even though she's wearing tension lines around her eyes and mouth, she still looks positively beautiful. I can tell working with this asshole is taking a toll on her, and I hate it. If I could somehow pull her away from him forever, I would. But she doesn't need a knight in shining armor. She needs a friend who stands by her side, and if needed, steps in front of her to protect her from the Lances of the world.

Lance heads my way. "Wish I could say this wasn't going to sting a little, but it will." And he smiles.

"I can handle a little *prick*," I reply, grinning smugly, just as he did when he entered the room.

Oaklee coughs, but I'm pretty sure she did it to cover a laugh. She keeps her focus on what's on the counter, and her shoulders are drawn up and shaking just a little. Oh, yeah, she's laughing, and I fucking love it.

Lance rubs an alcohol swab around the wound, and yes, that doesn't feel so great. Then, he sticks the needle into the tender skin and pushes the syringe. There it is. The burn. I hold completely still, refusing to so much as flinch or tense as he pulls the needle out and moves to the other side of the wound and does it again. I get a third shot, which is just as uncomfortable as the first two.

"Now we wait a few minutes for it to numb up."

"Great, you got a TV or a Mad Libs book?"

His eyebrows arch up. "Mad Libs?"

"You know, a fun book to keep me occupied while I wait."

"It's going to be three minutes."

"Yeah, you're right. I need a little more time. I do my best work when I'm not rushed and can really take my time and savor the *fun*." I go ahead and give him a Cheshire cat grin just to goad him a bit more.

His ears turn red, and his mouth is in a tight, straight line. I almost laugh out loud.

Good, asshole. Serves you right.

Oaklee spins around, holding a stack of papers tightly against her chest. "Dr. Williams, I have the paperwork filled out and ready for you to finish."

He nods, reaching a privileged hand out for her to walk closer and give him the papers, which she does. He scans the documents, but I pay no attention to him. My gaze is on the beautiful nurse. She's a bit more relaxed now that we're getting down to business.

"How does it feel?" Lance asks, scooting beside the table once more. Before I can reply, he reaches out and taps the skin around the wound. "Can you feel this?"

"Naw, I'm good," I reply.

"All right, Nurse, let's flush it out with saline," he instructs.

I watch them work, mentally noting how they work decently together, but more because their professionalism has taken over, not because they have chemistry. When it comes time for the stitches, Oaklee brings a tray on wheels over and positions it right next to Lance.

"Ready, Mr. Miller?"

"Yes—no, wait, Doc. I need something for comfort." Extending my hand toward Oaklee, she nibbles her bottom lip to keep from smiling.

"There's a teddy bear in the other room I can grab for you," she teases, earning a smile from me.

"No need, beautiful. I've got something better than a teddy bear," I insist, taking her hand and holding it tight. Not because I truly need the comfort, and not because Lance's beady little eyes are shooting daggers at me. I take her hand simply for the fact it's an opportunity to hold it. "Ready, Dr. Williams."

I watch as he puts six stitches in my leg, closing the wound up nicely. He actually did a good job, if you ask me. Looks clean and straight, and I won't have a jagged scar across my shin. "All done?"

"Yes," he replies, removing his gloves and tossing them in the trash. "We'll cover it for you, and you'll want to keep it dry for forty-eight hours. Wrap it in Saran Wrap when you shower and try not to let water pour on it or down your leg. After that, you can remove the cover and wash it with clean water two times a day but no scrubbing or submerging it in water like tubs or pools. Take pain reliever as needed. Watch for redness or infection around the wound. Return in seven to ten days to have the stitches removed." He spoke monotone, as if he was reciting instructions he read from a handbook.

"Thanks, *Dr.* Williams. You did a great job. You've got a real gentle hand," I compliment with a smile.

He just stares at me, trying to gauge my sincerity, I'm sure. There's not much of it in my statement. I mean, the guy did a good job, but he's still a douche. "You should take the next twenty-four to forty-eight hours off work."

"Nope," I reply, as Oaklee pushes the footrest back in, so I can lower my legs. "I'll be fine. I'll keep it clean, but I need to work tomorrow."

"It's Saturday," he states unnecessarily. I'm well aware of what day of the week it is. We're pushing to finish up a state job before layoff season hits. Lance just stares at me for several seconds, and I can tell he's ready to argue. Why? Simply because this is something I want, and he can deny it.

"Listen, I've had stitches before. I know what to do and not to do. I'll be fine at work."

He sighs. "If you notice any changes in the wound site or you develop a fever, get it checked out right away."

I nod. "I will. Besides, I have a personal nurse to help take care of me."

I don't look her way, but I can imagine the blush on her face.

"I'll finish this paperwork and take it to the front," Lance states before basically hightailing it out of the room like his ass was on fire.

"That was fun," I say the moment the door is closed.

"You were goading him."

I shrug. "Maybe, but everything I said was true."

She steps over and covers my stitches with a bandage. "So, you have a nurse coming over to take care of you?"

"Well, not officially, but there's someone I'm hoping wants the task."

When the bandage is secured and she rolls my pant leg down, she stands up between my legs and asks, "What does this job entail?"

I can't help but grin. "Sponge baths and hand jobs."

She barks out a laugh, just as I expected. "Oh my God."

"What? I'm serious. I'm injured and won't be able to do it myself."

She shakes her head and presses her lips to mine. Then, she removes her second set of latex gloves and tosses them in the trash with the rest of the used materials from my stitches. "Come on, Romeo. I have work to do."

"You do," I agree, getting up from the table and walking to the door. "Wanna stop by later?"

"Yes. I'll bring dinner."

"And then we can get to the sponge baths and hand jobs."

Shaking her head, she presses her lips to mine and turns the knob. "I'll see you after work. Grab the workman's comp paperwork at the counter."

"I will," I reply, watching as she walks toward the back of the clinic, my eyes glued to her ass every step she makes. Just as I go to turn and head to the front, Lance steps out of the room across the hall. His eyes are full of tension as he stares me down.

I could stand here and glare back all day long, but I won't make it any more difficult on Oaklee than I'm sure I already have. Instead, I throw him a friendly wave and head for the front reception area.

Lance walks into the office and hands Becky my paperwork. "Have a nice day," he says to me, even though I know he doesn't mean it.

Becky turns around and smiles. "Well, he seems a little grumpier than he was earlier. You wouldn't know anything about that, would you?"

I give her an innocent grin. "Of course not."

She chuckles and types on her keyboard. "I bet you don't." She looks at the screen before taking a quick glance at me. "I might be stepping out of line here, but I just want to say, we all like Oaklee. She's a great nurse and a sweetheart."

I nod, catching her meaning. She's referring to whatever this is between Oaklee and me. I'm sure everyone in town is talking, and I could not give two shits. "Agreed."

"And she seems…happy. Your little gifts make her smile a lot."

My heart is doing a little jig in my chest at her words. "I'm glad."

"Anyway, I just thought I'd mention that. Here are your discharge papers and the stuff you need for work. I have a few availabilities for suture removal next Friday, or I can do next Saturday morning."

"Honestly, do I have to do that in the office?"

She grins and glances over her shoulder. "Technically, no. Anyone with a medical degree can remove them," she says, answering my unasked question.

"Good to know. I'll call you if I need an appointment."

"Sounds good, Cade. Take care," she says, handing over my paperwork and sending me on my way.

I step outside and head for my truck, everything that's transpired in the last thirty minutes spinning in my head. I officially met the asshole ex, even if I had to get injured to do it. But if you take him and our exchanges out of the equation, I got to see Oaklee in her element. She's everything Becky said, but so much more. Her caring and calm demeanor is only part of what makes her a great nurse.

As I climb into my truck, I think back on the conversation we had about the future she wanted and gave up.

Well, fuck him.

It's not too late.

I can vividly see her holding a newborn baby, caring for expecting mothers before and after delivery. Yeah, I did a little research on midwives, and it's a perfect fit for Oaklee's nurturing and caring personality.

Of course, I'm man enough to admit that's not the only vision I see.

That baby?

It's hers with her dark hair and eyes, gazing up at her with so much love and trust.

And me?

I'm standing right there too, looking on in awe, my chest so full it fucking hurts.

What does that mean?

I have an idea, but now isn't the time to dive into it. Right now, I need to head home and change my clothes. I should shower, but the idea of having a certain nurse provide a little assistance later outweighs the need to shower now. I also need to put my leg up and rest, because as much as I try to pretend it doesn't, my leg kinda throbs. Not bad or anything, and not the wound itself, since ol' Doc Lance numbed it before he stitched me up.

I fire off a text to my foreman, letting him know I was taken care of and will be back to work in the morning. Then, I pull out of the parking spot and head for home, Oaklee on my mind the entire way.

CHAPTER TWENTY-FOUR

Oaklee

I GRAB THE SARAN WRAP AND HOLD IT UP. "COME ON, MR. MILLER. Let's get it wrapped up so you can shower."

Cade flashes a cocky grin. "New kink unlocked."

Shaking my head, I can't stop the chuckle from flying. He's been like this all evening. Incorrigible is the word that comes to mind. Everything he says is laced with a sexual innuendo, but it doesn't bother me. In fact, I've enjoyed this evening with him more than any previous spent together. It just feels…different. Natural, laid-back, and, well, fun.

"Stop it."

"I didn't do anything," he insists, heading down the hall to his bedroom.

He strips out of the shorts and T-shirt he was wearing when I got to his house and stands there in his boxers looking positively edible. He snaps in front of my face. "My eyes are up here, Nurse Oaklee."

I giggle and shake my head. "Sorry. You're very distracting."

He presses his lips to mine and says, "As are you. Now, wrap me up so we can take a shower together."

"I'm not taking a shower with you," I counter, grabbing the Saran Wrap and starting to pull it out.

"What? Why not? What if I fall?"

I roll my eyes and drop to my knees in front of him.

"Now we're talking."

"Stop it," I holler through my fit of laughter. He doesn't say anything as I wrap his leg, making sure to keep it as tight as possible so no water gets in. "All set."

When I look up, he's just staring at me, a touch of annoyance mixed with his normal humor-filled eyes. "I can't believe you're not showering with me."

I roll my eyes dramatically. "You'll be just fine. While you shower, I'm gonna get the ice cream and brownies ready."

That perks him up a bit. "Fine, but only if I get to eat mine off your wet pussy."

A gasp fills the room. "Knock it off," I insist, hitting him gently in the chest.

We walk into the bathroom, and he cranks on the hot water to let it heat. I make sure his towel is within reach as he carefully drops his boxers on the floor. His cock is erect, and when he points down to it, he says, "I can't believe you're going to ignore him in his time of need. How rude!"

He's something else, I tell you. Cade has made me laugh more in the short time we've known each other than all six years I was with Lance. Sad, isn't it? But it's the truth. I've never felt this carefree, and I know it's because of the naked man before me.

"Get in," I insist, pulling open the shower curtain and stepping to the side.

He adjusts the water and tests it with his hand.

"Remember to try to keep your foot up on the ledge of the tub as much as you can. That'll help keep the water from running down into the cling wrap."

"Or you could just get in here with me," he grumbles, the cutest pout on his handsome face.

"That would not help at all. In fact, I think it would have the opposite effect."

"We'll never know until we try."

Shaking my head, I point to the water. "In."

He points down at my crotch. "There?"

"Later, tiger," I reply.

He touches the water again to check the temperature before reaching over and grabbing my boob. Of course, it leaves a big handprint on my scrubs top and is quickly soaking through to my bra. "You're wet. You should just get in," he states right before reaching for my arm and dragging me toward the water.

"No!" I bellow just as the front doorbell rings.

"Ignore it."

"It could be something important," I counter.

"Anyone important would have let themselves in the back door," he says.

I shake my head. "I'll go check. Take your shower, and when you're done, we'll discuss ways to eat the ice cream and brownies."

He steps inside and pulls the curtain closed. "I already know how I'm eating it, beautiful. Off your naked body," he hollers.

"I'll be back."

"You better be naked," he demands.

I make my way to the living room just as the doorbell rings a second time. I release the lock and pull open the door, finding a beautiful older woman with blond hair and blue eyes smiling at me. "Hello," she says, and even without asking, I instantly know who this is.

Cade resembles his mother so much.

"Hi," I squeak out, my throat suddenly dry. "Would you like to come in?"

She glances down and grins knowingly. "I don't want to interrupt."

I look down, feeling the mortification burn my entire being when I see the big wet handprint on my chest. "You're not interrupting," I insist, pulling my shirt away from my body and stepping back. "Please, come in."

She does, and that's when I catch the scent of something in the bag she's carrying. "I'm Linda Miller, and you must be Oaklee Daniels."

"I am," I reply, a bit surprised she knows my name.

"It's a small town, Oaklee," she says, as if confirming how she's heard of me. "Well, and Cade has mentioned you a time or two when we've talked."

"Oh."

He has?

She glances around the living room, as if looking for her son. "Cade is in the shower. I had to wrap up his leg so he didn't get his new stitches wet," I say, feeling like the word vomit is flying.

Mrs. Miller smiles politely. "Oh, I understand that. Between Cade, Collin, and Camden, I'm very familiar with stitches and the proper care."

Chuckling, I reply, "I can only imagine."

She leans in and whispers, "They were menaces, don't let him fool you. Cade could find mischief without trying."

I find myself grinning from ear to ear. "I bet."

She holds up her bag and pulls out a bowl. "I made him some chicken and dumpling soup. It was his favorite when he was little, so I thought I'd whip some up. There's plenty for two."

"Oh, thank you," I reply, taking the container from her and putting it in the fridge.

"You know, even though I wanted to throttle them more times than I could count, they were great kids. Cade, he tries to hide it, but he wears his heart on his sleeve and loves with his whole heart. He doesn't think I've noticed, but he secretly wants what his brother has found with Lizzie. I've noticed the way he watches them. It's not out of spite or jealousy, but appreciation. I know the way he acts around town and what he's known for, but I see more than that side. He's looking for a future, whether he admits it or not."

My eyes are a little wide as I listen to her talk about her second born son, who even though he is a twin told me he was born five minutes after Collin. The one who's a little silly and charismatic. The one I can see myself falling for.

"I apologize for just dropping by unannounced. I saw the extra vehicle in the driveway and knew he wasn't alone. I was really hoping to get to meet you though. Not only has Collin met you, but Charli has talked so positively about you too. I wanted to finally meet the woman who is stealing my son's heart."

"Oh, we're not—I mean, it's not like that…"

Stop talking, Oaklee.

The last thing I want to tell his mom is I'm just the woman he's sleeping with right now, that this isn't what she's suggesting.

But if I'm being completely honest with myself, something that feels an awful lot like hope takes root in my chest and blooms.

You know, for someone who wasn't looking for a relationship, I sure as hell want this to turn into one.

"Well, nonetheless, I see the change in my boy, and I'm sure you have a lot to do with it. I won't stay. I'm sure you two have plans," she says, giving me another polite smile.

"Not really," I reply. "He's supposed to be resting his leg, but you know how he is."

She chuckles and nods. "I do, yes. So I guess I need to wish you luck then. That boy of mine will definitely keep you on your toes."

"You better be in the kitchen and you better be naked!"

Oh. My. God.

Before I can say anything, like warn him to the fact his mom is standing right here, Cade comes around the corner. Praise the Lord above he's wearing a towel. Oh my word, it just hit me he could have very easily walked around the corner wearing nothing but a smile.

"Mom." Cade stops in the doorway, his gaze darting between me and the woman standing next to me. "Hi."

"Hello, Cade," she replies with a grin. She steps forward and kisses his cheek. "I was just having a lovely chat with Oaklee."

"Yeah?" he asks, turning his attention to me and giving me a slightly worried look.

I give him a reassuring grin, letting him know I'm okay. "Your mom brought you chicken and dumplings."

He looks her way. "My favorite."

"Well, I thought you could use some comfort food after cutting your leg and having to get stitches."

"How'd you hear?" he asks.

"Charli. She heard it from Quinn, who heard it from Camden. I assume he talked to Collin after he ran into one of your coworkers at the bar."

"Ahh," he replies, as if it were no big deal that half the town was talking about him getting injured at work. "Well, thank you for the dumplings. I'll have it for lunch tomorrow."

"I made plenty so Oaklee can have some too," his mom says. "Well, I'll leave you two to get back to your evening together. I'm glad you're feeling okay."

He waves her off. "Nothing a good needle and thread couldn't fix."

She shakes her head and glances my way. "More stitches than I could count, and two broken bones."

"Two?" I ask. The nurse in me is very much intrigued to hear the details.

"Arm and a nose."

"And not at the same time," his mom adds. "You two have a good one. Oaklee, it was lovely to finally meet you. I hope to see you again soon." She steps forward and gives me a warm hug.

Something causes my eyes to burn at the friendly gesture. Maybe it's because my grandparents weren't huggers, nor was my mom. I don't recall a lot of exchanges like this growing up, and for some reason, having this woman give me a simple hug is almost too much for me.

"It was nice to meet you, Mrs. Miller," I finally croak out, clearing the emotion from my throat.

"Linda, please. I'll see you both soon. We'll be celebrating Cade's dad's birthday in a couple weeks, and we'd love to have you join us."

"Oh," I spit out, not really knowing what to say. Hanging out with friends is one thing, but going to a family function is an entirely different animal.

"I'm sure Oaklee will be there if she can," Cade says, catching me by complete surprise.

"Good. I'll keep you posted on the date and time," she says, going back over and hugging her son. She's quite a bit smaller than he is, especially when he wraps his arms around her and squeezes.

"Love you," he tells her, walking her to the front door.

"Enjoy your night," she says before throwing me a final wave and walking out the door.

He watches to make sure she gets to her car safely, not even caring he's standing in the doorway wearing a towel. When she backs out of his driveway, he finally steps back and closes the door. Turning my way, he places his hands on his hips and says, "You're not naked."

"Uh, no. It would have been very rude to answer the door for your mother wearing nothing but my birthday suit."

He takes a step toward me and snakes his arm around my waist. "You can wear your birthday suit *now*."

"Your mom was just here five seconds ago, and you're already thinking about sex?"

"Baby, I'm always thinking about sex," he replies, leaning down to kiss me. "She likes you."

"She's very friendly. I bet she likes everyone," I retort, slipping my arms around his waist and sliding through a few water droplets.

He snorts. "And you'd be wrong. Mom is very fair and tough, and while she usually has a very sunny, friendly disposition, she most definitely doesn't like everyone. In fact, she wasn't a fan of Whitney."

"Whitney?" I ask, knowing I haven't heard that name before.

"Collin's ex. She cheated on him when he was in Washington in the Air Force. She was friendly to her face, but I knew she didn't really like her. I think she knew Whitney wasn't the one for my brother."

"Possibly," I reply.

Reaching behind him, I hear the click of the lock moments before his hands are back on me as he lifts me up. "Let's go, Nurse Oaklee. I believe you owe me a little *personal* attention."

My legs are wrapped around his waist as he carries me toward his bedroom. He slaps me on the ass, making me giggle. All thoughts of meeting his mom and what she said are forgotten.

For now.

The music isn't very loud, but the atmosphere is electric.

Charli and Sommer invited me to join them for Lizzie's Saturday paint night at the bar, and so far, I'm having a blast. We're painting a pumpkin sitting in a field, and even though I'm far from an artist, I admit mine doesn't look half bad. Of course, that could be the alcohol talking, thanks to the Drunk Ghosts.

That's the name of the drink.

Drunk Ghost.

It's a mixture of coconut rum, vanilla vodka, coconut cream, and lemon-lime soda, with a cute little ghost Peep on top, and it is delicious. I think I innocently hugged Collin when he handed me my third drink.

"I don't know about you, but I'm well on my way to being a little intoxicated. These drinks are yummy," Charli murmurs to me before taking a long sip from her straw.

"Definitely yummy." Glancing to the bar, I find the bartender's yummy twin brother sitting on the bar stool in the corner, keeping an eye on me and my friends. Every time I stand up, he's moving in my direction, wanting to know if I need something, if I've eaten enough food, if I'm having a good time. He's very attentive, even when I'm out with friends, and it feels good.

"Stop ogling my brother. I already have to deal with that shit from Collin and this one," she says, pointing to Lizzie, "But now you and Cade? It's nauseating."

I roll my eyes. "I can't help it. He's as yummy as this drink."

"Eww," she replies, grabbing her paintbrush and giving her attention to the front once more.

"Don't mind her. She's just jealous because she doesn't have anyone yummy to ogle," Lizzie states loudly.

Charli points her brush at Lizzie and says, "You're right. I wish I had someone yummy."

As if on cue, the door opens, and a small group of guys walk in. I recognize them immediately, especially since the one in front is Cade's youngest brother, Camden. His friends Quinn and Robby are with him, and admittedly, I don't know them as well.

"Single guys, four o'clock," Sommer announces.

"Eww, what the hell is wrong with you? He's my brother!" Charli bellows, pretending to gag.

Her friend rolls her eyes. "Obviously, I wasn't talking about your brother, silly. The other two are good-looking and single."

Charli glances over to the trio, who are now sitting at the bar with Cade. "Robby is seeing Sierra Harrison. He's not single."

"Okay, *fine*. But Quinn is."

"Quinn is...no. He's immature and annoying. And he's practically a brother to me. That's just gross."

But her eyes don't match her words.

Something in the way her gaze lingers a little too long over there catches my attention. I don't comment on it, just file it away for later.

We keep painting, laughing, and drinking, and by the time my portrait is about complete, I'm exhausted in all the best ways. I've had the most fun I've had in a long time, and it's because of these people. And not just the ones sitting at the table with me. Allison and the girls I work with. Cade, Collin, and the rest of the guys at the bar.

This is comfortable.

This is home.

Cade catches my eye and offers a smile. It's full of promise and makes my core clench with need.

Need for him, and not just a sexual demand.

I need his smile, his light, and his warmth. I need his strength when I'm weak and his touch when I need to be grounded.

I watch as he laughs with his brothers and takes a sip of his water. He's not drinking, and that's because I am. Because he cares enough to make sure I get home safely. He's a natural protector, even when he doesn't have to be.

And I've fallen in love with him.

The realization hits me hard in the face, like a glass of cold water thrown at me.

This wasn't supposed to happen.

It was meant to be fun…a fling.

But here I am, realizing I'm helplessly in love with the one man who won't ever love me back.

It's like history repeating itself, but that's not fair either, because Cade is nothing like Lance.

Except, like Lance, I'll never have the one thing I've always wanted.

The one thing I refuse to live without moving forward.

The one thing not on the table.

His heart.

CHAPTER TWENTY-FIVE

Cade

"You gonna tell her?"

I look over at my twin and narrow my eyes. "Tell her what?"

He flashes one of his rare smiles. "Come on, man. You're not obtuse."

I take a sip of my water and grin over the rim of the plastic cup. "You severely underestimate my obtuseness, my man."

He shakes his head before catching sight of one of the regulars placing his empty beer can at the front of the bar. Cade walks over and retrieves a fresh can from the cooler and places it on the bar. He says something to the other two men before tapping on the computer screen for the register system. Then, he makes his way back to me and leans against the bar casually.

"Well?"

I sigh, knowing exactly what he's talking about, but wishing he weren't pushing the topic. I don't want to talk about my feelings for Oaklee, especially when they're all a little jumbled and scattered in my own head. "You're annoying."

He chuckles. "That's rich, coming from the twin who used to hang from the top bunk and pretend he was Spider-Man at all hours of the night."

I bark out a laugh. "I couldn't help when the Spidey senses would start tingling."

"The only thing tingling was your body when I punched you. Now, quick deflecting."

I sigh, knowing there's no getting around this conversation. If it doesn't happen now, it'll happen next time I see him or the time after that. No one knows me the way Collin does, and there's no hiding the fact something is bothering me. Or when *someone* is bothering. That includes pesky feelings I've tried to keep out of my relationship with Oaklee but now can't deny.

"Why are you bothering me?" I ask.

"Because you're troubled. I can tell. I lived with your ass for eighteen years, and quiet means you're thinking. And the way you keep looking over at Oaklee tells me you're thinking about her. The dopey smile you're trying to hide speaks volumes too. It's not the drop-your-panties grin you normally wear, which means this is serious."

"I'm staring at her because she's beautiful."

"And because you've found someone you actually want more out of life with." His pointed look and the fact he's one-hundred-percent right pisses me off.

Exhaling slowly, I decide to level with him. "We're not looking for the same thing."

He leans both elbows on the bar. "What do you mean?"

I shrug and take a sip of my water. "She's just wanting fun after a particularly disappointing relationship. That's it."

"She told you that?"

"In so many words, yes," I reply quietly.

"When?"

I give him a confused look. "When what?"

"When did she tell you that?"

"A few weeks ago. Why?"

"What if that's changed?"

My heart starts to beat a little faster. "It hasn't."

"And you know this how?"

He's really starting to piss me off now. "What could have changed in such a short amount of time?" I ask.

Collin shakes his head and sighs. "You really are dumb. Keep up with me here, will ya? If your feelings have changed, don't you think there's a possibility hers has too?"

I open my mouth and shake my head in resignation. "I really don't think so."

"I do," he proclaims, reaching over and popping a piece of popcorn into his mouth.

"Why do you say that?" I ask, hope starting to bud in my chest, like a bloom after the first spring rain.

"Because she hasn't stopped looking over here either," he informs me, tapping his hand on the wood and standing up.

The front entrance door opens, and, like the rest of the bar, we both look over. Camden and his friends are here and heading this way, so the conversation I'm having with Collin abruptly ends.

Camden, Quinn, and Robby sit down at the bar and order drinks. "How you doing?" my younger brother asks from the seat beside me.

"Fine. You?"

He shrugs. "Not bad. Getting new neighbors," he informs me.

"Yeah? That couple who argued all the time moving out?"

"Yep, thank the Lord. I've been more than done listening to the yelling," he says, his attention turned to the main part of the bar where twenty women are painting fall pumpkins. "Can you believe this shit is still going strong? Collin said she sells out every month, almost immediately, and has a waitlist."

"Definitely crazy," I comment, not quite understanding it myself. But the women who take the paint night classes always seem to have a good time. From themed drinks, including nonalcoholic options, and snack food, Lizzie does her part to ensure it.

"You here with Oaklee?" he asks innocently, but all I can think about is the conversation I just had with my other brother.

"Yeah."

He nods and takes the beer Collin sets on the bar. "Is that like…a thing?"

I roll my eyes. "Does it matter?"

"No," he replies immediately with a shrug. "I like her. I think she's good for you."

"Yeah, well, it isn't like that," I insist, the truth burning my gut.

He doesn't say anything else, essentially ending the conversation, which makes me grateful. I'm done explaining to everyone that Oaklee and I are just a "thing." A fling. Friends with bennies. Whatever you want to call it.

What you wouldn't call us is boyfriend and girlfriend. Even if we spend a lot of time together in the evening, that's all it is.

Sex.

And friendship.

Period.

"No?" he asks, watching me closely.

I turn my attention to the ladies—or more accurately, one specific lady—and find those beautiful dark eyes watching me. She offers a smile, and even though it's small, it lights up her entire face. She's a fucking angel on earth, and all I want to do is bathe in her goodness and light.

She whispers something to Lizzie, who's sitting beside her, and gets up. My eyes remain locked on her as she heads toward the hallway where the restrooms are located. Without thought, I slide off my stool and start to move her way.

"The apartment's locked," Collin hollers, earning a middle finger as I pass by. I know what he's insinuating, and even though I'd love to take her up there and have my wicked way with her, now isn't the time. I'd never want to interrupt her paint night like that, not when she seems to be having a good time.

But that doesn't mean I can't steal a kiss or two…

I reach the door to the women's restroom and stand outside. I'm about to push inside when the door opens and a woman a few years younger than me steps out. "Uhh, hi."

"Hey. Is anyone else in there?" I ask casually.

She gives me a weird look and replies, "One woman in a stall."

"Okay, perfect. Thanks," I reply, leaning against the door as she slowly walks away, giving a quick glance back in concern as she goes.

When she exits the hall, I push the door open and step inside the restroom. I glance under the stalls and only see one pair of legs, recognizing the pants and boots. Then, I reach behind me and lock the door. The toilet flushes and the stall opens; revealing a surprised Oaklee when she spots me standing here.

"This is the ladies' bathroom, isn't it?" she asks, a smile on her lips as she walks to the sink and washes her hands.

"It is," I confirm, stepping closer.

When she dries her hands on a paper towel, she gives me her attention, shaking her head. "You're not supposed to be in here."

I shrug, wrapping my arms around her waist and drawing her into my chest. "Needed a quick kiss."

"And you had to go into the ladies' room to do that?"

I casually lift a shoulder before pressing my lips to hers. "I have to take what I can get," I insist.

"Because I hold out on you?"

"No, because I never want to miss an opportunity to steal a kiss or two."

I claim her lips, my tongue delving inside her mouth. I can taste the fruity concoction she's been drinking all night, and even though I'm not a huge fan of coconut, it's driving me wild. Of course, that could just be her too. When we break apart, I grin and whisper, "Just a simple hello."

"I rather love your hellos."

And there it is. The one word that sends my mind spinning and my heart racing.

No, she didn't declare her undying love the way I'd prefer, but just the use of the L-word has me picturing a future that doesn't match hers.

"What's wrong?" she asks, concern flooding her face.

"Nothing. Why?"

"You just suddenly looked…sad."

"Me?" I reply with a little chuckle and a grin, doing everything I can to mask the hurt I suddenly feel. Realizing we're on two entirely different pages is a hard pill to swallow.

She watches me, trying to get a read on me, but I make sure to shut down any emotion or feeling other than the normal carefree, laid-back vibe I usually carry. "You'd tell me if something was bothering you, wouldn't you?"

"Of course," I insist quickly. "Now, come on, let's get back out there. I don't want them sending a search party for you and finding me in the women's restroom."

I take her hand, release the lock, and pull open the door. Only to come face-to-face with Lizzie. She has her arms crossed over her chest and gives me a look that lets me know she's not impressed. "A customer just came to tell me a man may have cornered a woman in the restroom. How did I know this is exactly what I'd find."

I lift my shoulders and bring Oaklee's hand to my lips, placing a gentle kiss on the soft skin. "I can't help she finds me irresistible."

Oaklee whacks me on the arm. "All is well, Lizzie. This one followed me into the restroom for a quick kiss."

Lizzie shakes her head and points at me. "Steal your kisses in a public place, not designated for restroom use, buster."

"Yes, ma'am," I give her a wide, charming grin.

She sighs and steps back, allowing us to exit the restroom.

We walk back into the main bar, and I can feel everyone's eyes on us. I don't care though. I just press a kiss to her cheek and watch as she returns to her table with Lizzie to finish painting her masterpiece.

And me?

I return to my stool to watch.

Like the lovesick sap I am.

"Come on, beautiful. Let's get you home," I say as I help a buzzed-up Oaklee into the passenger seat of my truck before slipping her painting over the headrest and into the back.

"You're pretty," she says, running her palm across my cheek as she stares up at me from the seat.

I can't help but smile. "Thank you, sweetheart. I think you're pretty too."

She grins as I shut the door and run around to the driver's side and climb in. As soon as I have the truck started, she leans over and lays her head against my arm. Since she's buckled in, she can't get any closer, but I sure do like the feel of her lying against me regardless.

I drive toward her house, a Faith Hill song playing on the radio. I don't know when I start humming along to the tune, but I only notice when I sense her eyes on me. Glancing to my right, I give her a grin. "What?"

"Even when you hum, you have a nice voice. I think you should come over every night and sing me to sleep," she says, yawning.

"Yeah?" I ask, returning my eyes to the road while my heart pounds like a snare drum in my chest.

"Oh yeah. You sing me to sleep, and you'd get lucky every night," she vows.

I'd be *lucky.*

She starts to hum along to the end of the song and jumps right into the next one. Her eyes are closed and there's a faint grin on her lips. She doesn't say anything else, just sits there quietly and contently as I drive her home.

When I pull into her driveway and park, I release my seat belt and climb from the driver's seat. I make it to the passenger side and open her door before she's made a move to exit. I help her out, slinging my arm around her shoulder as I escort her to the door. "Got your keys?" I ask.

She pulls them from her bag and dangles them in front of me.

"Thank you," I reply, finding the one that unlocks the front door. "Come on, beautiful. Let's get you inside."

"I had the best time tonight," she says, stepping into her house.

The second I cross the threshold, she moves. Like a cheetah, she leaps at me, knocking me back against the door and almost sending us both to the floor. But I'm able to right myself to keep standing. "Are you okay?" I ask, hoping she didn't injure herself in the shuffle.

"I'm fine," she declares, leaning her head against my shoulder. "Thanks for catching me."

I chuckle. "You leaped into my arms."

"Yeah. Because I knew you'd catch me."

I press my lips to her forehead, the words I long to say on the tip of my tongue. "I'll always catch you."

She sighs, her eyes closed. "I'm tired."

"We should get you to bed," I state, walking toward the hallway that leads to her bedroom.

"Yeah."

When we reach her bedroom, I slowly lower her to the floor. She keeps her arms wrapped around me, holding me tightly. All the things my brother said come flooding to my mind, and I can't help but wonder if maybe, just perhaps, she actually feels the same way I do. Of course, she has no clue how I really feel because I've never told her.

What if…

"I have an idea," I start, causing her to look up at me. "What if I stayed here tonight. With you."

I don't know what I was expecting, but confusion wasn't it.

She watches me, as if trying to figure out what I just said. "You want to…stay? Here?"

I shrug, as if it's *no big deal*, all while my heart is pounding so loudly, I'm sure the neighbors can hear. "Why not?"

"Because we're just…ya know, fooling around."

My heart drops to the floor. "I know, but—"

"No, buts. You wanted casual, right?" she asks, releasing her hold on me and stepping back. The distance is excruciating. "You always do casual."

"I do, yes," I confirm.

Until now.

"We have to keep it that way," she insists, her arms crossed over her chest as she looks anywhere but at me. "That's what we agreed to."

I don't argue with her. No agreement was really made. It was just assumed, in my opinion, which is part of the problem. I haven't really communicated well because I knew she was nursing a wounded heart and didn't want anything serious.

At the time, that arrangement was perfect.

I usually don't do serious either, but somewhere along the way, it started to feel different, and I never told her. Hell, I didn't even see it myself really, not until someone else slapped me upside the head with their observations. All I know is she wants to keep things casual, and I don't want to lose her and the friendship we've built just because I've started to have feelings.

Oh, who am I kidding. Definitely not my brother. Collin saw it. Camden too.

I fell in love with her.

"Okay," I reply, shoving my hands in my pockets, agreeing to whatever she wants because she means too much to me.

A plethora of emotions cross her face, everything from hurt to shock to anger, but it's when I see the tears in her eyes, I realize I really fucked this up. I want to kick my own ass for putting those there.

Stepping forward, I take her in my arms. "I'm sorry, just forget I said anything."

She sniffles and whispers, "Yeah, okay."

"I'll head home and let you get some rest."

She nods and doesn't say anything, just stands rooted in place.

I press a kiss to her forehead, not wanting to push it by kissing her lips. "I'll lock up behind me."

There's so much emotion swimming in those dark brown eyes, and I know I can't fix this now. Not after she's been drinking with the girls most of the night and is buzzed up. Any further conversation needs to happen when we're both sober and able to talk like adults.

"Good night, beautiful."

I walk out of her bedroom, praying it's not the last time I'll be there. And I'm not talking about the sex, even though that's pretty fucking amazing. I'm talking about being here, with her.

I glance around the living room before stepping outside, ensuring the door is secured as I go. My feet are heavy as I return to my truck and climb inside. I start the engine and sit there, watching her bedroom window. The light never turns on, so I can only hope she climbs into bed and passes out.

As for me, I pull from her driveway but only make it as far as the road. I stop along the curb and put my truck in park, wishing I had a magic wand to fix this. I shouldn't have said anything about spending the night, even if I truly wanted to stay. Now, because I tried to potentially take this thing to the next level, I may lose her completely.

See?

Nothing good comes from falling in love.

CHAPTER TWENTY-SIX

Oaklee

I DON'T KNOW HOW LONG I LIE HERE, BUT IT'S ENOUGH THAT MY buzz is gone. In its place is a slightly broken heart that is consuming me.

Why did he want to spend the night?

Man, I wanted that so much. I want him lying beside me more than I want my next breath, but I can't let it happen and then just magically go back to being friends with benefits. My heart is invested, and if he stayed here, it would only bring heartache. I can't keep the two separate when he's in my bed. I can barely tell the difference between friends and what feels like a real relationship at this point.

If I can't keep a firm line between the two, I'm going to lose him forever, because at the end of the day, he doesn't want what I do.

I want to find someone to spend the rest of my life with.

He wants a good time.

When the clock on my phone hits three in the morning, I crawl from bed and use the bathroom. Once I've washed my hands, I make my way to the kitchen. I need a glass of water and some ice cream. Flipping on the light, I retrieve a glass first and fill it up from the tap. It doesn't taste the greatest, but it's liquid, and I'm dying of thirst.

After draining the glass, I head for the freezer and pull out the carton of mint chocolate chip and a spoon and have a seat at the table. I peel off the lid and dive in, not even caring to be eating straight from the container. No one else lives here, so it's not like I need to worry about germs or backwash or anything like that.

My mind immediately goes to Cade.

I can picture him sitting across from me, spoon in hand, and scooping out a big bite of the minty chocolatey goodness for himself. He's got a sweet tooth, even though you wouldn't know it. His body is hard, his abs pronounced. He's gorgeous and fit and would still sit right here and eat ice cream in the middle of the night with me.

Just as I scoop a second spoonful out, there's a knock on the door.

I sit completely still, wondering what I should do. Obviously, I shouldn't answer the door. It could be anyone at this time of night, and usually that person is up to no good. I set my spoon down, wondering where my phone is.

Shit, I left it plugged in on my nightstand.

A second knock sounds, this one a little louder and more insistent than the first one. "Oaklee? Are you awake?"

Cade?

I get up and quietly move to the front door, peeking through the little hole in the door. My heart is hammering in my chest, and I'm pretty sure I'm not breathing. I confirm with a second look through the peephole and unlock the door, slowly pulling it open.

"Are you all right?" he asks, his face full of worry.

"Yes, I—what are you doing here?"

Is it the alcohol still in my system causing my head to spin like this?

He looks exhausted. There are bags under his eyes, and his hair is sticking up in a thousand directions. "I never left."

My mouth drops open, and I realize we're standing in the doorway.

I step back and wave my hand, allowing him inside. "You didn't leave? Why?"

He stands in my living room, still looking like the most gorgeous man he is. My chest is tight as I stare at him, waiting.

"Because I didn't want to leave you. What are you doing up? Are you okay?" he repeats.

I blink once. Twice.

I open my mouth, but nothing comes out.

"Oaklee? Are you all right?

It takes several seconds before I'm able to formulate a single word to say, "Yes."

"Okay, good," he replies, visibly relaxing. "That's good. I freaked out that something was wrong when I saw your lights go on."

"Cade," I say, reaching out and placing my palm against his arm. "Why were you still outside? It's three in the morning."

He glances down, a sheepish look on his face. "I, uh…can we sit?"

I nod, turning to move to the couch, but then remember my ice cream. "Let's go to the kitchen. Do you want something to drink?"

"No thank you," he replies, stopping when he sees my middle of the night snack sitting on the table. "Ice cream?"

I shrug. "I got snacky and it sounded good."

He slides onto the chair opposite the one I was sitting in earlier and reaches for the spoon. Without asking, he dips it into the ice cream and takes a small bite. "Good stuff."

I nod, waiting.

"You're feeling okay? After drinking?"

"Yes, Dad," I reply with a small grin. "I feel fine."

"Good." He hands over my spoon and levels me with a gaze. "I have to tell you something, and I'm scared."

"You're scared?"

He nods, watching as I take a small scoop of ice cream, just to give myself something to do with my hand. "I'm scared to tell you the truth."

"About?" My voice doesn't even sound like my own. It's barely a whisper and hoarse.

"How I feel about you," he confesses, watching as I lick the spoon.

Handing over the utensil, he takes his own small bite before continuing.

"I know my history screams hump and dump. I've never had a real relationship. I've kept women at arm's length my entire adult life. But the truth is, I've always wanted what my parents have. I want the life, the house, the kids, everything. However, I knew it wasn't just going to fall in my lap, so I've continued being me, while keeping my eyes open."

"Okay," I say, trying to understand what he's saying.

"I was content just having fun. Until I met you."

My eyebrows pull up in question as he takes another small bite. "I wasn't any fun?"

"No, you were more than fun, Oaklee. You changed the game. A game I didn't even know I was playing until it was too late."

"Stop speaking in metaphors," I insist, reaching for the spoon and grabbing a big bite.

He grabs my wrist holding the spoon and stops my movement. "I lied about my reasoning for wanting to spend the night, and the reason I'm scared is if I lay my heart out there, you might not feel the same. But I don't know that I can go back and pretend I'm not completely in love with you, beautiful. It's too hard. So, if you tell me you're not ready for a relationship, that you just want to be friends, I'll do it. But you need to know my feelings are more than that, and I'll be working my ass off to not only prove it to you, but to show you until you realize you love me too."

My vision becomes blurred as tears fill my eyes. "You...love me?"

He takes the spoon and sets it in the carton before standing up and moving to where I sit. He squats in front of me, using the pads of his thumbs to wipe the wetness off my cheeks. "Yeah, I love you."

I bring my hands up to my face and cry.

Realization washes over me. Not that I want to think about my ex at a time like this, but when was the last time I heard him say those three little words? He was always too hurried to get off the phone, and he'd never text me just to let me know he was thinking of me and loved me.

But here's this beautiful man, laying his heart out there. He's exactly what I didn't even realize I was looking for, and I'm so damn lucky to have found him, despite how quickly it might have happened.

"Oaklee?" he whispers, carefully moving my hands off my face. "Are you okay?"

"I love you too," I blurt out. "So much."

His smile is slow but lights up his entire face. "Yeah?"

I nod. "Yeah. It's a recent realization, but I thought you only wanted the friends with benefits thing. That's why I didn't want you to stay the night with me. I knew if I had you in my bed all night, I'd never want you to leave or never recover when you did."

He moves, lifting me off the chair and taking my place, setting me down on his knees. "So, let me get this straight. You love me but didn't want to say because you didn't know how I felt, and I love you for the same reason."

"That sounds about right," I agree with a chuckle.

He claims my lips, and it feels so different this time. It's like the first kiss all over again, but so much better. Real. Deep. Meaningful.

Love.

I don't know how long we sit here, making out, but it feels like only a few seconds. However, by the way we're both gasping to catch our breath, I'd say it was much longer. I slide my palms up his jaw, my fingertips dancing at the edge of his hairline. "I can't believe you love me," I whisper.

He threads his hands into my hair, holding me close as he gazes into my eyes. "Best day of my life was when I hit on you at the bar."

"I turned you down," I remind him with a grin.

"Yeah, but I got the woman in the end." His smile is cocky, just as I'd expect it to be.

"Yes, yes you did," I agree, brushing my lips across his. "Now, take me to bed, and promise you'll spend the night."

"I promise."

Lifting me up, he carries me into the living room where he stops and makes sure the door is locked before walking to my bedroom and laying me on top of my bed.

We're awake for the next thirty minutes, and when we're both naked, sweaty, and spent, we curl up together and close our eyes. It's the best night of sleep I've ever had, with the man I love sleeping right beside me.

It's the start of something amazing.

EPILOGUE

Cade

One month later

I SMILE AS I OPEN THE DOOR AND STEP INSIDE THE CLINIC. "GOOD morning, Cade."

"Hi, Fiona," I greet, walking toward the counter where Becky usually sits. On Saturday's, the front-end ladies and the nurses rotate and work every other weekend.

"Go on back. She might be in an exam room, but you can wait in the hall by the nurses' station."

"Will do," I state, nodding to the mother and child sitting in the waiting room.

I can hear voices in one of the two exam rooms with the doors closed, so it doesn't surprise me when I pop my head inside the nurses' station and she's not there. I set the flowers on the counter and step back outside the space.

It takes a couple minutes before I hear a door open and watch the woman I love walk out of the exam room. She's a sight, her scrubs hugging her curves and her hair piled high on her head in one of those messy bun things, as she places the chart in the plastic holder beside the door.

Then, she turns my way and notices me immediately.

"Hey," she greets, a big smile on her gorgeous face.

"Good morning," I reply, holding up her favorite iced coffee as she approaches.

"Thank you." She takes the offered beverage and sips. "So good. I don't even care that it's cold outside."

Just then, the second door opens in the hallway, and Dr. Houston walks out. "Oaklee, Isiah is ready. We're going to send a prescription into the pharmacy," he says politely, nodding to me.

"Absolutely, Doctor. I'll do that right now," Oaklee responds as the good doc grabs the chart at the other door and knocks before entering.

"I know you're busy. I'll let you get to it. I just wanted to say hello." I step forward and press a kiss to her lips.

"I appreciate the visit and the iced coffee," she replies.

"You can show me how much you appreciate it later when we're alone," I state with a wink, making her laugh.

"Will do, big guy," she says.

"Here, let me set your drink on your desk so you can go prep the next room," I state, extending my hand.

She takes a quick drink before handing it over. I set it on the counter next to the flowers and return to the hallway. We walk together and pause outside the room she needs to step inside.

"I'll see you at my place in a bit," I say quietly, bending down and brushing my lips across hers.

"Yep. I'll run home, change, and grab my bag. Should be there by one."

"And then we're running to grab a bite for lunch?"

"Yes," she replies, leaning in and placing a chaste kiss on my lips.

God, I love it when she does that.

"See you in a bit, beautiful. Love you."

I head for the front entrance with a smile on my face and love in my heart. I knew the night we met she was going to change my life. Even in such a short amount of time together, I already know it to be fact. Everything is better with her beside me, and even though it's still too early to make major declarations, I can see where this is heading.

Someday, I'll make her mine forever.

Until then, I'll spend every moment of every day proving to her she's always first to me.

ANOTHER EPILOGUE

Oaklee

ONCE THE ROOM IS READY FOR THE NEXT PATIENT, I STEP OUT into the front waiting room and call the patient back. We've seen an influx of sick kids, thanks to the colder weather and a brutal strand of strep throat that's hit the schools.

I run through the process of getting his vitals, including taking his temperature, since his mom reports he's been fighting a fever for more than twenty-four hours. "All right, Dr. Houston will be in shortly."

I leave them in the room and drop the chart in the holder before making my way back to the nurses' station. I need to send the prescription for Isiah and check the messages for any additional refill requests. It never fails, Saturdays are flooded with requests the moment patients realize they'll be without until sometime Monday.

Rounding the corner, I stop in my tracks when I find the vase of flowers sitting by my computer. The smile is automatic. Not only did he bring my favorite iced coffee, but a vase of pink and white lilies too. I take the few steps forward and bend over, inhaling the fragrant scent of the blooms. They smell amazing.

Something shiny catches my attention.

I sit down on the chair and reach for what's hidden inside the bouquet. The moment I see it, my eyes fill with tears, and I can't fight the smile. It's a small, gold-framed photo, taken last weekend at The Tipsy Lizard. I'm standing in front of him, leaning against his chest, and laughing at something someone said. Cade has his arms wrapped around me and he's laughing too, but his eyes are on me. He's watching me laugh, just like I catch him doing a lot. His eyes always seem to be on me.

I dig the frame out of the bouquet and pull out the little stand before placing it next to my computer.

There.

Now I can see him—us together—all day, every day while at work.

It's surely going to help make my workdays better.

Not that my days aren't fine as they are. I mean, I'm not working alongside Lance anymore, so there's that. We still work for the same hospital company, so there's always a chance we'll run into each other or work together again at some point, but that's nothing I want to worry about now. I've proven I can be in the same building with his cheating ass for thirty days and not injure him with my stapler.

When I pictured my life here in Cooper Town, this wasn't what I saw.

Dating Cade, spending my time with his family and our friends, is better than anything I could have expected.

I love living in this small town, and if I have my way, I'll never leave.

This is where I found myself.

Who I was meant to be.

This is where I found real love.

And it all started with a simple hello.

THE END

BONUS SCENE

Cade

April

"SHOW ME."

Oaklee rolls her eyes. "Why are you so impatient?"

I cross my arms over my chest and narrow my eyes. "Because I've been dying to see what you got since you returned from your appointment." Hell, since the moment she told me she was getting a tattoo about two months ago. I've been anxious to know what she settled on, and even though we discussed many different ideas and potential placement locations on her beautiful body, what she ultimately decided on today has been kept a secret.

"I told you I'd show you," she counters.

"You said when we got here. We're here," I remind, repeating what she told me earlier today before she left for her tattoo appointment. And after, because I've been begging to see it, even going as far as to try to coax it out of her with the promise of orgasms so I could get her clothes off her.

Win, win.

"You're being extra."

I bark out a laugh. "I'm always extra, beautiful. Now, take off your clothes and show me your new tattoo."

But again, she rolls her eyes and continues toward the creek, where I already have the fishing gear deposited by the chairs. When she left for her tattoo appointment this morning with Charli and Lizzie, I came out here to my favorite spot on Wyatt's property to clean up the timber a bit and to prep for our afternoon excursion.

It's a gorgeous, sunny day for early April. With the afternoon highs in the low seventies, we decided it was a perfect time to fish. Even though it's slightly cooler under the canopy of trees, it's still a better day than we've seen lately. Winter was a bitch and hung around much longer than anyone wanted, but now it seems spring has arrived, leaving us warmer days and more sunshine.

I stand back and watch. Oaklee moves to the tackle box and starts to remove everything she needs to bait her pole. She still doesn't remove the fish, but she has no issues hooking the worm or whatever we use for the catch. Oaklee does her thing, and I can't help but smile with pride. She's so fucking strong and determined, not to mention gorgeous as all get out. She's one tough woman, and I'm damn lucky she's mine.

She goes through the entire process, from baiting the hook to casting. It's not until the pole is placed in the holder in the ground that she turns. "Why are you over there?"

"Because the sight of you doing that made me so hard, I can't walk."

Her head flies back, and she laughs. "Oh my God, you're incorrigible."

I finally take the remaining steps toward her and pull her into my chest. "I'm a man in love."

She grins, a faint blush creeping up her neck. "You're a smooth talker."

"I speak the truth. Not only are you the most beautiful woman in the world, but your heart is pure gold. I'm the luckiest son of a bitch on the planet."

She gives me a slight shake of her head as her fingers dance up my arms. "A little cheesy but keep talking."

Now it's my turn to laugh. "I'm more of a man of action, beautiful."

She laughs in my face once more. "Actually, I've pegged you more as a man of many words, but I do admit, the action part rates pretty high on the list too."

"Thank you." I'm preening like a peacock.

Then, my lips find hers, as they always tend to do anytime she's near. I could kiss this woman all day, every day if I could figure out how to still work. The boss might not approve of her riding along throughout my day, just so we could make out.

Before the kiss gets too carried away, she rips her lips from mine and steps from my arms. I want to pull her back to me, but I notice her hands move to the bottom of her crewneck sweatshirt and lift.

"That's what I'm talking about," I mutter, my vision glued to action of her removing the sweatshirt.

She holds what she took off in her left hand and pulls down the low-cut tank top with her right. That's when I see it.

Her tattoo.

The dark, yet delicate lines across fair skin is mesmerizing. It's covered with Saniderm, the thin protective shield to keep it clean and protected, but you can still see the beauty of the piece. It's some sort of lamp, like a genie one, but I'm certain that's not what it is. "Tell me about it."

She glances down to the fresh tattoo and smiles. I can tell by the light reflecting in those dark orbs, there's great meaning to whatever it is she chose to have permanently imprinted on her body, especially at the location she chose.

Over her heart.

A place of pride and love.

And I know, whatever she's about to tell me will hold great significance, and despite it sounding cheesy, make me love her even more.

I find myself holding my breath as I wait.

Oaklee

"This is the Lamp of Knowledge," I tell him, returning my gaze to his curious eyes.

"What does it mean?" he asks, knowing this wasn't one of the options we discussed when we talked about me getting this tattoo.

"The Lamp of Learning and Lamp of Knowledge was first introduced to me in nursing school. The Lamp of Knowledge is used as a sacred symbol of life by the nursing profession. It represents the nurturing, guidance, and dedicated care of nurses, often associated with Florence Nightingale. It is said she used a lamp like this throughout the night to check on the patients she cared for."

"And the date?" he asks, stepping closer and raising a hand. I don't move, knowing his touch will be gentle as he gingerly caresses the fresh ink.

"My graduation date."

His blue eyes shine brightly as he smiles. "I fucking love it, Oaklee. It's perfect and so very you."

"Thanks," I reply. I glance down once more and ask, "Do you think it's silly? Having something that symbolizes my profession inked on my body?"

"What? Hell no. Being a nurse is a calling. It's what you do, who you are. It's an achievement, a symbol of everything you put into your education, just so you could give everything back to someone else. I can't think of a better reason to put this on your body."

My heartbeat slows and I take a deep breath. He gets it. "I know I had mentioned using a nursing hat, but when this idea popped into my head, I guess…well, it just felt right."

"And it is. It's perfect," he insists.

Reaching for his arm, I push up the sleeve of the long-sleeved T-shirt he's wearing, exposing the tattoo I'm looking for. I glide my thumb over the detailed ink. "I remember that night you told me about this tattoo, the deep meaning behind it. That always stuck with me," I tell him, recalling that particular conversation.

Cade and Collin have matching tattoos on their forearms. Two interlocking puzzle pieces, representing their bond as twins. Each piece of the puzzle contains a symbol of their military careers. Collin's, flames for firefighting and the Hap Arnold Wings of the Air Force, and Cade's, bricks with the Eagle, Globe, and Anchor for the Marines. There was something so impactful about hearing of why they chose what they did, how their time in the service affected their lives in so many ways. It made me realize how my past shaped my life too, and that's why I chose what I did.

"It's absolutely perfect," he repeats, a smile on his lips. "I can't wait until it's healed and I can lick it." He wiggles his eyebrows suggestively, making me laugh.

I adjust my tank top and bring the sweatshirt up to slip it back on. Cade reaches out and stops my hand. "What do you think you're doing?"

"Putting this back on. It's a little chilly," I state, referring to the shaded timber.

He gently pulls me against his body, his warmth wrapping around me like a comfortable blanket. "I have a few ways we can warm you right up."

I glance around. "I don't see a tent."

"Not this time," he says, his voice laced with sadness. "Soon, the weather will be decent enough to go camping again."

"Good. I like camping with you."

"Mmm," he murmurs," kissing my neck and sliding his nose against the shell of my ear. "I rather enjoy camping with you too. Naked camping."

I giggle, wrapping my arms around his waist. "Hmm, so no tent. Whatever will we do?"

"I have ideas," he proclaims, rocking his hips forward, his cock hard and ready.

"Well, we should probably just go back to fishing. You know, since there's no tent to provide...privacy."

Suddenly, I'm being lifted into the air. I'm not exactly thrown over his shoulder, but it's pretty damn close. He turns and walks back to where his truck is parked. We almost brought the side-by-side, but since the temperature is supposed to drop as the sun sets later, he wanted to have an enclosed cab.

Or so I thought.

Something tells me *this* was his master plan all along.

No that I mind.

Sex in the back seat of his truck is usually pretty damn hot, and if there's one thing I know for certain, it's that Cade Miller will make sure I enjoy it.

My heart is already pounding out of my chest as he places me on the ground and opens the driver's side back door. "I promise there'll be a tent next time," he starts, running his hand up my bare arm and causing sparks of heat to race through my veins.

"I'm counting on it," I say, jumping into the truck and giving his hand a playful tug.

He climbs inside, closing the door. His mouth is on mine immediately, the fire I feel for him turning into a full-force inferno of need. "I love you," he whispers without breaking the connection of our lips.

"I love you."

And he shows me just how much.

Twice.

THE END

BOOKS ALSO BY LACEY BLACK

Rivers Edge series

Trust Me, Rivers Edge book 1 (Maddox and Avery) – FREE at all retailers

Fight Me, Rivers Edge book 2 (Jake and Erin)

Expect Me, Rivers Edge book 3 (Travis and Josselyn)

Promise Me: A Novella, Rivers Edge book 3.5 (Jase and Holly)

Protect Me, Rivers Edge book 4 (Nate and Lia)

Boss Me, Rivers Edge book 5 (Will and Carmen)

Trust Us: A Rivers Edge Christmas Novella (Maddox and Avery)

~ *This novella was originally part of the Christmas Miracles Anthology*

With Me, A Rivers Edge Christmas Novella (Brooklyn and Becker)

Bound Together series

Submerged, Bound Together book 1 (Blake and Carly)

Profited, Bound Together book 2 (Reid and Dani)

Entwined, Bound Together book 3 (Luke and Sidney)

Summer Sisters series

My Kinda Kisses, Summer Sisters book 1 (Jaime and Ryan)

My Kinda Night, Summer Sisters book 2 (Payton and Dean)

My Kinda Song, Summer Sisters book 3 (Abby and Levi)

My Kinda Mess, Summer Sisters book 4 (Lexi and Linkin)

My Kinda Player, Summer Sisters book 5 (AJ and Sawyer)

My Kinda Player, Summer Sisters book 6 (Meghan and Nick)

My Kinda Wedding, A Summer Sisters Novella book 7 (Meghan and Nick)

Rockland Falls series

Love and Pancakes, Rockland Falls book 1

Love and Lingerie, Rockland Falls book 2

Love and Landscape, Rockland Falls book 3

Love and Neckties, Rockland Falls book 4

Standalone

Music Notes, a sexy contemporary romance standalone

A Place To Call Home, a Memorial Day novella

Exes and Ho Ho Ho's,

a sexy contemporary romance standalone novella

Pants on Fire

Double Dog Dare You

Grip

Bachelor Swap, A Bachelor Tower Series Novel

Perfect Kiss, Mason Creek Series book 9

Waiting For Love, The Love Vixen Series book 11

Quarterback Keeper, a surprise baby novella

Kissing A Stranger, book 4 in the multi-author

The Kissing Games series

Burgers and Brew Crüe Series

Kickstart My Heart, book 1

Don't Go Away Mad, book 2

Same Ol' Situation, book 3

Wild Side, book 4

What's It Gonna Take, book 5

Home Sweet Home, book 6

Too Young to Fall in Love, book 7

Without You, book 8

Time For Change, book 9

You're All I Need, book 10

Pine Village Series

Pretty Remarkable, a free prequel short story

Pretty Incredible, book 1

Pretty Dependable, book 2

Pretty Drunk, book 3

Pretty Relentless, book 4

Pretty Wild, book 5

Cooper Town Boys Series

A Simple Request, book 1

A Simple Hello, book 2

A Simple Mistake, book 3

A Simple Regret, book 4

Co-Written with *NYT Bestselling* Author, Kaylee Ryan

It's Not Over, Fair Lakes book 1

Just Getting Started, Fair Lakes book 2

Can't Get Enough, Fair Lakes book 3

Fair Lakes Box Set

Boy Trouble

Home To You, a second chance novella

Beneath the Fallen Stars, Never Too Far book 1

Beneath the Desert Sun, Never Too Far book 2

Tell Me A Story

Royal

Crying Shame

Watch and Learn

ABOUT THE AUTHOR

USA Today Bestselling Author Lacey Black is a Midwestern girl with a passion for reading, writing, and shopping. She carries her e-reader with her everywhere she goes so she never misses an opportunity to read a few pages. Always looking for a happily ever after, Lacey is passionate about contemporary romance novels and enjoys it further when you mix in a little suspense. She resides in a small town in Illinois with her husband and two children.

Website: www.laceyblackbooks.com

Email: laceyblackwrites@gmail.com

Newsletter: www.laceyblackbooks.com/newsletter